Third Moon Chemicals

Third Moon Chemicals

Adventures of a Jump Space Accountant Book 3

Andrew Moriarty

Andrew Moriarty

Chapter 1

"What's our status?" Jake asked.

"We are tumbling through space, and our main engines are out. One thruster is leaking, forcing a clockwise roll. The roll is increasing steadily and will soon hit 4 g's," Riley said.

"Life support?"

"Life support is offline. Breathable air for about twenty minutes until CO2 increase causes unconsciousness. There is a small fire in the engine room. One engineering airlock's outer hatch is open to space. Uncertain why."

Jake frowned at the screen in front of him. First, he needed to stop the roll. But before he did that, was he going to collide with anything?

"What's in front of us?"

"There is a group of asteroids ahead. We may impact them, we may not. Unsure. Details on your pilot's console," Riley said.

Jake looked at his console. Should he change course? How far away were they from the asteroids? Not that far. But the roll kept increasing—if he didn't fix it soon, centrifugal force would pin them in their seats. Nonetheless, firing the thrusters would complicate things for engineering. What should he do? He had to do something.

"Firing thrusters two and five." Jake toggled the power. The roll stopped increasing, slowed, stopped, then reversed. Too fast. He dropped the power of the thrusters until the roll was barely decreasing. Time enough to fix it later.

Now, to fix the pitch. He fired a combo of thrusters again, which lessened the pitching. He spun the ship so that it pointed in the direction of travel, rolling slowly and with a bit of yaw. Now, get out of the way of the inbound asteroids, or deal with the fire.

"Main engine?" Jake asked.

"Still offline. No response from engineering on repairs," Riley said. "Fire in engineering increasing. It may damage lock integrity. Should I vent the atmo?"

"How many crew are back there?"

"Several. They report being trapped behind the fire."

"Are they in skinsuits?"

"Not all of them."

The collision alarm bonged again. They were headed straight for the asteroids, and their ship rolled slowly in a full circle perhaps once every twenty seconds.

The fuel button lit on his screen. Jake smelled hot plastic. Then he saw smoke. Crap.

What now, Jake Stewart?

No main engine. The fuel leaking from the damage acted

like an extra maneuvering thruster, pushing the ship off-course. But in what direction? Out of danger or into it?

The collision gong bonged again.

"Time to impact?"

"Computer says two minutes on this course," Riley said. "Engineering fire is still out of control." Sweat was starting to run down her face, and her long red hair had become unscrewed from her bun.

"Right. Firing four and five," Jake said, stabbing the thruster controls. Four stopped the roll. Five stopped the yaw. They were now floating dead in space. He eyed the fuel gauge. They were burning fuel holding this aspect. Jake waited.

They were thrusting backward.

Backward didn't matter. What mattered was that they'd generated a vector at a right angle to their current course. Now they should miss the upcoming asteroids. He touched the yaw controls so that the ship spun a bit. Now, the leaking fuel was propelling them sideways.

"How long to impact?"

"One minute. The fire in engineering is spreading. We need to vent atmo."

Jake looked at her. "We'll kill them all back there."

"If thruster control goes, we'll lose the whole ship," Riley said. The cabin reeked of hot plastic. The collision alarm bonged again. The smoke thickened. Jake could see it. He coughed and wiped sweat off his face.

The fuel light started flashing faster. Jake killed the thruster that canceled the roll. Without the offsetting counter-thruster, the leaking fuel rolled them faster and faster. Jake felt himself slide to the side of his seat as the roll increased. It was approaching a 2-g roll. He wanted to stop it, but he needed the fuel to spill out to give him the necessary variance in their course to avoid crashing into an asteroid. The vector generated by the leaking fuel was the only thing stopping them from crashing into a rock.

"Thirty seconds to impact."

"Will we clear it?"

"Not yet. A few more seconds of side thrust."

Jake slid into one side of his chair and felt himself straining against the straps that secured him to his seat. Their spin passed 3 g's and was on its way to 4. Jake felt himself pressed into the corner of his seat. He loaded up the roll and began typing a series of commands onto the screen, but he kept his hands away from the execute button.

"Fifteen seconds to impact...."

"Will we clear?" Jake said, glancing to the side.

"Uncertain," Riley said. She sounded cool and relaxed, but her face was plastered with sweat. "It will be close. We'll know shortly."

Jake felt the urge to be afraid, but had no time for that. He had a splitting headache, his knees hurt from being crammed together, and he could barely move his hands. His vision began to go. He pushed his arm out toward the thruster control on the console in front of him. He couldn't quite reach it. He strained as hard as he could. The roll was still increasing and would soon hit 5 g's, at which point he wouldn't be able to move at all. Again, he stretched out his arm, and this time, Jake felt his hand reach the console. He tried to pulse his finger up and down on the thrusters, but he couldn't. His finger was locked on the screen. He needed to stop the roll.

His vision was rimmed with black. It was like he was looking down a tunnel that was darkening. He couldn't see his hands at all, just what was in front of him. With a convulsive heave, he threw his hands up as high as he could and let them flop back down. As high as he could was probably a quarter inch, but it was enough. One of his fingers hit the 'engage' button on its descent.

The pre-programmed counter-roll thruster fired at full throttle. The rolling stopped increasing and then began to slow. Jake had programmed it to dump maximum thrust out right from the start. He needed that roll to be canceled.

"The fire has reached the fuel lines, next to the damaged airlock," Riley said. "It will—"

BANG.

Jake felt a whoosh as air and smoke began to stream out of the cabin. The explosion must have blown the airlock open, and the ship was venting. In thirty seconds he would pass out from lack of oxygen. Jake tried to reach up to close his helmet, but the g-force was too strong. The roll was increasing again. He pushed the thruster button, but nothing happened. He realized the control runs must be severed.

I wonder which will knock me out first, Jake thought. The increasing g-spin or the lack of air.

He was still pondering this when he passed out.

"Simulation ended," the lieutenant announced after the blowers removed the smoke and the room stopped spinning. "Everybody back to the classroom."

The sixteen students in TGI pilot training returned to their assigned seats and then reviewed the results of each simulation as a class.

Just under half of the students had died nobly—not quite managing to get things together before impacting the asteroids—distracted by the fires they were fighting or while fixing something else. Most of the others had missed the asteroids, but they had either passed out due to the increasing roll or when the smoke or oxygen deprivation got them. Four of the students, not including Jake, had solved all the problems and finished with a functioning, not-on-fire spaceship at the end of the test.

"So, some of you need to practice more, obviously. Those that crashed out, pay attention to the decisions others made. Especially in the rings, your course can get you in trouble pretty quickly. Oxygen is a problem as well, but most of the crew usually wear a skinsuit in flight, and they can survive without room O for a quite a while. And fire is bad. But easy to fix—no oxygen, no fire."

Everybody got up and trooped out of the classroom. Jake paused to collect his comm. He dawdled a bit, shuffling things. There were five women in the class. At least four were about his age, and he planned to involve some of them in his new 'Jake-needs-a-girlfriend' project. He had already ascertained that two of them were married, and the other two were not. One of the two unmarried girls was his cockpit partner, Riley. The other was Chantelle, a tall brown-haired girl in braids. He slipped between them as they walked out.

Chantelle stomped toward the door.

"How did you do?" Jake asked.

"Screwed the pooch. Hugely. Total canine copulation."

"Oh." Jake didn't know what to say to that.

"I spent too much time on the fire, fired the thrusters in reverse order, and passed out with the g-forces. Impacted the asteroids like a comet."

"Sorry."

"They said the largest piece of me would have fit in a bucket. I'm so angry with myself. I feel like hitting somebody." She narrowed her eyes and looked Jake up and down, as though she was measuring him for a beating. "I'll go and beat up a punching bag for a while. That will make me feel better. And it doesn't matter that much to me."

"It doesn't?" Jake asked.

"No, I'm in security. Pilot was for secondary training. As long as I'm willing to hit people, I'll still have a job. What about you?"

"Crashed. Burned."

"This is your second simulation, isn't it?"

"Third."

"So, you failed?"

"Probably."

"You work for one of those orbitals—TGI, isn't it?"

"Yes."

"That's not good. Lose your job then?"

"Maybe. I'm not sure."

"I'm sure you'll figure it out," Chantelle said. She stomped off.

Jake turned his head. "Riley, can I ask you a question?"

Riley had stopped at the side of the corridor and was looking into a viewport. She reached into her pocket and produced a hair elastic with a jewel in the center, then unwound her hair bun and rolled it into the elastic. She patted it down and examined her reflection in the viewport.

"Sure," she said.

"How did you fix everything without venting the compartment?"

"Oh, I did vent the compartment. I did it right away. But I wanted to make sure the fire was out, so I kept it vented for five minutes."

"Wouldn't that kill everybody?"

"Sure, but the ship would have been safe. Besides, that's why you wear skinsuits and keep your helmet with you."

Jake took a good look at her. Like him, she wore a practical skinsuit. It had fittings for hard gloves and boots, a collar for a helmet, and an emergency pack with a collapsible helmet strapped to her shoulder. She wouldn't be hurt in a blowout.

Unlike Jake's, Riley's skinsuit had tailored coveralls with an elaborate FREE TRADER patch over it. She sported patterned slippers, and a green scarf and matching headband. With that getup she wouldn't be out of place at a party.

"Seems a little ... harsh, don't you think?" Jake said.

"It is. But that's life in a small ship."

"You have a ship?"

"My family."

"That's interesting. Maybe I can buy you a beer sometime, and you can tell me about it." Riley looked at Jake, then gave his outfit the once-over, noticing the scuffed hard suit Jake wore. She frowned, and shook her head. "Maybe not today. My dad is waiting to drop as soon as I get back. Ships in dock aren't making money. Free trades, Jake."

"Free trades," Jake said as she walked away.

He sighed. Well, that didn't work. As usual. And now he had to tell his boss that he had failed his exam.

Chapter 2

The monorail station waiting room was still on fire when Salvatore Mascellon arrived for the council meeting. He had stopped outside the office container on the square. He shook his head.

"Henk," Sal yelled through the door. "What are you doing about this?"

A short bald man appeared. "About what? The station?"

"Yes, Henk. Emperor's balls. The station is still on fire. Why aren't we putting it out?"

"We don't have enough water."

Sal turned around and looked at the other side of the square. Beyond a single row of office containers, a concrete bank ran down to a huge reservoir filled with water. He turned back to Henk and jerked a thumb over his shoulder.

"What's that over there? Ice cream?"

"I meant pressure. We don't have enough water pressure for three hoses. Sorry, I've been up all night." Henk wiped his face, and his hand came away smeared with ash. He was covered with gray grit. "The pump isn't powerful enough."

"Sorry, I'm tired too," Sal said. "And I shouldn't shout at you. You're the emergency coordinator, and you're doing a damn fine job of it."

"Thanks. That's praise I could have done without."

"Henk, where are the kids?"

"What kids?"

"The ones that started the riot. The ones that started the fire. The ones that I have to do something about."

"I don't know what you are talking about," Henk said.

"I left them chained to a heating pipe in the council office. They're gone now."

"Oh, those kids. My fire crew clipped the chains. We were worried that the fire might spread and they would be caught in it."

"Henk, the fire wasn't anywhere close to the council room."

Henk shrugged. They both turned to look as a 'pop' sounded from the train station, and a group of sparks shot up into the air. The smoke puffed briefly, and then settled down. Henk sniffed the air. "Doesn't smell as bad as it did before. More like burned wood than stinking plastic."

Sal slumped against the door. "Where are the kids?"

"GG security wants to shoot those kids, Sal," Henk said.

"I'd like to myself, especially Ross's eldest boy. I've never met a kid more in need of an ass-kicking than him."

"Sal, I'm not kidding. And I'm not being figurative either. If we hand them over to their security department, they might not come back." Henk rubbed both hands on his face. They came away covered with gray ash. He began to wipe his palms on his coveralls. "We can't let GG shoot them, Sal. They were bored and angry."

"I'm bored and angry, Henk. But I didn't set fire to the company store."

"It was an accident. They're angry about the pay cuts, and the store price increases. They weren't trying to burn the place down. It was an electrical short."

"An electrical short after they ripped the cooler from the wall," Sal said.

"It was just a bunch of kids being kids," Henk said.

"It was a riot. GG wants prisoners. And they won't re-build until we pay for the whole store we burned down." Sal pointed at a group of smoldering containers up the road.

"We don't need GG. We can open our own store," Henk said. His voice had gotten louder.

"Not while they own the monorail, we can't."

"We'll take our business to the other corps."

"I'm sure they will be happy to take on mighty Galactic Growing over perceived unfairness to tiny Land and Ocean Enterprises." Sal sat down and leaned against the wall. Henk sat down beside him. They watched the station burn.

"What are you going to do?" Henk asked.

"What do you suggest?"

"I'm not suggesting anything. I'm the emergency coordinator. You're the council chair. Negotiate. Pay them off."

"With what? Buttons? My hidden stash of inter-company credit tokens?"

"You'll figure it out, Sal. Everybody trusts you to do the right thing."

"Gee, thanks. Just what I need—more pressure." Something popped from the waiting room, and flames roared up. Sal watched a piece of burning paper rise up on the hot air, then it drifted down to land in the square in front of them.

"What's our status then?" asked Sal.

"No injuries at all, luckily. No serious damage to the plant production lines. We've got both water lines hosing down the warehouse annex. It burned. There was paint in there, so everything burned hot, and it's still smoldering. The smoke is toxic. I'm worried that it might flare up, and if the wind changes and the smoke gets into the plant...."

"Right. The production line will fail quality checks. No sales for us."

Henk nodded. "I made an executive decision. That waiting room is isolated, so it can burn. It's just an empty container. We have lots of those. But there is more bad news. Production isn't affected, but we lost two containers of ready-to-go food trays, and one of shop supplies."

"What type of shop supplies?"

"Shari says supplies we need for maintenance."

Sal rubbed his head. "Shari would know. We can defer maintenance. Again. But we need to get production back on-line. How long till we can restart the plant?"

"A month."

"A month? We can't wait a week. We need the money. You have to get it up and working now. Why a month?"

"Maybe sooner. But we'll have to do a structural survey to see if the heat damaged any of the frames."

"And if it did?"

Henk shrugged again.

Sal shook his head, stood up, and turned toward the door. "I have a meeting to chair. Where are the kids now?" he asked.

"You think I'd tell you?"

"Your sister is married to my cousin. If she won't tell me, somebody else will," Sal said. "Where are they?"

"The youngest ones I sent home. I've got the rest down at the fish plant."

"The fish plant?"

"We don't have a jail, Sal. Where else would I put them?"

"You can't leave them there. GG security will be here sometime, possibly on the next train. They'll take them."

"Take them? Won't you stop them?"

"Officially, I have five shotguns and ten revolvers in the council armory. They'll send fifty."

"I could probably find a hundred people with shotguns in town."

"So then they'll send two hundred, with Gauss rifles."

Another 'pop' sounded, and they looked back at the burning station.

"So you're going to let them go?"

"Have you heard from your second cousin—whatshis-name—the one who took that contract in landing?"

"Nizeen? Yes, but what does that have to do with these kids?"

"How's his new job—the orbital one?"

"He complains, but he was always a wimp. He gets paid for a change."

"That guy who set up that contract, can you call him?"

"Why?"

"Those kids can't hide here. GG will find them. They need to leave. To disappear. Fast. Now, I have to go into a teleconference with Don Ortega and haggle about how much a company store and its goods are worth. And find somebody who wants to buy some food."

Chapter 3

"I hear they're all going to stop passenger service to the end stations," the thin man said as he waited across the street from the monorail station. He wore utilitarian office clothes: gray pants, white shirt, long charcoal jacket, with Galactic Growing sub-contractor colors.

The second man was taller than him. He wore a blue trench-coat-style jacket, buttoned up to the collar, without flashes. He turned to look at the thin man, but didn't say anything.

"The magnets on the cars are starting to wear out. Oxidizing or something chemical. So they all want to reduce the load on the trains and take them apart for parts. They will still let cargo down," the thin man said. He pulled an apple out of a pocket and took a bite of it.

The tall man didn't respond.

"How long does the air in a sealed container last?" asked the thin man, chewing on his apple.

"What?"

"It's not the oxygen, right? It's the buildup of CO2 that kills you, I think."

"What does that have to do with anything?"

"Aren't you in the Militia?" the thin man asked.

"Yes," said the tall man. He turned to face the station door as the train halted.

"So, you know about spaceships and air and oxygen. How long till ya run out of air in a space cutter?"

"I don't know."

"I thought you Militia guys all went out and did orbital inspections and rescued lost ships, and stuff like that."

"Not me. I work in water scheduling."

"You schedule water? How do you schedule water?"

"We pump H and water into the orbital shuttles. They use it for fuel and reaction mass after they are boosted off the mass driver. We want them to arrive in orbit with just enough to dock."

"Don't the computers do that?"

"Yes. But I handle other things as well." The Militia man removed his comm from his pocket and checked the time, then resumed watching the station.

"Right. The recruits. You have the tickets?"

"All of them. You have the money?"

"One hundred credits for each ticket. Will there be any problems with these 'recruits' not showing up at the recruiting depot?"

"Some recruits sign up and then chicken out at the last minute. It happens."

The thin man stopped eating his apple. "Chicken out?"

"Don't show up," the Militia man said.

"I've never seen a chicken, except in vids. What's a chicken have to do with showing up?"

"No idea. Just an Old Empire expression. It means that they don't show up. But nobody cares."

"Good," the thin man said. He went back to eating his apple.

"What are they going to do?" the Militia man asked.

"Work in one of the stations. And you never answered my question."

"What question?"

"About that talk of shutting down the monorail."

"I don't know anything about that. The Militia doesn't have any ground-side presence other than the launcher. Ground operations are you guys and your corporate buddies."

"Not my buddies. I just work for Don Ortega. For GG. Food for the masses."

"I've eaten your trays," said the Militia man. He grimaced. "They taste horrible. Why is everything potatoes?"

"Best caloric density per hectare," the thin man said.

"What in the Emperor's name is caloric density?"

"If you plant a hectare of wheat, your yield should be, I don't know … eight million calories' worth of food. With potatoes you get sixteen million calories or thereabouts. If calories are all you are worried about, potatoes are your best bet. Potatoes are efficient. And they even have all the essential amino acids. Just mix in some insect-generated protein and you have the perfect food."

The Militia man gave him a puzzled look. The thin man

smiled and shrugged. "I took a year at the university. Agricultural science."

"But why just potatoes? Why not a little variety?" the Militia man asked.

"The corps who built the colony wanted lots of cheap food for passing ships. For rice and wheat, you need seeds, special harvesting gear, more people, and for rice, lots of water for irrigation. We're not set up for it. Potatoes are easy to plant and harvest. Harvest is easy to mechanize. They tolerate the cold temperatures and the rain. We'd have to remodel the operation if we decided to use rice or wheat. Irrigation. Fertilizers."

"I get bored of potatoes," said the Militia man.

"I hear you. At the university, they have a test farm. They grow all sorts of stuff, for research. I had rye bread once when I was studying there. It was the best food I ever tasted. I wanted to plant it on the ranch, but the family nixed it. 'Not enough market,' they said. 'We can barely feed the workers we have. We need to get rid of some of them.'"

"Get rid of them?"

"We released 'em and sent them to Landing. They can get jobs in orbit. Or something."

A train finally appeared, and the two watched it slide silently into the station.

"How will you get your workers to Landing without the monorail, if it all goes to cargo?" the Militia man said, watching the station door.

"We treat 'em like food trays. Put the workers in a cargo

container. Seal them in. They'll go directly to the launch pad for orbital jobs."

"It's 5 g's during liftoff. People will get crushed. And even if you put food in there, there isn't a bathroom."

"Not my problem. They put in temporary nets or something. They want the work, give 'em work."

"Do you tell them the conditions?"

"Feel free to tell them yourself, if you think it's important."

A stream of people began exiting the station and proceeded down the connecting streets. Many had packages under their arms. Probably food. Many city dwellers took a day trip to the country to buy black-market food trays. A group of about twelve young men had stopped outside the station's entrance and huddled around a man in office garb. They were dressed as farm workers—gray coveralls, green boots, heavy jackets, and gloves. The office-garbed man curtly addressed them. Some of them stood still, and others leaned against the station wall. They all seemed tired, but most looked around with interest. Moments later, a booming noise filled the square. They all stood up, trying to locate where the sound was coming from. One of them yelled as a shuttle rocketed overhead. The nose of the shuttle began to glow red as the air compressed in front of it heated up.

The tall Militia man hadn't bothered to look up at the sonic boom. "Not exactly sophisticated city people, are they?" he said.

The thin man shrugged and sauntered across the square to speak to his colleague. They conferred for a moment, and the thin man returned.

"Thirteen one-way tickets, one two-way," he said, producing five large credit tokens.

"Wait one," the Militia man said. He checked the credit tokens one after the other. "This one is GG credits. We need inter-company ones."

"I don't have any," the thin man said. "That's all I was given."

The Militia man shrugged and extended his hand with the credit tokens. "Sorry. No can do."

They stared at each other for a moment, then the thin man reached into a pocket and produced a different token. "One-third inter-company, the rest GG."

"OK. But you are buying round-trip tickets for everybody."

The thin man shrugged. "Fine, here," he said, offering him a different token.

The Militia man collected the token and examined it. "I'll have to call this one in. Stand by." He put the new token in his comm and punched some buttons, then waited. It took almost thirty seconds before his comm beeped and flashed green.

"Close enough for government work." He reached into his pocket for a different token and inserted it into his comm. Then he punched a few settings and handed it back.

The thin man checked it and nodded. "Pleasure doing business with you. See ya in a month." He turned and walked away.

"Wait," said the Militia man. He had opened his trench coat, revealing his Militia captain's uniform and the revolver tucked away in the holster by his belt. His hand was on the revolver. "You have some numbers for me."

"I almost forgot to give them to ya."

"Forgetting would be bad."

"What if I give ya the wrong numbers by mistake?"

"That would be worse than forgetting."

The thin man smiled. "Says you. Here's your numbers." He checked his comm and read off a string of six different eight-digit numbers. The Militia man typed them into his own comm and read them back.

"That's it. Free trades," said the thin man.

"The Emperor will return," said the Militia man, turning and walking away.

"So will spring. Every thirty days." The thin GG man strode toward the station and the group of young men. He handed the ticket token to the office man, then he disappeared inside the monorail station. The escort turned and spoke to his crew. It was loud enough to be heard across the square. "Guess what, everybody—now you get to go into space! Here's what is going to happen."

The Militia man straightened his uniform as he walked back toward the shuttle dock. There was a group of youths lounging on a street corner ahead.

"Need directions to the shuttle, sir? A guide, perhaps?" said one.

He didn't make eye contact but did glance at their collars. Mostly mixed dark and light green, but at least one girl had yellow collar flashes. Not good. He carried on.

"Help looking for something, sir? Want to buy something to relax you?" another youth said.

"He's Militia," said a woman's voice behind him. He glanced down and cursed. He had forgotten to close his jacket. His captain's uniform was visible. He heard a general stirring but didn't look back or change his pace. He needed to get off the main street.

To his right were actual buildings made of concrete. He angled across and ducked underneath an arcade separated from the street by a line of pillars. He kept his tread steady but turned into the first street.

As soon as he rounded the corner, he broke into a run. He swerved left off the regular route toward the shuttle station, and pounded down an alley between two blank-faced warehouses into a service alley.

"Come on! Let's get him," echoed behind him.

At the end of the alley, he turned left and followed four black pipes that ran along the ground. After another block, another four merged in from the right, and the whole mess intersected a mass of valves and wheels on a larger pipe. He climbed up an inspection ladder until he was almost two meters off the ground, and boosted himself onto the top of the largest pipe then began to run along it.

"He's on the steam pipes. Get him." The words sounded behind him.

"Run around the side and catch him before he's through the berm. We'll never catch him in the shanties!" shouted a different voice.

He emerged from the buildings and could now see a field

of containers. The pipe ran along the top of them and into the distance.

A shape ran in from the side, between two containers with stick figures painted on them. Schoolchildren scattered as she ran to the pipe and began to climb it. The Militia man maintained his pace and kicked her as he ran by. She dropped to the ground with a yelp.

He continued sprinting along the pipe and passed an earthen berm that marked the end of the regular town. Past the berm, he hopped off the pipe and onto the top of a container. He cut left and jumped from one container to another, then to another—but landed on a blue awning instead.

He rolled off the awning and crashed onto a table, knocking over a frothy beer. He kept rolling and hit a bench, then flopped onto the ground. A waiter with a tray of beer stood frozen. Other patrons stared at him.

He rolled to his feet and ducked left before anybody could do anything. He ran under a blue tarp between two containers and knocked over a pile of used clothes. Shouts sounded behind him, but he ignored them.

Around the next corner was a pile of steel beams. He ran up to the top of the pile and down the far side. He ducked around another corner and ran down a long row of crushed and cracked containers. A campus of buildings rose up behind a metal fence at the far end of the road, along with a steam plant and a very large fusion power plant. Large cables ran out the side of the building and into buried conduits. Even larger cables ran to the monorail switching yard that stretched next to the building.

He slowed down and began to walk, breathing heavily. Almost there.

A young man and a young woman stepped around the corner of a battered container several meters ahead of him. They wore standard corporate coveralls, except there were no corporate color flashes on the collar and breast. He had a wooden club of some sort, while she had something else in her hands.

"Hey, mister," the man said. "You ran away before we could negotiate a passage fee." He brandished his club threateningly, and the women extended her weapon.

"The Emperor's scrotum," the Militia man said. "Is that a sword?"

"Doesn't matter," the man said. "Makes no difference to your passage fee. I'm thinking … a hundred credits? Payable now."

"Where in the Eternal Empire's name did you get a sword?" the Militia man asked the woman.

"Technically, it's not a sword," the woman said. She swung it from side to side.

"What?" the Militia man said.

"Only one side is sharpened. Swords have both sides sharpened, and swords are longer," she said.

Both men stared at her. The Militia man raised his eyebrows.

"It's a cutlass. An Imperial Marine boarding cutlass," she said. They still didn't say anything. "What? I looked it up on the net. They used it on ships. Works in all atmospheres and in a vacuum. Very low maintenance. Wouldn't damage the hull or equipment. Just people."

Her companion shook his head. "Thanks for the history lesson, Pak. Now, how about you empty your pockets there, buddy."

"Sure," said the Militia man. He reached under his jacket, drew the revolver and pointed it at the woman. "Let's start with this. I call this a gun, but I guess you'd call it a shipboard officer's revolver. Uses chemical propulsion to fire a bullet. Works in all atmospheres and in a vacuum. Low maintenance, won't damage hull or equipment. Just people." He swiveled the gun to point at the man. "You two look like people to me."

They stepped back and the weapons wavered, but then the man raised his club.

"There's two of us. You can't shoot us both," he said. He started to edge forward.

"Maybe not, but by the Emperor's royal anus I can surely shoot you first. And I don't think your friend there can finish the job by herself."

The two wavered again. "Pak, run and get the others," the man said.

"Blaze, he'll shoot you as soon as I go."

"Not true," the Militia man said. "I don't need to wait for you to leave to shoot him. I can do it anytime. I can shoot him and be gone before you get back with your friends."

"Blaze, let's go. We can't do it," she said.

"Stop your whining, girl. Don't tell me what to do," the man said. He began to advance.

The Militia man pulled the hammer back with a click.

"This isn't a game, kids. We're not on the net here. If I shoot you, it's real."

The man looked at the gun, wavered, then shrugged. "Guess it's your lucky day, mister. We don't need no more money today, so we'll let you go, rather than call our friends."

"Yeah," the woman said.

They retreated back down the alley. Before disappearing, the man turned around and extended his middle finger. The Militia man followed their progress with the gun still aimed at them, and when they were out of sight, he slowly walked forward, pointing the gun down the alley they had escaped to. He couldn't see anybody.

"Well," he said, and lowered the gun. His hands were trembling. He changed his grip and flipped the cylinder out of the revolver. It was empty. "Well," he said again, then loaded the gun and returned it to his holster.

Chapter 4

It took the Militia captain three tries to unlock the door labeled 'MASS DRIVER ORBITAL OPERATIONS.' His hands were shaking badly. He took several deep breaths before he went inside. After the door, he climbed three flights of metal stairs and entered a control room. A pudgy lieutenant sat at a console in front of a dozen screens and as many camera views. "How did it go?" the lieutenant asked.

"I made them buy round-trip tickets," said the captain.

"I'll bet they aren't happy with that."

"I don't really care if they are happy or not. Do you know the difference between a sword and a cutlass?"

"Sure. A cutlass is usually curved, and it's sharpened only on one side. Swords are sharpened on both sides."

"How in the Emperor's name do you know that?"

"Haven't you ever played *Sword and Sorcery* on the net?"

"Not enough, apparently."

"Why do you want to know that?"

"Never mind. Here." He flipped a credit chip toward the lieutenant, who glanced at it and put it in his pocket.

"Thanks, commander, oh wait— Thanks, captain. I didn't say congrats on your promotion."

"Thanks."

"Captain now, huh. That's great. I bet that cost a bunch."

"It did. I'll be paying that loan back for years."

"Loan. Oh, it was one of those deals."

"I suppose. I want you to find this container," the captain said. He read out one of the eight-digit numbers he had. The lieutenant typed the numbers into his console.

"It's just come in on the monorail." He punched some buttons, and a camera view highlighted a recently arrived maglev train. It contained perhaps thirty containers on flatcars. "It's set for TGI Main transfer orbit. The next window is in thirteen minutes. And after that, the next one is twenty-seven hours."

"Can you put it in the next window?"

"Sure. Watch." The lieutenant typed rapidly. On the screen, a robotic crane rolled over the monorail, dropped four locking arms, and snatched the container upward, then backed up till it was clear. Afterward, it slid down the end of the yard, then rolled forward and dropped the container on a different train. The train had slightly different flatcars, a little more aerodynamic ones.

"I've never seen this done before," the captain said. "What happens next?"

"We attach the launch cones on them," the lieutenant said.

"The mass driver launches them, they pass near the stations, and their tugs pick them up."

"Yeah, I want that not to happen."

There was silence for a moment. The lieutenant glanced at the captain. "Look, I did that once before, and I told you it was a one-time thing."

"Well, it's a *multi-time* thing now."

"Look, taking some money off stupid kids who want some orbital adventure is one thing. Sabotaging critical shipments is different. I won't do it."

"That's an order. This is Militia business."

"Screw your Militia business. I'm not career. I'm only here on loan for a year."

"I'll court-martial you."

"Which means that I'll get kicked out, and then I go back to my happy place, running a cargo deck at my station. And I'll never have to do this stupid duty again, ever. Try again."

"Or I can let this go and then tell the Officers' Council. They can take care of the matter, unofficially."

The lieutenant grimaced.

"Why do you care, anyway?" the captain said. "Your folks are no friends to TGI."

"We're no enemies either."

"They won't find out. And if they do, they'll blame the regular Militia, not some obscure short-timer."

"What do I tell my corporate people?"

"Tell them that you didn't want to fight the Officers' Council. Tell them that you were just following orders. Tell them it was none of your business. Tell them you had a hangover and felt mean. Or don't tell them anything."

The captain walked over to the window and looked outside. "Of course, you'll be compensated for your work. What we paid you for hiding those kids' records? We'll do that again. Every time. From now on."

The lieutenant looked at his screen. "I hate this job," he said. He looked up at the captain. "Do you know how my station picks who fills the Militia slot each year?"

"No. Tests?"

"We cut cards for it."

"And you won?"

"I lost. From now on, whenever I hide records, I want double what you paid me before."

"Okay," the captain said.

"And if I do a container for you, I want the same. In advance."

The captain reached into his pocket and pulled out a credit chip. "I've got that right here, with a little bonus for you."

The lieutenant took a deep breath, then he turned back to his screen. "Okay, hang on." He typed some more. "We need the new nose cones." The robotic crane on the screen moved off. A second robot rolled over to a pile of rounded metal cones. The cones were aerodynamic, with fittings on the back side that matched the container's. A set of four small canards extended back from the cone. The robot used four locking arms to select one, then it rolled back until it was above the special flatcar with the new container. It spun the nose cone ninety degrees and lowered it in front of the container.

"How are they special?"

"This cone isn't as strong. It deforms under launch pressure."

"So?"

"So, that doesn't matter on the mass driver launch, 'cause the train just takes more power to accelerate it up to speed. But once it's launched off the edge, the deformed nose cone slows it down. It doesn't go as fast, meaning it doesn't go as high, meaning it doesn't make transfer orbit."

The robot had maneuvered the spun cone in front of the container and pushed it firmly onto the front.

"And there it is," said the lieutenant. His display flashed green. "Train is ready to go."

"What happens now?"

"Computer takes over. You can see it out the window if you want to look." They both turned to look out the window. Nothing happened for a moment, then the loaded train began to move out of the yard, then it switched to the mainline. The train accelerated as they watched.

"Come on, the light's about to go. If we go up to the roof we can watch it launch," said the lieutenant.

"Is it okay to leave the boards empty?"

"You're the boss, what do you say?"

The captain shrugged and walked to the door. Outside the control room, they climbed two sets of stairs and then went through an exit, which took them to the building's roof. They walked around until they had a view of a mountain directly to the east. It was starting to get dark, so they couldn't see the train, just shadows on the mountain.

"There." The lieutenant pointed. A series of bright lights launched from the mountain and rose into the air. The captain tried to count them, but they were so close together.

"Thirty?"

"Should be forty-two. But we always lose some."

"Always?"

"A couple percent. Sometimes more."

"Losing one won't be suspicious."

"Nope. Happens all the time."

"Even for the shuttles?"

"We don't lose shuttles. Well, just that once. But shuttles have engines. They can adjust. Containers can't."

"What happens if the containers don't make orbit?"

"Burn up on re-entry over the south. I guess. We never go look for them."

"Good," said the captain. He reached for his comm.

Several hundred kilometers above, and about one-third of the way around Delta, a Militia tug loitered in orbit. There were two crews in the control room at the front. The commander of the ship, whose rank was actually commander, typed some notes into his screen. "Okay, it's on its way up," he said.

The pilot, a spaceman second class, looked at him. "Can you give me the orbital characteristics?"

"What?"

"When it launched, semi-major axis, eccentricity, all that sort of stuff?"

"Do you need that?"

The spaceman closed his eyes and shook his head. "What did you take at that fancy university again?"

"Finance. Which is why I'm a commander, and you're not."

"You are a commander because your family had the money to buy the slot, and I'm stuck with doing all the work because I didn't."

"I can do this myself."

"Go ahead," said the spaceman. He folded his arms. "I'm sure you are great at orbital rendezvous. Lots of classes in it at the university, huh?"

The commander stared at him for a while. "Fine. I *need* you to do it. Happy?"

"Not quite. Promotions are coming up."

"So, you want to be first class? Fine."

"Nope. I want to be a sergeant."

"I'm not sure I can manage that."

The pilot looked down at his folded arms, then back at the commander. "This isn't a standard maneuver, you know? We're not just picking up containers passing a station. And we have to do it right the first time because we can't be seen in this orbit when we swing round."

"Emperor's balls. Fine. With that sort of attitude, you'll make a great sergeant. Just pick it up."

The pilot smiled, then reached for the controls. The commander felt the tug pivot, and then start to fire backward in relation to the orbit.

"What are you doing now?"

"Relax, just dropping lower." The pilot switched screens

and turned on the radar. They watched a line of objects behind them approach and then overtake them. The pilot brought up the navigation screen to his right and began to type into it.

"Just need to drop between them…," he muttered. The commander said nothing.

The pilot pulsed the engines again, and the pursuing devices appeared to slow down.

"Are we speeding up?"

"Sort of. We're going lower, so we need to go faster. If I time this right … there."

The tug dropped below the line of pulses and then held there. They both watched the radar closely.

"Gotcha," the pilot said. He waited as the lower container sped toward them on the screen. It looked like it was going to overtake them, but the pilot pulsed the thrusters a few times, and they dropped toward the oncoming container.

"There." The pilot pointed. "Think you can work the box and grapples?"

"I can work the grapples," agreed the commander. He grimaced. "If you get us in close, and there's not too much velocity difference."

The pilot didn't respond. He kept his eyes fixated on the approaching container. It was tumbling slowly, and the nose cone appeared to have been shredded.

"Shouldn't you get out of its way?" asked the commander.

"Not yet … not yet…," the pilot said. He positioned the tug in the path of the tumbling container.

The commander looked out the viewport. "It's going to hit us. It's coming right at us."

"Not if I do this," the pilot said.

He pivoted the tug upward, exposing a large, gridded metal box just below the viewport. The container smashed into the steel frame, and the tug lurched backward with a thunk.

"Close the box. Now."

The commander had been waiting, and he punched a button on his screen. Powerful hydraulics swung heavy metal grids up from the bottom and the sides of the box, capturing the tumbling container and holding it.

"Done like dinner. Dinner for ten thousand."

Chapter 5

"We're in trouble, sir. We need to do something."

"Is that so, Jose," Dashi said.

Jose leaned toward the window and stared down toward the water a hundred meters below. The monorail was attached to the side of the cliff with brackets, but they didn't hinder the view. He turned back to Dashi.

"Inflation is way up. We're seeing sustained price inflation of over 10 percent per month. And adjusted food prices have risen another 30 percent in the last two months. Production is down across all companies according to my research," Jose said.

"Fertilizer," Dashi said.

"Yes, sir, I agree—we need more fertilizer," Jose said. "But Fourth Moon Chemicals isn't taking additional orders."

"Why not?"

"Shortages of phosphorus and potassium. Only one mine on the surface provides it, and production is declining."

"Orbital sources?"

"Two problems: We haven't had much success with our exploration, and second, we sell what we do find to them—that doesn't guarantee us more food. They use what they buy from us to meet other orders and don't provide us with more."

Dashi checked his tablet. "Turn on the heater, please, Jose," he said. Jose opened the vent on the wall.

Air conditioning was rarely necessary in this part of Delta. The moon orbited Sigma Draconis IV, otherwise known as 'the Dragon,' near the innermost part of the system's Goldilocks zone. Delta had almost no inclination relative to its orbital plane, but the Dragon often eclipsed the sunlight, so things stayed pretty cold—at least in the Northern Hemisphere where all the settlements were. Delta was about 30 percent water. Both poles were very mountainous and glaciated. A world ocean circled the base of the Northern Hemisphere. Cold deserts rimmed the south of the ocean. To the north, massive mountain ranges reached down to the water, pieced by giant river valleys that drained from the glaciers. Habitation existed in a few dozen fjord-like river valleys separated by sawtooth mountains. A single Old Empire monorail train line stretched east and west from the town of Landing.

Dashi smiled as the warm air started to hit him. "And if we stop selling it to them, we don't get any more food, and we forgo revenue that we would otherwise have. I see," he said.

The sun flashed off the green water as the passenger car swung around a curve, then the outside view went black as they ran through a tunnel for a few seconds. Now they were on the opposite side of the knife-ridged mountain, and the ocean to their left had been replaced by a sheer rock wall. The view to their right opened up, and they could see a long, narrow valley with a river down the middle, framed at the far end by giant snow-capped peaks. Herds of domesticated buffalo roamed up and down the valley, right up to where the bottomland gave way to steep hills and the cliffs.

Dashi looked out the window. "Good ranching land," he said. "Pastures and water. Just what you need for cattle."

Jose's boss, Mr. Dashi, was small, neat, and brown. What he did for TGI was somewhat nebulous, and his titles were innocuous, but he held real power. When he said come, they came. When he said go, they went.

"You know cattle, sir? I thought you grew up in orbit," Jose said.

"My grandfather had a ranch."

"How do they get the buffalo out for food processing?" Jose asked.

"They have to stop the main line and lift a container onto a flatcar. Very expensive and disruptive to the schedule."

"That explains why the meat is so expensive," Jose said.

They flashed out of a tunnel along another cliff. The valley river reached the sea here. Dashi pointed out the window. "There is a tidal bore. I have never seen one in person before," he said. A two-meter wall of water was thundering up the river as the rising tidal force overwhelmed the river flow to force its way up between the rock walls. The algae growth of the ocean made a thick, dark contrast to the clear, blue river water.

"That's moving fast. Faster than I could walk, sir," Jose remarked.

"Faster than you could run, Jose," Dashi said. "There are about twenty deaths every year from people who venture too far out during low tide and can't get back to safety when the tide turns."

Jose contemplated the water. "Planets are dangerous."

"Danger is everywhere. What's happening with our food shipments to orbit?"

"Loss rate from the mass driver is up, but only very slightly. It's 1.2 percent rather than 1.1 percent. However, losses are concentrated in containers for us, and mostly food trays. Sir, I believe the Militia is stealing our food containers."

"Yes, yes they are," Dashi said, examining something on his tablet. Jose waited, but Dashi didn't say any more.

"Yes? That's all you have to say, sir—yes?"

"Yes, they are stealing our food."

"Sir, we need to do something."

"What is our food status?"

"As I said before, we're in trouble, sir. We do have supplies of basic. Tons of the mixing powder. But operations on two stations had to break into their emergency reserves of trays."

"How much of a problem is that?"

"They have ninety days' worth of reserves normally, sir," Jose said. "They can hold for now, provided we can get future shipments into those stations."

"Good. Let them hold."

"Should we confront the Militia?"

"How? Where? Do we have proof that they have taken anything?"

"Not proof per se, sir, but a strong suspicion."

"'Per se'?"

"Sorry, sir, I saw that while reading some of those books you recommended."

Dashi looked up from his tablet. "How do you find them?"

"*The Prince* is my favorite so far, sir."

"Mine too," Dashi agreed.

Jose took a deep breath. "Sir, I purchased several dozen containers of trays on the market. I had to pay a massive premium, but we'll be able to keep everybody fed and replenish our reserves. I've also contracted extra shipping to carry it where necessary."

Dashi looked up. "You did it without asking me?"

"Yes, sir. I did."

"Why?"

"We needed the food, sir. And you, well, sir—"

"Yes?"

Jose took a deep breath. "Sir, you are not paying attention to things. Small things, I mean. I know that you have many important things to keep track of, sir, but you are missing some of the smaller things, like this food issue. The details. There is too much going on."

"There are a lot of things that are going on right now, Jose. Important events."

"I agree, sir. But these other decisions need to be made. And you haven't been making them. Somebody needs to."

Dashi usually smiled. Dashi never got upset. He just smiled different smiles. But for the first time ever, Dashi was frowning. This was an expression Jose had never seen on his boss's face. It made Dashi look dangerous.

"To summarize, Jose, you think I am missing things. That I am not doing my job properly. Are you trying to do my job for me, Jose?"

"Sir, I—" Jose swallowed. "Yes, sir, I am. Part of it."

Dashi nodded. The smile came back. "Good. Carry on, you can take care of those details from now on."

"I'm sorry, sir, but I— wait what?"

Dashi grinned. "Don't apologize. That's your job now. If you see something I've missed, fix it. So, we're in good shape for now."

"Yes sir."

"Provided our ongoing shipments continue to arrive."

"Yes sir. I've cleared warehouse space for the containers coming in. I'm aiming for six months of supplies."

"Sounds like you have the current situation under control."

Jose was silent. Mr. Dashi looked out the windows. Small valleys and rivers flashed by the monorail. At one point, they passed over a large hydro dam that impounded a river. Snow-covered mountains ranged to the north, open sea to the south. The land curved and the track turned southwards. They spun around a final headland as they reached the valley containing Point 37. The setting planet burst out in front of them, framed on the horizon between two valley walls. The estuary had widened, and a series of fishing boats could be seen bobbing up and down on the water. A very long lake fell ten meters over a rock ledge to splash into the ocean below. The ocean swell flooded up and down against the rocks. Buildings were visible at the up-valley end of the lake.

"Where do the boats dock?" Jose asked. "How do they get into the harbor?"

"The tide range is about thirty meters here. The sea rises up until it floods over that waterfall. Then the boats have about a half hour to get up into the river on the flood tide, into that giant lake. They dock at the processing plant at the end. They stay tied up for a tidal cycle then race out on the next falling tide. They can only get in and out during those times."

"That sounds difficult," Jose said.

"It is. The boats aren't corporate. They are personally owned, and the crews are usually family."

"Rough life."

"Yes. But they make good money on the wild fish. Some people think it's tastier than the farm-grown ones."

"Do you like it, sir?"

Dashi shrugged. He didn't like any type of fish. "It's certainly tastier than algae." He stood up. "Jose, switch seats with me, please."

"Sir." Jose got up. Mr. Dashi had barely noticed the scenery before. Jose had enjoyed the window seat the entire trip. Why did he want to change now?

"Do you have a geo-compass on your comm, Jose?"

"Yes sir, that is, if I have satellite service at this time of day."

"One of them is overhead right now. Start a track, please, and log it. As much precision as you can." Mr. Dashi pointed his comm out the window across the valley and watched it closely.

Jose did as directed. For the next few kilometers, they traveled due west, with no deviation at all, as far as the precision on Jose's comm could tell. Jose found himself being pushed back into his seat as the maglev accelerated on the long straight stretch.

"Due west, sir."

"Thank you."

"We're lucky that we have satellite coverage here today." Delta's satellite constellation was incomplete, reliably covering only the main city of Landing. Satellites were expensive, and the founding corporations hadn't seen the need for a mining colony to have a full set. Outside Landing, it was catch-as-catch-can. Ground-based repeaters provided public communication services for the monorail and attached settlements. Corporations could use private networks based on their orbital infrastructure, but they weren't optimal, and they didn't share.

Dashi smiled. "Do you think so, Jose?"

Jose smiled back. "You timed our trip for when there was satellite coverage, didn't you, sir?"

Dashi didn't answer. He smiled some more instead. "This lake is never less than two kilometers wide. Good." The monorail began to slow down.

"Sir, what do you want me to do when we get to Point 37?"

"See to our accommodations. Accompany me to the meetings. Ask questions of everybody about everything, and take note of the answers. Stay away from the senior people—hang out with the younger folks. Play the rube from the big city. I will be the senior executive with gravitas, and you will be the eager young assistant."

Dashi stood up and began to re-tie his neck scarf. He wore

a tailored business suit over a custom-fitted skinsuit. The skinsuit was not strictly necessary in atmosphere, but it could serve as extra warmth when the weather got cold. His wrist ruffles were subdued, but high quality.

"That's a very handsome scarf, sir," Jose said. "Those synthetics are so good. You would almost think they were real silk."

"Yes, one would almost think that," Dashi said with one of his patented smiles.

Emperor's balls, Jose thought. It must be real. That scarf cost more than the whole outfit. A lot more.

"Let's meet our potential new business associates," Dashi said, heading for the door.

They were climbing out of the train when Jose spoke again.

"Sir, what about the thefts?"

Dashi had reached the grab bar to swing onto the steps. He held on with one hand and turned to Jose.

"Ignore them," Dashi said.

"Sir, I don't understand how you can be so sanguine about this."

"The Militia is doing this to hurt us. Either on their own behalf, or on somebody else's. Who will gain if we lose?"

"Everybody needs food, sir. Us, the Militia, Castle Transport, all the other corps."

"Yes, but not all of them need it equally. Some produce their own, like Galactic Growing. And those with ground-to-orbit traffic, like the Militia, can be fed from Downport."

"We don't produce our own food, sir. Not yet, unless you buy a plant."

"Food is just the symptom. If it wasn't food, it would be something else. Rare earths. Hydrogen. Oxygen. We need all of those things. Some are available in orbit, and some are not. That's not the whole problem." Dashi stepped down onto the platform and began to walk toward the station's waiting room.

"What is the whole problem, sir?"

"Production, of course, but mostly transportation. We don't have secure methods of moving things from ground to orbit."

"The Militia has a monopoly on the shuttle, sir."

"Yes, but they can't operate without us. We provide them H and O in orbit, as well as a lot of metals, and quite a few of their rare earths."

"They can access other sources, sir."

"Not enough of them, Jose. Not enough of them. What's changed that they feel they can dispense with our cooperation at this time? Why now?"

Jose stepped into the waiting room and held the door for Dashi.

"You think they have other supplies, sir?"

"Absolutely. I'm not sure where, or how. The other corps can't make up the shortfall if we stop trading with them. The food is the key. Where is it going? Once we find the where, we'll know the why and the how. We need to find out where that food is."

"How do we do that, sir?"

"Exhaustive checks of records. Analysis of sales patterns. Checks of payments and balances. Computerized modeling of storage location fill rates. Boring, tiring, exhausting, under-appreciated drudge work."

Jose smiled. "I'll contact Jake Stewart right away, sir."

Chapter 6

"When will I be flying this?" Nadine said. She was a curvy blonde girl and wore a corporate office skinsuit and jacket in a muted charcoal-gray hue. If observing closely, one would note that the suit was custom-made, and the office jacket was some sort of expensive fabric—not silk, but some sort of industrial analog. The message had said to wait by herself in the bar, and she would be approached. She hadn't expected it to be the daily Militia courier. Nor that he would be so ugly.

"Soon. But we'll pay for you to go up to Orbital-16 right now. We'll pay you and put you on a regular short route out of there so that you are available when we need you. Probably a few weeks, maybe a month, then we'll send you out," the sweating Militia man said.

"What's the cargo, then?" Nadine asked.

"None of your business. You are being paid to fly a ship. Just drop it and don't ask questions," the Militia officer said. He shifted uncomfortably on his seat and tried to tuck his tunic back into his pants. His gut hung out over his belt, and the top buttons on his shirt stretched. The low gravity had caused his tissues to collect fluid, and he sat like a giant piece of steaming dough.

"Why me? You have your own pilots."

"We did. We do. But you have some unique skills."

"You did? As in you don't have it now? What happened?"

"Nothing. Never mind."

Nadine raised her eyebrows and looked at him. "What unique skills? You should tell me in case I forgot them."

"We are told you can fly a glider?"

"An unpowered glider? Like an aircraft, not a spacecraft?"

"Yes."

"I can do that."

The bartender arrived with a tray. He put a large plastic cup in front of the man, and a small shot glass in front of Nadine.

The Militia officer took a drink from the cup in front of him and immediately spat it back. "What is this?"

"It's reconstituted basic. Vitamins, nutrients, sugar, salt, all in one easy, mixable package. We use it on ships 'cause it lasts forever, and all you need is water. You can live on it for weeks."

"It tastes like rancid apple juice and motor oil had a baby."

"You don't see me drinking it."

"Where do you get the water?"

"Water is infinitely recyclable on a space station provided you have electricity. We just distill it out."

"You mean it comes from...?"

"Yeeeuup. That's why I drink vodka." She popped the shot. "Now tell me about the cargo."

"This is a need-to-know operation, and you don't need to know. That's good tradecraft; you should understand that."

"What I understand, you posturing idiot, is that you probably came direct from Militia HQ, so anybody who wanted to follow you would have no problem."

"I wasn't followed. I took precautions," he said, looking around.

"Don't look around, twithead. Look at me. You are supposed to be picking me up. Stare at my boobs or something."

The man reddened. "Sorry. I mean, yes— I mean, sorry." He stared at the bridge of her nose.

Nadine stretched her arms back, accentuating her bust. "There, that's for free. Did you have to wear your uniform?"

"Couriers always wear their uniform. I delivered the courier box to the station manager, and I'm staying overnight till the drop shuttle tomorrow. Standard procedure. I just went out for a drink in the bar, and I met a pretty girl, and we talked and went back to her room. I'll give you the nav chip there."

"Nobody will believe that."

"Why not?"

"Because you are a fat slob who is drinking crappy basic, and I'm a gorgeous blonde girl who drinks expensive vodka shots. Why wouldn't you at least order booze?"

The man looked down at his drink and mumbled.

"What?"

"I said, it's a religious thing."

"Oh no," Nadine said. "You're not one of those, are you?"

"I'm not ashamed. We swore a holy oath to the Emperor. We will uphold his laws until relieved. We are always on duty. We uphold the old truths."

"The old truths?"

"Honor and loyalty to the Empire."

Nadine shook her head. "We haven't heard from the Empire in eighty years. We need to go our own way, make up our own laws. And what does that have to do with no alcohol?"

"We have the imperial edicts from my grandfather's time. That's enough for any imperial officer. And we can't drink on duty. We are always on duty."

"You grandfather was *not* an imperial officer. At least not here. There was no base here. He was some sort of logistics person who bought processed algae for the fleet."

"He was not." His grandfather had actually been a baker in the cafeteria of the purchasing department. He still had the recipes. "The Emperor will return. There is no need to change anything."

"Just keep going this way till we all starve? Doesn't matter. The Militia won't be in charge for long—half of your ships don't work. Does your room have a shower?"

"That's a lie, Our ships are fine."

"You're right—it is a lie. Do you have the chip with you?" Nadine asked. She turned toward the bar, lifted her hands to call the bartender's attention, and then gestured with her hands. The bartender nodded and began to fill a pitcher of beer. "I think the number is more like three quarters, but I don't care. The nav. chip? You have it?"

"Yes, I do. It's clipped to my breast pocket." Nadine looked down—and there was indeed a nav. chip case clipped to his pocket. He continued, "We'll finish here, and then we'll go to your room together. Once we are alone I'll give the navigation chip to you, I'll stay for two hours and leave. Nobody will suspect anything. There will be no risk."

"Everybody in this bar will suspect I've lowered my standards and lost my mind. I'm not prepared to risk that. You never said if your room had a shower."

"It doesn't."

"Outstanding." The bartender arrived and dropped a full pitcher of beer. "Jeem, this military gentleman will be paying before he leaves," Nadine said. The bartender nodded and walked away.

She scooted around the table to her left and leaned in toward her contact. "There is one thing that would make your plan more believable."

"What's that?" he said, leaning in.

"Two hours is too long," she said. Nadine pulled him close with her left hand and held him tightly. Very deliberately, she used her right hand to pour the entire pitcher of beer over his head and uniform. As he sputtered, she released his shirt and carefully palmed the nav. chip. "You are more of a two-minute type of guy," she said, stepping back.

"Bitch. When the empire is restored, I'll come looking for you."

"Really? Well, in that case, remember this," she leaned back toward him, "screw your empire. You can be first against the wall when the revolution comes."

She strode out as the bar clapped for her.

Nadine arrived back at her rented room. She closed and locked the door, and began to read the information on the nav. chip. As she read it, she frowned several times. She finished reading it and stared into space for about a minute. Then she shook her head and grabbed her comm. After a few tries, she connected to the station system. It took quite some time before her encrypted channel opened up and the far side answered.

"What?"

"The Militia want me to hire me. What were you thinking, giving them my name? I hate the Militia."

"When? Where? Do you know what time it is?"

"In two weeks. A ship I'll meet at transfer 7. Why were you asleep? It's mid-afternoon in Landing."

"I'm not in Landing, I'm supervising something elsewhere. It's the middle of the night here. Where are you?"

"Orbital 3."

"What are you doing there? I told you to stay in landing."

Nadine rolled her eyes, even though the expression was useless since the voice couldn't see her.

"I was bored. I talked some friends into bringing me up on the shuttle."

"You bought a ticket. They track that."

"Nope. Flew in the cargo hold."

"The cargo hold? That's dangerous. You could be killed."

"Bite me," Nadine said. "It's pressurized. I'm not one of your idiot subordinates that you dictate things to."

The voice laughed over the radio. "I should have known.

That's your mother talking there. But I'm concerned about your safety. You should listen to my advice."

"My mother took your advice, and it killed her and Dad. I'm not going to make that mistake. I don't want your advice."

There was a long pause. "They were too hasty. That's what got them killed."

"They didn't—wait." Nadine put both palms to her forehead and rubbed her eyes. She shook her head once. "Let's not talk about my parents. Why did you give the Militia my name? You know I never want to work for them."

"I didn't give them your name. They must have gotten it some other way."

"Oh."

"They and I don't exactly get along either, you realize. If I was stuck in an airlock without a suit during evac testing, well, too bad. Tests are important, right? Why would they ask me for help with anything, especially something as obviously unofficial as this?"

"Don't get along is an understatement. That's why I called. I wanted to know what you were thinking."

"Well, for that matter, you saying you don't like them is also a considerable understatement. And they know it. How were you contacted? Who was it?"

"It was one of those Empire Rising guys. Salute the Emperor, braid his hair, all that stuff."

"They are a joke. What do they want you to do?"

"Fly a glider."

"A what?"

"A glider—an aircraft without an engine."

"I know what a glider is, child. I can fly one, and better than you. Not a cutter, or a ship?"

"Nope. I didn't know you could fly a glider."

"There are lots of things you don't know about me." The voice on the other end was silent for a long time. "You can fly a glider, I know that," he said.

"Yes, apparently they do too."

"But how would *they* know that you could? Aha. You learned in Militia cadets, at that boarding school."

"Yes. When I was fourteen. So?"

"You never said why you joined."

"It seemed like a useful skill to have, and I wanted it to round out my resume for future corporate jobs."

"Try again."

"There was a cute boy. He had a girlfriend, she was older, and had money. Good clothes. It sounded kind of fun and gave me an excuse to spend time alone with him. After a while, he forgot about her and her clothes. I had fun, and I discovered I liked flying."

"That's how they found you. They decided they needed a glider pilot, and that's the only place in the system that does gliding. They just went through the school records until they found somebody who had kept it up. They don't know you work for me and the others. They don't know any of that."

"What do you mean?"

"They don't know who you work for. To them you are just a slightly shady commercial pilot who also has a glider license."

"But what about my history with the Militia?"

'You never talk about that, do you?"

"I don't."

"I wouldn't talk about it to them. They probably don't make the connection between somebody's daughter and a slightly sketchy courier pilot called— What name are you using now?"

"Nadine."

"Right, slightly sketchy courier pilot, Nadine. So you are probably safe. I'll bet the initial question came from one of your smuggling contacts. Somebody who knows that you will take a package or two on your regular route and not declare it in customs."

"That's true. It definitely wasn't one of your people."

"So that's all they know. That's what they think they are hiring. It's best to keep it that way as well. If there is something slightly off for them, and they find out who you really are, then you might be out the lock without a suit."

"I'm not worried about that. So this wasn't your plan?"

"Not till now. Now I'm interested. What do you need a glider for?"

"No idea."

"I know how to find out."

"How?"

"Go out there with them and fly one."

Chapter 7

"Welcome to Land and Ocean Enterprises. I'm Salvatore Mascellon. Call me Sal." The man was dressed in standard corporate coveralls with his corporate flash above his breast pocket, rather than on his collar.

"Dashi. This is my assistant, Jose. Pleased to meet you, Mr. Sal," Dashi said.

"Just Sal, please."

"Of course, Mr. Sal."

Sal frowned at the correction but decided to ignore it. "No assistant for me. We're a small operation. Shall we go? I've arranged a small tour, and then we can go into my office over here?"

"I understood that we were going to be met by a GG official," Dashi said.

Sal shrugged. "I was told Don Ortega was not available. I'll take care of you."

"He was the primary shareholder. I would have expected him to be here to do the handover."

Sal stopped and looked at Dashi for a moment. "Don Ortega may have been the primary shareholder, but he never visited here. Nor did any of his family."

"Never?"

"Not even once."

"Are there any GG staff left at all?"

"Not now. They all left two weeks ago, except two who work with the glass printer."

"Two weeks ago. Right after the fire, then," Dashi said.

"How did you know about the fire?" Sal asked.

Dashi just smiled. "Who is doing their work?"

"Well, honestly, it's always been Land and Ocean staff who did the real work. The GG staff was mostly for administration."

"Of course," Dashi said. He smiled again. "I'm sure you'll miss their valuable contributions in planning and organizational tasks."

Sal didn't say anything, then nodded. "They were useless. Fourth sons of third-level stockholder families. They spent as little time here as possible, drank their paychecks when they were here, and got transferred as soon as they could." Sal shook his head. "Perhaps we can skip the tour and just go to my office."

"If you don't mind waiting a moment, I'd like to watch the unloading. I spend most of my time in orbit, and I rarely get to see ground activities in operation," Dashi said. Without waiting for an answer, he turned and watched the monorail. Passengers had already disembarked from the passenger section, and new passengers had rushed on. The doors locked and the train slid forward to the first flatcar. Magnetized bolts unlocked, and robotic rams pushed the shipping containers off the train onto a loading dock. Built-in rollers facilitated the movement. New containers slid in, replacing the loaded ones, and were pushed onto the train. The process was very efficient, taking less than a minute to empty a flatcar's worth of four containers. Only six containers came on and off, after which the train halted momentarily, then it began to reverse, gathering speed slowly. It was moving fast enough to generate a wind as it left the station.

"Marvelously well organized," said Dashi. "Let's take your tour now."

The small group began to cross the platform toward a road. On one side was a long row of containerized buildings, while on the other was the factory and its automated machinery, followed by a standard medical prefab, three school prefabs, and storage containers. A second road ran off at right angles to the first, heading up-valley. Jose looked around—all he saw were containers.

"Are there no buildings here, sir?" he asked.

Sal looked at Jose, frowned and looked back at Dashi, who had a bland countenance. "No, only the colony prefabs. Even the workers' quarters are rows of Class D housing. Uh, we have a Class A for you, of course, Mr. Dashi. And your assistant has a room in a Class B. We don't have that many luxury accommodations here—not like in Landing."

"What's the population here, sir?" Jose asked.

"We have just under five hundred in the town. There is

an out-station up-valley for the hydro plant, and there is the silicon mine up-valley as well, but it's mostly automated."

Jose began to count the containers. A Class D container had a single restroom and bunks for forty people. A Class C had five rooms with four bunks each, and a restroom. Class B had two restrooms, and four rooms with double beds. A Class A took up an entire container—had a sitting room, dining/workroom, bedroom, and a private bathroom.

Sal saw Jose darting his eyes around the town and guessed his thoughts. "If you think we have too much housing, you're right. The plant never expanded like it was supposed to, and we've been losing population over the last five years. A lot of the younger people have moved to Landing. We have lots of extra container housing. Especially Class D. We could probably house four or five times the number of people here."

"Why no expansion, then, sir?" Jose asked.

"Transport costs. We're too far from Landing. Slots on the monorail cost money."

Ahead of them, on the right side of the road, a group of young men and women hung around under a grove of birch trees. Several of them carried sticks or batons of some sort. They began to saunter toward them. Jose saw them approaching and swung his head to the left. Another group with the armbands of Council Police were nearby and saw the youths, but they turned their backs, ignoring the budding confrontation. The group of youngsters spread across the road and blocked access to the plant. Sal, Dashi, and Jose stopped in front of the group.

"Wassup, Sal?" asked the short, shaven-headed youth who stood in front.

"Just showing these folks around, Evan. Tour of the factory, then to my office."

Evan and his friends didn't move. "We hear they are going to close the plant, Sal," he said.

"Evan, they are not GG. We're exploring our options," Sal said.

"Any word on the back pay?" Evan said.

"Not just yet."

"It's been two months, Sal. We've been patient like you asked. But we can't wait forever. A lot of us owe money."

"I'm doing what I can, you know that. It's not in my hands."

"But when are we going to hear something?"

"I need to talk to these gentlemen. I'll know more when we're done."

Nobody said anything for a moment. They didn't get out of the way either.

Sal walked up to Evan and leaned into his personal space. "This is not helping. I need to talk to these two. If you need work, your cousin's friend is always hiring."

Evan backed up a step, but Sal didn't take his eyes off him. "Okay," Evan said finally. He stepped to the side and made a sweeping gesture. "These guys can't be worse than Ortega, right? Enjoy your visit. We'll be here when you are done, Sal."

"Thanks, Evan," Sal said. They began walking into the factory.

"What was that all about?" Jose asked.

"Just boys and girls being boys and girls," Sal said.

"Do you have any Militia here, sir?" Jose asked.

"Nope. Just corporate security." Sal coughed. "Sometimes. Mostly, the council does its own policing."

"We heard that there was a bit of a scuffle here a few weeks ago," Jose said.

"Not really," Sal said. "A group of kids were drinking and got out of control. But no harm done." He looked at Dashi. "Like I said, just boys and girls being boys and girls."

"An insignificant event then," Dashi said. "Our information must be exaggerated. We heard that a warehouse was looted, and some fires started. And several youths left town for Landing in a hurry, before GG corporate security arrived. We'll mark that as incorrect in our files."

Sal stopped and stared at Dashi. "That wasn't on the news," Sal said. "Where did you hear that?"

"We're the research department for TGI. We research a lot of things. By the way, where is the new store going to go?"

Dashi turned away and continued walking. Sal stared after him.

They arrived at an office with corporate flashes that matched Sal's breast flashes. Sal led the way into a conference room and closed the door behind them. He poured glasses of water for Dashi and Jose and then they all sat down.

"Right. Who are you guys really?" Sal asked.

"We work for the TGI research department," Dashi said. "We're researching a potential purchase of some of your assets here."

"I don't believe you," Sal said. He gestured at the glass

of water. Dashi shook his head. Sal continued. "First, there was never any talk of a sale here until the fire. And until you called yesterday to say you were coming, I'd never heard of you. I tried to do some of my own research, but you guys are a mystery. TGI is orbital. This 'purchase' would be your first primary resource industry investment. Everything else is insurance, finance, and shipping. Nobody has heard of a Mr. Dashi. The ground-side sales vice president is Simon Kim. He's got a good reputation, but you are a mystery. So, what gives? Are you shutting us down? Closing the plant?"

"We're exploring our options," Dashi said.

Sal sat back and crossed his arms. He looked from Dashi to Jose and back. He shook his head.

"All right, I'll put my cards on the table. You saw what happened outside. Lots of kids with no work. We're in a pickle here. The food plant is really the only game in town —other than the fishing, and that's not much. We've been making a little money, then losing a little money for years. Galactic Growing, meaning Don Ortega, put up with that, but they never made any investments in the place. We've been scavenging parts to keep all four processing lines going, but we couldn't make it work last quarter. And we lost one in the fire. We've only got two left in operation, and no chance of getting number three or four sorted out without spending more money. Money that our local corporation doesn't have."

Sal paused and poured a glass of water for himself, taking a drink. "Then the tariffs went up on the monorail. Even with four lines running, we wouldn't make money. And they changed from paying in cash to paying in kind. And like you figured, the costs at the store went up. People were having problems making ends meet."

He took another drink of water. "We had to idle one of the lines, so we had to cut the workforce. We did it by seniority, and now, a lot of the kids have nothing to do. The fire was the last straw. One night they were drinking, got into it at the store. The store was GG-owned but locally staffed. Harsh words, some shoving, a few punches. Things got out of control, then there was a fire.

"I haven't told anybody, but I know GG is not rebuilding. No new store. Which means we'll have to send to Point 33 for goods, or all the way from Landing, and pay the new tariffs. Either way, we're screwed. We can't afford that. We'll all end up in debt to them, with nowhere to go. I figured they would do something, but I didn't think they would offer to sell the whole operation that quick."

Sal tried to take another drink but realized the glass was empty. His hand shook, just a bit, as he put it down.

"So, I figure you're here to shut us down. Buy up the assets from GG, sell what you can, scrap the rest."

Sal looked at the water glass for a moment and banged it sideways off the table. It shattered against the wall. Jose jumped, but Dashi didn't move.

Sal continued. "I want you to know, though, you corporate guys, you won't just be shutting down a plant—you'll be killing a community." Sal leaned over the table. "There are almost five hundred people left in this town. If the tray plant closes, the farms will close. If the farms close, there will be nothing here except that silicon mine. There will be work for twenty people, tops. Everybody here will have to leave, or starve. And if they leave, they'll come looking for the likes of you. And I want you head office bastards to know that. You are ruining the lives of everybody here. Hardworking people who've worked for the company for years—low pay, bad conditions, no extras. No scholarships to the university, no funded trips, not even monorail credits. Nothing but work and time off in the bush. Nothing at all from you bastards."

Sal looked at the two of them. His mouth was a thin line.

Dashi smiled broadly. Jose swallowed. That was his going-to-war smile. "Thank you for that information, sir," Dashi said. He paused and took a drink from his glass of water. "Jose, bring up the numbers, please."

Jose pulled out his tablet and typed. Figures appeared on the tablet. Dashi glanced at them, then focused on Sal. "Productivity here is some of the lowest in the GG group," Dashi said. "This settlement is too far south. The growing season is too short, and these farms have the worst soil on Delta. GG attempted to automate the plant several years ago, but abandoned the attempt after they realized the cost. And there were some labor disruptions as well—"

"They would have thrown half the workforce out of work," Sal said.

Dashi ignored the interruption and continued with his account. "There was widespread sabotage and destruction of GG property. Acts of vandalism. GG, meaning Don Ortega, still had contracts to deliver to suppliers, so they were forced to run overtime, and the locals benefited substantially with additional overtime payments. Headquarters' assigned management and staff were threatened."

"They were idiots. Just collecting a paycheck," Sal said.

"Oh, I agree," Dashi said. "But there are two sides to every story. You cost Don Ortega a lot of money and prestige. So he decided to bleed you white. But he was so slow and so patient about it, you never realized it till now."

"That's your viewpoint," Sal said. "Or that's what corporate reported. We're all alone out here, and we have to look out for each other. Sometimes things aren't as simple as they appear from a distance." Sal stared into space. "Some people get out of control, sometimes. But they are still our people."

Dashi paused, leaned back in his chair, and steepled his hands in front of him. "You, personally, along with most of the management that remains here, are local. You were born here, correct? And your family is still here, yes?"

Sal nodded.

"Your second cousin is the chief of security."

"Yes."

"He sold those rioters to an off-planet firm as indentured workers. And that's not the first time he's done it."

Sal looked surprised. "I don't know what you mean."

"Yes, you do. You got the rioters out of here before GG security arrived. Sold them out as indentured workers."

"They can earn out their contract, as long as they pay off the transportation costs."

"The rates they have to pay are at an unparalleled level of usury."

Sal's forehead crinkled. He looked from Jose to Dashi.

Jose quickly registered that he didn't know the word. "Usury means 'expensive, pricey,'" he supplied.

The crease on Sal's face cleared, and he nodded. "Again, says you," Sal said. "Maybe some stock does disappear, and maybe there is some pilferage. But you've seen the town—do you see me in a mansion with ten greenhouses full of grapes? You don't. But if you want to come by the school, it's fully equipped—screens for every class, computers. Everything they need. GG didn't pay for that. I'm okay with a little graft."

"Are you okay with indentured servitude?"

"You know, I've heard on some of the outer stations that, if they catch somebody stealing from his friends, or causing problems, they don't put him in jail. They just put him out an airlock," Sal said.

"I have heard that as well. I do not see that it is relevant," Dashi said.

"We don't have airlocks here, Mr. Dashi. What do you think would happen to somebody who stole stuff from a fellow worker if we let them stay here? And the money from the work contract goes to the victims. And as regards the rioters, GG wanted them turned over. I'm not sure we would have gotten them back. Indentured servitude is better than a shot in the head."

"I see." Dashi pondered for a moment. "Now, as regards your five hundred people here, they are mostly employees and their families. GG offered them work at other sites as part of the realignment, and a bonus. After they cleared their debts, of course. Almost without exception, they turned that offer down."

"Work? Slavery, more like it. Contracts at other plants where the pay doesn't cover what they owe the company store. Those kids who moved to Landing didn't move. They ran off to escape debts. TGI charged for water, for school, for everything. They were never going to get ahead, so they did a midnight run. I wish them well."

Dashi shrugged. "I do agree there are two sides to every story. From GG's point of view, they are finally fed up with trying to find a solution for people who, in their opinion, are borderline criminals who don't want to help themselves, and they have jumped at the opportunity to offload it to TGI. That deal is done. TGI is your new boss now."

Mr. Dashi took another drink of water. "TGI, in this case, is me. This is my idea. And I don't have five hundred that I'm responsible to. There are forty thousand working at TGI. If you include families and dependents, there are almost a hundred thousand people that are our corporate—and in my opinion, my personal—responsibility. All of these people are TGI stockholders. For most of them, almost all of their savings are in TGI stock. The money that we spent here is their money, their savings, their hard work hoarded against need. I'm betting not just my livelihood on this, but theirs as well."

Dashi stopped and leaned back for a moment, regarding Sal.

"So, you are correct about things being tight. Tariffs are going up on the monorail. They have already gone up on the orbital shuttles. We're paying almost twice as much for food this year as we were three years ago. We need to feed our people, so I convinced the board to acquire this beat-up, clapped-out, broken-down plant at the end of the line for a song. Why? So that we can supply at least part of our food needs."

Sal stretched his arms. "So what?"

Dashi raised his eyebrows and flexed his fingers. "Of course, if that doesn't work, we have another option. Shut this place down. Sell off the production lines for parts, burn the crops as bio-waste to generate steam in Landing. Sell the containerized housing for metal reclamation. Sell the magnets in the monorail to a repair company, and yank the stanchions out of the mountains behind us as we pull out."

Dashi stood up and walked over to the wall and examined a production flowchart. "I don't want to do that, but I have limited time, and I can't afford any problems. Problems like physical assault, sabotage, labor disruptions, strikes, or just general lack of cooperation with my agenda."

Dashi turned back. He smiled a broad smile. "Do you have any questions at this point, Mr. Sal?"

Sal contemplated the shattered glass on the floor, then shook his head.

"Good. Now, the good news. We are not closing the plant. We have put a substantial line of credit into your operating account in Landing. It should be there already. That was the reason for my delay in coming here. We needed to ensure our financing was in place. I expect to modernize the plant and bring lines three and four into full production. You also have room for expansion in the plant. We will be adding additional farming acres and some more lines. Probably two more for superpotatoes and radishes. And I want to have a more formal arrangement with those fishermen—I want all of their surpluses, and I'd like to buy all their catch. I want a regular contract for hiring them. And I want some new construction between their wharf and the monorail line, to move some other goods I have in mind."

Sal's mouth dropped open. "Oh."

"Furthermore, I want this done quickly, and quietly. We need to get this sorted out before GG discovers what is happening and cancels the deal, or before any other corporation causes issues. Can you guarantee that this can be done in secret?"

Sal nodded. "Of course. Everyone here can keep a secret."

"You can guarantee that? What about those rowdies outside?"

"I'll speak to them."

"That's it? You'll speak to them."

"I should have said, I'll have somebody speak to them. Several somebodies."

"Good. Let's begin. First, Jose will be my agent here. You probably won't see me again. Jose will oversee everything. We will need to close one of the outlying stations, but we anticipate moving those people to a new waterfront processing plant. Next...."

They finally left the meeting as it was getting dark. Sal couldn't have been more helpful. He had lunch brought in, called in his staff, and issued instructions. He also had a few quiet words with the plant people. Dashi had laid out his plans, and Sal and his crew looked to be working all night to get the figures Dashi needed. The attitude seemed to be 'Let's get the money out of these guys before they learn better.' Dashi didn't mind. He preferred the new attitude to the old one.

The lounging youths had vanished when they walked back to their guest containers, and the few security personnel walking the road smiled at them and wished them a good evening.

"Are you coming out for dinner, sir?" Jose said.

"No, I will be eating in tonight," Dashi said.

"Yes, sir. I have to say, this is quite impressive. You have outdone yourself."

"How so, Jose?"

"Well, sir, given how much money you are putting into more production here, the board of directors are showing a great deal of confidence in your judgment."

Dashi just smiled. It was a whimsical smile. Jose watched him closely. He was an expert in Dashi's smiles.

"Sir, you did tell the board of directors, didn't you?"

"Jose, here is a piece of unsolicited advice: Don't ask a question you don't want to know the answer to."

"But, sir, all that money. You stole it?"

"I think 'misappropriated' is more accurate, Jose. After all, it's not going into my pocket. I'm using it for this project." Dashi stopped and looked up at the Dragon covering half of the night sky.

"You will be in charge of this project. You know what needs to be done. Make it work. I will be wrapped up in some other operations for the next few weeks. Draw what resources you need."

"But what if it doesn't work, sir?"

"You're in charge. Goodnight, Jose," Dashi said and walked away.

Jose watched him go. "I'm in charge? The Emperor's balls."

Chapter 8

The crowd on the balcony watched as the fireworks exploded in the sky over Landing. Each burst of light illuminated the waterway below. In the brief flash, Dashi watched a shuttle being cranked out of the lake. It had just been placed in the cradle that would attach it to the mass driver. An engine hummed, and the cradle pulled the whole shuttle out of the water.

The fireworks flashed again as the crowd cheered. Oooooh. Ahhhh. Ehhh. Dashi wondered why there seemed to be some pattern to it. Surely everybody just picked the noise they were most comfortable with. Why the repetition?

A figure looked up next to him in the dark.

"Happy Discovery Day, Dashi," the tall man said.

Dashi couldn't see the man in the dark, but he knew the voice. "Happy Discovery Day to you too, Mr. Kapur."

"You have a lot of nerve coming down here."

"I do? Why? If the Militia didn't want me as a guest, they shouldn't have invited me."

"Everybody gets invited. Even those who aren't supposed to come. If I thought I'd get away with it, I'd stab you to death with a sharpened buffalo rib."

"And waste that good food? Surely not." Dashi picked up one of the ribs and chewed on it.

A man in a Militia commander's uniform stepped out of the gloom and stepped between them. He addressed Kapur.

"Is everything all right, sir? Do you need help with this gentleman?"

"No, everything is fine, Ian," Kapur said.

"You must be Ian Danson," Dashi said.

The commander glanced briefly at Dashi. "I am. I don't believe we've been introduced, sir."

"Dashi. TGI. Special Projects. Congratulations on your retirement, Commander Danson."

Danson whipped his head toward Dashi. "What makes you think that I'm retiring?" he asked.

"You sold your commission to Belt Mining, effective next month."

Kapur turned and stared at the commander. "You sold your commission?"

The commander drew himself up to attention and faced Kapur. "Sir, I did. Yes sir."

Dashi smiled. "Mr. Danson will be a new station head for Belt Mining. And a stockholder as well. Everyone over there is very excited to have somebody of his experience on board."

Kapur's gaze was still concentrated on Danson. "You're retiring? You're leaving the Militia?"

"I've been grounded for nearly two years, sir. I've been

put in charge of every garbage detail there is. I'll never be promoted again. It was time to go."

Kapur continued staring at him. The commander went on. "Admiral, it's all been downhill since I was your aide. They're systematically hunting down the old crew and removing them."

"I'm not an admiral. Not anymore."

"You'll always be the admiral to me, sir."

Kapur stared at Danson, then his shoulders slumped. "I hope you charged them a fortune."

"I did, sir. They offered me a whole block of stock for my commission, and this job as well. Angela was ecstatic. We'll be wealthy, and in orbit where we belong."

Kapur grimaced. "The Militia will be sorry to lose you, Ian. We'll miss you. I'll miss you. Good luck." He extended his hand, and they shook vigorously.

Dashi smiled. "Good luck from me as well, Mr. Danson. Could you excuse us, please? Your former boss and I need to discuss a few things."

Danson looked at Kapur, who nodded and smiled, before moving away.

Kapur looked at Dashi. "He was one of my best officers."

"Yes, that's why they trumped up those charges against him."

"A commander's commission is worth a lot of money."

"There was quite a bidding war."

"Belt Mining is too small. They can't afford to buy it," Kapur said.

"They gave him stock instead. Lots of stock."

"Why would they do that?"

Dashi smiled at Kapur. "Because I asked them to. And I loaned them a lot of money."

"Why?"

"Because he's competent. Because I didn't want him as an enemy. Out in far orbit, he'll be away from all this mess."

"He won't ever be your friend."

"The enemy of my enemy is my friend. Whether he knows it or not."

Kapur thought for a moment. "Smart. Militia Council appointments are coming up. One of the Belt Mining officers is due, the unaligned spot on the council. Then they spring this other commission on the board. They go from a minor player to somebody to be reckoned with. They've never liked the Militia much, and they know Ian was treated poorly. Everyone over there will be well-disposed toward TGI, and anti-Militia. Well played, Dashi."

Kapur reached down, picked up a buffalo rib, and began to chew on it. "You know, Dashi, I really hate you, and your company, but you never do anything without reason. Why are you here?"

"I'm here for the food. TGI provided a ton of buffalo meat. And I only charged half price."

"Half price," Kapur said. "Anybody else and I would say they were foolish. But you, Dashi, there will be some scheme. You'll be ripping us off somehow."

"Just a lot on the market right now. Transportation issues."

"Transportation issues? The Emperor's scrotum. What do you really want?"

"I want the Militia to stop stealing our orbital shipments, before you start an inter-company war."

Kapur turned to Dashi. "It's come to that?"

"Almost. It has to stop, or our board will want to do something. I need you to tell your people that."

"They're not my people, not anymore. I'm off the council." Kapur chewed for a moment. "You'll lose. The war, I mean. We have all the armed ships. Those piddling weapons you have hidden away aren't enough. We can cut off your orbital access. You'll starve."

"We'll cut off your fuel and air. And we can wreck the financial system. Inflation. The markets will grind to a halt."

"Even so, it would be worth it to get rid of you leeches."

"From your point of view, perhaps, if it was just the two of us. But you know it won't stay that way. There will be riots. Deaths. Some of the GG stations are barely under control. There are a lot of unaligned corps out there. Lots of them hate the Militia. They might not jump the way you think."

"Let 'em. We'll blast them too."

"And the Free Traders will get involved. And they're crazy. You never know what they'll do."

Kapur looked at him. "Like what?"

"Like running a far trader into a shuttle dock."

"You'd let them do that?"

"I can't stop them. I have no armed ships, remember?" Dashi was silent for a moment. "Do we really need to wreck our orbital infrastructure and destroy our industrial capacity right now? We're already suffering shortages as it is."

"As much as I'd like to see you bunch of weasels gone,

no, it's not worth all that. And it's all hypothetical. Even the Officers' Council isn't stupid enough to start things now."

"Something has changed. They've started intercepting our shipments in orbit."

"I don't believe you. They wouldn't be that stupid. What makes them think that they can get away with that?"

"You tell me."

"I haven't heard anything."

Dashi was silent, smiling at Kapur.

Kapur looked back. "What?"

"You haven't talked to me since the funeral."

"That's not a good topic to bring up."

"But you've seen me since then. We've been at different events together, but never spoken."

"So?"

"So, why, tonight of all times, did you actually come over to talk to me?" Dashi asked.

"To tell you how much I hate you?"

"I already know that. You made sure of it. Something else is bothering you."

Another set of fireworks fired off with a crackling sound, and a waterfall of light appeared over the river. Kapur watched them. "Even if it was, why would I talk to you about it?"

"Because you dislike conflict. You prefer order. And you are patient. Not like those Empire Rising people. You suspect something. Otherwise, you wouldn't have come over," Dashi said.

Another light flashed, but Kapur ignored it. "You would be much easier to hate if you weren't so competent, Dashi."

"Yes, I suspect that is the case."

"I have seen some things that concern me. The Officers' Council is getting—"

"Bolder? More adventurous? More willing to take exceptional risks for uncertain results?"

"I was going to say 'stupid,' but your vocabulary, as usual, exceeds my requirements. They are doing something stupid."

"Go on."

"I have an agent, a pilot, that was approached by the Militia under suspicious circumstances," Kapur said. "She is on Orbital-16. Some things are going on that concern me. Perhaps they are related to your issues. Perhaps not."

"I have someone investigating unusual circumstances as well. Some of these circumstances are on Orbital-16," Dashi said.

"Perhaps we could pool our resources. Exchange information."

"What would you give us?"

"I still have some friends in the Militia who can pass on some information. Deployment information, for example."

"Deployment information is public."

"I'll get you the non-public part."

"What would I be expected to provide in return?"

"I need you to take messages from her, and provide backup for her operations."

"Why don't you just ask your friends to help her?" Dashi said.

"She can be a little unpredictable. My friends might not approve. I still want her to have some help. I know you have contacts. And I need a way for her to communicate with me without my Militia friends knowing."

"You don't trust your friends anymore. I can do that. But she'll have to meet with my agent on a regular basis to exchange information."

"Can you get her out if she gets into trouble?" Kapur asked.

"My person is surprisingly resourceful. If he can get out, she can get out."

"And if he can't get out?"

"She can't get out either."

Chapter 9

"They always lie to us," the man next to Jake said.

"What?" Jake said.

"I said they always lie to us." He slumped even lower in his seat. He had close-cropped graying hair and a neatly trimmed graying beard. His clothes were neat, and his shirt was ironed. Everything about him was neat. Jake felt wrinkled just looking at him.

"First, it was Traffic Control delaying us, then it was the late cargo, then it was the launch window, and now they say they are waiting for another first officer. Doesn't it bother you?"

"Well, what do you expect, really?" Jake said. He turned back to his tablet.

"I mean, do they think we're stupid? They always make stuff up. Why don't they just say that they hate their customers and don't care if we wait, that they were waiting for more expensive cargo, or they wanted to save fuel?"

"I guess they could do that," Jake said, flipping the tablet open.

"It's the disrespect that bothers me," the man said. "Like they don't care what we think. Do you feel disrespected?"

"Um, sure. But there's nothing I can do, you know."

"We should do something. We should walk up there and tell them what's what. That they can't just keep us waiting here without an explanation."

Jake tipped his tablet up and tried to ignore his seatmate. The drop shuttle was now an hour late, and he needed to get to orbit. This was not going well.

"There she is."

"Sorry, who?" Jake said. He sighed and put down his tablet.

"The first officer must be that skinny girl in the Castle Transport uniform up there. Nice view from this angle."

"Yes. Yes, it must be," Jake said, appreciating her from behind as she stormed into the cockpit. She looked familiar somehow.

"Nice-looking girl from the back. I like that. What about you?"

"She does look very fit," Jake said. He looked more closely. A horrible suspicion grew in him.

The intercom boomed. "Your first officer speaking. Sorry for the delay. We'll drop for Transit-16 in a moment. Apologies for the late departure, but we were delayed by the late arrival of an inbound shuttle."

Oh no. That voice. He knew that voice.

"They should have to make up new excuses every time, don't you think?" the man said.

"Yes," Jake said. "They absolutely should."

"What excuses would you make for the first officer being late?"

"Well, I would say that the first officer was late because she had been involved in a scheme to defraud her employer of insurance payouts. And she had kidnapped the main investigator, shot him in the chest, then held him hostage until he helped them steal a cache of black-market Old Empire weapons. And as a side effect, she had the auditor shoot his best friend." Jake shut off his tablet and continued. "Or, perhaps she had been busy pirating a spaceship that this auditor was on and stealing rare metals off it. And when everybody got sick in a measles epidemic, she helped the auditor escape off it, yet tried to steal all of his money so that he would lose his job and be left destitute. But it didn't quite work out because the auditor tricked her into taking the less valuable stuff, and she's probably here because she wants to exact some terrible revenge on that auditor—like spacing him, or putting him in jail for murder, or dropping him off on some station with no food or water or air or hope."

The man next to Jake looked at him with wide eyes. "Wow. You have a great imagination. What do you do, write fiction for a living?"

"No," Jake said. "I'm an accountant." *Nevertheless, what I just said,* Jake thought, *was reality, not fiction. Hello, Nadine.*

Nadine stormed onto the bridge. She hadn't paid any attention to the passengers, and hadn't seen Jake. "Let's get this show on the road. We still have a few minutes left to catch our drop." She began flipping switches. "Control, this is Castle Transport Drop-6, do we have clearance to go?" Nadine tapped a different screen. "Steward, this is control. Why aren't the hatches sealed?"

"Control, this is steward. I have a name. And they are not sealed because nobody from the bridge told us to seal them."

"Are all the passengers on board?"

"Yes."

"Then by the four and twenty testicles of the Imperial Council, seal them and let's get out of here before we miss our launch window," Nadine said. She shut off the squawking from the steward and changed channels. "Control? What's the word?"

"Any time, Castle Transport 6."

"Outstanding," Nadine said. She pressed the warning gongs and began to drop the magnetized grapples. "Steward, as soon as you get that hatch closed we're gone. Speed it up," she said and shut off the channel, then pressed the zero-g gong.

"Hi," she said, turning to the man to her left. "I'm Nadine, who are you?"

"I am Timothy Desmaries. Acting second officer. I am the pilot-in-command."

"Good for you, Timmy. Command away while I get us out of here." She watched the board turn green. "Control"—she hit the radio—"dropping now. Free trades."

"That's a nice sentiment from a corporate ship, Castle Transport 6. Free trades yourself."

Nadine grimaced. *Oops. Stay in character.* She maneuvered the ship away from the truss and began to decelerate to push into a higher orbit. They started to move away. She sat back and watched her board. She had agreed to do these runs until the Militia contacted her, but now she had to learn as much as she could about Militia activities on the station. Spy on them and pass her information to an on-station contact.

Oh, and not upset her contact.

She turned to Timmy. He was frowning. She flashed him a smile. "So, Timmy, what's a girl do for excitement on Transit-6?"

"Give me a beer," Jake said.

"Sure," the bartender said. He called something down the bar. A young woman at the other end filled a draft glass and walked it down.

"Here ya go. Three credits. Give me your corporate card for the tab," she said.

"I'll pay now. Here's some GG credit," Jake said, sliding one of the GG chips over the bar.

"No card?"

"No."

"More convenient that way."

"I've had problems with my corporate card before. You don't like GG credit?"

"It's fine. Just most people put a card up is all."

"I drink too much and spend too much money when I run a tab."

"Don't we all," she said. She winked at him.

Jake drank. "This is Belter beer."

"Yes."

"Why did you give me Belter beer? Does everybody here order it?"

"You're a Belter. Corporate logo on the skinsuit, but it's a semi-hard suit, equipment belt, and—"

"Belter boots. I know. They were my dad's."

"Expensive boots. Professional. Functional. Not very stylish, though."

Jake drank his beer and contemplated life. A figure sat down on the seat next to him. He wasn't the least bit surprised to hear a familiar voice.

"Hi, Jakey," Nadine said.

"Hello, Nadine."

The bartender returned and stood there expectantly.

"Are you going to buy me a drink?"

"Nope, I don't think so."

Nadine slid a credit chip across the counter. "Give me a shot of vodka," she said.

The bartender poured one shot and slid it to Nadine. She downed it in one go. "Another, please," Nadine said.

Nadine turned to Jake. "Wow, Jake. What a coincidence meeting you here, in the first bar I walk into."

"You're lying. There are six bars between here and the docks. I counted. You saw me on your passenger list. You were looking for me. What do you want?"

"After all that money you stole from me, you should at least pay for my drinks."

"I didn't steal anything from you. You stole it from me. Or from corporate, or something like that. Either way, it wasn't yours. And you shot up my ship," Jake said.

"Technically, it wasn't your ship. And it wasn't personal."

"Okay, shooting up the ship wasn't personal. From my point of view, taking all that metal wasn't personal. But how about shooting me in the chest? Was that personal?"

Nadine downed her vodka. "That's old news, Jake. Another, please," she said to the bartender. Their voices had risen a bit, so both bartenders had drifted down to listen.

"And for me. The green bottles. And give me a shot of vodka as well," Jake said. "Well? Was shooting me personal?"

"You were being annoying. I didn't know you drank vodka. And you let that stupid engine room guy shoot me with that shotgun and break my arm. Why did you do that, Jakey?"

The drinks arrived, and Jake drank some more. "You were being annoying. And I hate vodka."

Nadine glared at him. "What about my money?"

"What are you doing here, Nadine? Are you here to bother me? You going to shoot me again?"

"Not today, Jakey. No time. I've got work to do here."

"So do I."

"Well, I have no plans to shoot you again. But if you get in my way, I might just change my mind, so stay clear." She banged the last glass down, and collected her credit chip from the bartender. "Thanks. See you later," Nadine said. She sauntered out, taking care to put a wiggle in her walk.

The male bartender crossed his arms and watched her wiggle away. He looked at the female bartender standing next to him with her hands on her hips. "She likes you, doesn't she?" he said to Jake.

"What?" Jake said.

"She likes you a lot," agreed the female bartender.

"You two are both nuts," Jake said and shook his head. "Another beer."

He sighed as he sat at the bar. Another boring assignment. This was what happened when you screwed up at school—again, he reflected. He replayed the meeting with Mr. Dashi in his mind. He had been summoned to Dashi's office a few days before.

"Mr. Stewart. Good morning," Dashi had said. He smiled at Jake. He was at his usual place behind his large, expensive, wooden desk.

"Sir," Jake said.

"You look well, Mr. Stewart."

"Thank you, sir."

"Very well, for somebody who died four times during training."

"Ah. You know about that?"

"Piloting doesn't seem to agree with you, does it, Mr. Stewart?"

"Not at present, sir."

Dashi was silent for a moment, contemplating Jake.

"Sir, I would like another try at that simulator," Jake said.

"And why would I countenance that?"

Countenance? Jake wondered if Dashi looked up new words before every meeting. He coughed. "I think it's more a matter of experience than training, sir. I think with practice and experience, I could pass, sir."

"I'll reserve my judgment on that for now. Spots in those classes are in high demand. There won't be another one for some time. But you did well on the mechanical and electrical courses. A good feel for how ship systems work."

"Thank you, sir."

"But in the meantime, I have some duties for you."

"Yes sir."

"I want you to do an audit. I'm loaning you to one of our sub-corporations. They do business on Orbital-16. Fuel, consumables. There are some indications of unusual activities there. A few containers of food have gone missing. I want you to find out if there is something strange going on. Possibly illegal. Kickbacks or graft. We won't be taking any action at this time, but I want to know what is going on. Go there and nose around in the figures, the reports. Make sure the information that they are sending us is correct."

"I can do that, sir."

"But you can't let them know that you are doing it. You are going there as a worker, not as an auditor."

"You want me to keep under the radar, sir?"

Dashi cocked his head to one side. "Under the radar? What does that mean?"

"Old Empire term from some vids I watched, sir. It means 'quietly, without notice.'"

"Where does radar figure into it?"

"I'm not sure, sir. It's something from Old Earth."

"They had radar? I suppose they did—they got into space, after all. But radar goes in all directions, Mr. Stewart. How do you stay under it?"

"It's just an expression, sir."

"I see. Well, yes, I want you to be 'under the radar,' then."

"I will, sir."

"Good. You will share your notes with us in the usual way, of course, but there is also another on-station operation going on. Not one of mine, but we are temporarily working together. There is contact information in your chip. Please, meet with the listed contact regularly and share what you learn from that office as well."

"Yes sir," Jake said. Dashi nodded, and Jake recognized a dismissal. He got up and walked to the door.

"Mr. Stewart?"

"Yes sir?"

"Your contact up there is a bit unreliable. You should double-check any facts they give you."

"Of course, sir."

Two days later, when Jake arrived at the station, he went to meet his contact. He arrived at the caf early, pulled a cup of basic and bought a high-protein breakfast tray—two types of seaweed and a large block of processed and freeze-dried fish wrapped in bright green foil. It was so dry he had to pull an extra glass of basic. He had read that the Old Empire ate eggs for breakfast. He'd never tasted one, or even seen one for real. There were no chickens on Delta. He was careful to make sure that the bright green foil packaging was visible to anybody who walked by.

It was thirty minutes before shift change, so the place was packed. Large numbers of people came and went, some just pulling a cup of basic, then rushing off to work. This was a big station, and the coveralls reflected that—lots of different corporate logos, major as well as minor corps. There were almost as many office suits over coveralls as tool belts. The latest fashion style for the girls was bright scarfs and headbands.

To his considerable surprise, he saw Nadine walk in and go through the food line, collect a tray and sit down. She hadn't struck him as a morning type. He watched her for a moment, then shook his head. Focus.

The place nearly emptied out as the shift change hour approached. Only a handful of people were left, including Nadine. He glared at her across the caf. She glared back at him. People from the outgoing shift began to flood in. Jake ignored Nadine and continued to eat. People walked in and out of the caf, and some sat. None came near Jake.

After an hour, Jake had to admit defeat. His contact had missed the rendezvous. He'd try again tomorrow. He walked toward the disposal chute. Nadine was still there as well. That was odd. Jake very deliberately didn't look at her. Except, what was that color?

Crap. Nadine also had one of the expensive protein bars for breakfast. Could it be a coincidence? Probably not. The right time, the right place, the right color. Jake walked over to her table and sat down.

"Go away, Jakey," Nadine said. "I don't want to talk to you right now."

"If that's what you want. Are you sure?"

"Of course I am," she said. Then she looked at his tray. "Oh no."

"Yup."

"What did I do to deserve this?"

"You? What did I do?"

They stared at each other for a few moments.

"Let's make this contact official. I say the code words 'Gravity seems off today,' then you say—" Jake said.

"It's probably just the solar flares," Nadine said. "There, happy?"

"It looks like we're going to be working together."

"'Together' is a big word, Jake."

"Let's say we'll meet and have a few things to say to each other."

"Actually, I like that better, Jakey. Let's do that. I have quite a few things to say to you."

"A few ground rules."

"Ground rules?"

"No shooting each other."

"You were being annoying, but fine. No shooting. No stealing things from each other."

"It wasn't yours. But okay. No stealing." Jake shook his head. "I can't believe this."

"Believe it."

"Yes. Okay, I'll go first. My instructions say I'm supposed to inform you of any malfeasance I find."

"Malfeasance? Jake, just say people stealing things. It's easier to understand."

"Fine, I'm looking for people who are selling black-market food trays. Anything you find out about that, you're supposed to let me know."

"Who cares? It shouldn't be that hard to find that out. A task suitable for even your limited abilities, Jakey."

Jake gritted his teeth. "And you are supposed to inform me of anything you find out about unusual Militia activities."

"If I think it's relevant."

"Nadine, as much as we both dislike this, we are supposed to work together."

"We don't, really, Jake. I have no idea what my boss was thinking. And he's not here right now, so I'll do what I want."

"Which is figure out what the Militia is doing on this station," Jake said.

"You know that, huh? I don't need your help with that. And if you get in my way, watch out."

"Nadine, did it ever occur to you that I might be able to help you solve your problem?"

"Nope. I don't need your help. I'll be done and gone before you've filed your first report."

"If I find out something relating to Militia activities on the station, I shouldn't let you know?"

"No need, Jake. I'm way ahead of you. Like always." She got up. "I'll see you tomorrow morning, same time, same place." She smiled. "Maybe, if I'm back from my party yet. Later, Jakey." She flounced off.

Jake watched her go. Working with Nadine was going to be a chore.

But she did look good in that skinsuit.

Chapter 10

Even Jake thought his new job was boring. He'd been loaned out to the accounting department of the station's orbital services. There, he worked in cargo ops as a 'logistical sales specialist,' level three.

"So, Jack, basically, just answer the comms or emails. The ships want fuel, reaction mass, water, food, and a few other consumables. They either have a standing order or they send it in. Check the list of incoming ships against our orders, and make sure it's on the schedule for the shift," Jake's shift boss said. She was middle-aged and dressed older. A romantic soap opera was playing in the corner of her console screen.

"It's Jake."

"What?"

"My name is Jake."

"Right, sorry. Any questions?"

"Should I call the ships to see if they want anything special?"

"No."

"Just take the orders that come in?"

"That's right, Jack."

"Jake."

"Jake, sorry. Here's your terminal. If you have any questions, check out the manual."

"Can I ask you if I don't understand?"

"Um, sure. But check the manual first," she said. She turned back to her screen.

Jake pulled up the manual and began to read.

After a few days, he had settled into a routine. He did his regular day shifts with the rest of the office and volunteered for as many second shifts as he could. The office staff was lazy, so they were happy to have him pick up the evening work. Day shift was fully staffed, so whenever he pulled an overnight, he was allowed to go home and catch up on his sleep for four hours, then return to finish his full shift, which meant that his 'day' shift stretched into second and third shifts.

"You are doing well here, Stewart," his boss said. She couldn't seem to get the whole 'Jack/Jake' thing sorted out, so she opted for what was on his name tag.

"Thank you, ma'am," he said.

"Keep this up, and next year, I'll put you in for a promotion to level four. That's a 2-percent bump in pay."

"Two percent. After only a year? That would be great," Jake said. She didn't notice the sarcasm.

In addition to his potential 2-percent bump in pay in a year, working extra odd hours afforded Jake a lot of alone time in the office, so he was able to start running some reports and correlating information. Ninety-five percent of the operations seemed legitimate. From most of the ships, the orders were like clockwork—every week, corporate ship X would order one thousand kilograms of fuel, five hundred liters of water, a hundred mixed food trays, and two standard cleaning packs. These ships were on a regular route between different stations. The Free Trader orders were all over the map, of course, but they did come back from time to time.

Jake correlated consumption of supplies as they related to the types of routes and distance traveled. Ships of similar crew sizes should consume similar amounts of cleaning supplies, food, and water over the same time. Per-day rates should be similar. However, fuel consumption was more difficult to determine, because it was based on distance, not time, and he didn't always know where the ships went. There was a solution to that, he thought. Find the crew and ask them.

"*La Belle Chance*, huh," Jake said to the man sitting next to him at the bar, pointing to his ship patch.

"Yep, finest ship in the rings," the officer answered.

"Cleanest, anyway. I work at Orbital Logistics. You guys order more cleaning supplies than ships twice your size."

"We do? Well, the captain is death on dirt."

"What's your route?"

"We do all the lower stations—Orbital-46, Orbital-43, Orbital-37."

"Do you refuel at all of them?"

"Never have before. The prices are cheapest here, but you guys, your food is so expensive. Let me tell you...."

Jake nodded, bought the man a beer, talked some and made careful notes later. He also kept his receipts. It took only a few more days until he not only had routes, but also distances, times and all the information needed to locate fraud. Three ships stood out so far—a corporate ship and two Free Traders. The corporate one regularly took in more than 10 percent extra fuel for the distance traveled. The first Free Trader would load small amounts of cargo far more often than could be profitable. The other Free Trader kept coming back and ordering way more cleaning supplies than was necessary for such a small crew, but it never ordered food. Jake typed up a report for Dashi, but decided a personal investigation was in order.

He climbed up a set of spoke stairs, around the intermediate pedestrian ring, and then down to the docking ring to investigate. The docking ring was a double story with sets of airlocks piercing the wall at regular intervals. Arriving ships attached to a personnel airlock for passengers and small deliveries. Shipping containers bound for the station were detached, then replaced by new containers from the station. Detached containers were either connected to an airlock for unloading onto the station, or parked on the container level, waiting for the next ship to take them further on their journey.

The container level contained the huge cargo airlocks. Entire containers were winched inside and placed atop powered sleds, which moved containers and heavy equipment around the ring for delivery to other spokes. Station crew, passengers, visitors, corporate customs, and inspectors either walked or biked around on their errands. Jake wasn't as bothered by the chaos in the level as he would have been a year or even six months ago. He'd gotten used to larger groups of people and busier loading areas than those he had grown up with. He did make sure that his pockets were zipped closed and kept his hand on the credit chips in his front pocket. His three targets were latched right now, so he headed around the docking ring to see if he could meet some of the crew and get a personal feel for what was going on.

Jake ducked behind a bicycle to sidestep a passenger cart carrying people, and he nearly got squashed by a flatcar of dry goods. It carried boxes of cutlery, coffee pots, and kitchen supplies. He stepped behind a group of cleaners pushing brooms along the floor.

Jake stopped to organize his thoughts before approaching the three ships. He had to find out if they were smuggling. He was supposed to be a spy, but he wasn't very good at that. He couldn't shoot a gun to save his life, was a lousy pilot, had gotten beat up or shot at a lot—often by girls—and every spy-type thing he had tried had ended up in a fight, in jail, or both. But he knew cargo grunt work and paperwork. You could learn from what a ship was loading, how it was loaded, how the locking chains were attached, and suchlike. He had manifests for all three, so he knew how many containers were supposed to be loaded and of what type. He had arranged to have several shipments short-loaded so that the manifest would be wrong, and he was going down there to deliver the short shipment.

His first victim was the corporate ship. The first officer was friendly, helpful, and totally happy to receive his extra mops and cleaning fluid.

"We wouldn't have noticed it till we opened the box, and

the boss would have yelled at me. Thanks for bringing it down. This is great service. What was the problem?"

"Labeling error in the warehouse. We had a bunch of medium boxes listed as large, and it was picked from where the larges were supposed to be. We caught it in inventory and backtracked the orders. I saw you guys were here, so I thought I'd just bring it down and sort it out before you dropped. I'd end up fixing it anyway, and this way saves me a ton of work in the future," Jake said.

"Thank you. Not many people think that way. If you ever need a job in the cargo department, let me know. We could use a guy like you."

"Uh, thanks. But I'm up for a promotion and a raise this year."

"Hope it's a good one." One of the fueling techs approached and stood by their side.

"Uh, yeah. Hey, you can help this guy out while I finish my paperwork here," Jake said, gesturing to the fueling tech. He looked down at his tablet, but positioned himself so he could see and hear the transaction.

"Forty-four tons fuel. Thumb here," the fuel tech said, extending a tablet and a credit chip.

"Pleasure doing business with you," the first officer said as he thumbed the tablet, then pocketed the credit chip.

Jake turned to look at the fuel pump. It indicated forty tons, not forty-four. The fuel tech walked away and Jake handed his own paperwork to the officer.

The officer held the tablet but didn't thumb it yet. "Any questions here, buddy?" he said.

"Nope," Jake said. "I worked a fuel dock for a few years. Good job. Lucrative."

"Is this going to be a problem?"

"I don't sell fuel. And I currently specialize in minding my own business."

"Free trades then," the officer said, thumbing Jake's paperwork.

Jake walked to the edge of the fuel dock and looked back. The fuel tech now had four tons of paid-for fuel he could sell to somebody under the table. He watched the fuel tech saunter over to a Free Trader at the next berth.

Nothing sinister here. Just greed.

"Who are you again?" asked the Free Trader captain. He was short with greasy hair, twitching hands, and narrow eyes.

"Jake Stewart. I'm the sales clerk assigned to your account. I just wanted to double-check that everything was fine with your delivery."

"Our delivery?"

"Cleaning and environmental supplies. These pallets here. You order tons of it every time."

"Oh," the captain laughed. Or, at least, Jake thought it was a laugh. It was more like a snort. "Yes, we resell it at the outer stations. Your prices are high, but we make do."

"Everything okay with your order?"

"Yes"—*snort*—"yes"—*snort*—"it's fine. The station crews are just loading it into the containers now."

Jake looked at the crew in the cargo lock. In fact, the six tons of cleaning supplies were being broken up into six different packages, and each package was being loaded into separate containers—separate new, shiny, expensive containers. The external video showed one being towed with a chain onto the Free Trader's truss. All the trusses were empty.

"You are putting new containers onto your ship. Don't you have any to swap?" Jake asked.

"Oh, it's just easier to leave the containers at the stations when we drop the cleaning supplies. Faster unloading."

"Uh-huh. And of course, the stations get an extra container out of it. Which we pay for."

"It's part of your service. You bid free-on-board, after all. It's cheaper for you to just put on a new container rather than try to load it into ours. Faster, easier."

Jake nodded. "That's if the bid was FOB. However, my records show the bid, which you certified, is actually free alongside ship. We deliver it to the loading dock here, and you load it up."

The captain's look sharpened. He looked Jake in the eye. "There must be some mistake."

"Could be, I guess," Jake said. He didn't really care—containers were cheap, and they got a bulk rate from the station corp for loading. It was a tiny bit of embezzlement. "Either way, I have to investigate, check the paperwork."

The greasy captain took his comment as an opening. "How about I meet you for dinner sometime, and I'll bring my paperwork and you can reconcile things."

Jake smiled. He knew how this worked. "Well, sure, but cargo agents don't make much money. I can't afford to eat in the restaurants often."

"Oh, it would be my treat. It's work, after all."

Now act reluctant, and expand the stakes, Jake thought. "Well, I have to eat, but it would have to be away from the docks. I don't like to see my boss when I'm off work. All the cafs are too close."

"Why not the restaurant up a few levels? I'm sure your crew doesn't go up there much?"

"Well, I'm not sure. It's very expensive."

"Really, you would be doing me a favor by letting me take care of this during dinner. I barely ever have the time to have a meal, and if I can do that while filling out paperwork, that would be great. You'd be helping out the Free Traders."

"Well, okay, then. I have to eat anyway."

"Exactly."

"But before I go I want to see the container that we shipped you. I want to confirm what's in those containers before we load. If I don't have a reason for coming down here my boss will get on my case."

"Of course, just go over and ask them," the greasy captain said. "Let me know when you're free for dinner."

Jake set a date for his dinner. Afterward, he walked over to the station loading crew and asked them to open the containers. At first they were reluctant, but later agreed, after he piled documentation on them showing he was the shipper, referencing station regulations. He walked them down a line, opening up container after container, checking that they had cleaning supplies.

Yup, just more greed.

The next ship was another Free Trader, and Jake had to take the single lock to the chaotic Free Trader truss to view it. His corporate coveralls attracted a few looks but no comments. Jake surveyed the ship through the viewscreen. Totally standard, control cabin in the front. Three pods of six containers attached to trusses, a fuel module and then an engineering engine module at the back. The habitation module was double-sized. That was unusual. An access tunnel extended all the way down the center truss, reaching to the engineering sections at the back. The engine had only a single nozzle—slow acceleration, but simple to maintain, and cheap on fuel. The ship was docked nose-first, with the airlock under the control cabin plugged into the station. A chubby middle-aged man with a bushy red beard and a red-headed younger woman in a colorful dress stood in front chatting with the fuel clerk. Jake approached them and waited for the fuel clerk to leave.

"Master of the R&R?" Jake asked.

"That's me. I'm Rick Reece. You have the chip?" he asked, brushing some crumbs off his arms.

"Chip? No. I don't have a chip for you."

"Oh, sorry, I thought— I'm expecting a delivery."

"Not me, sir. We short-shipped you some items, and I've come to replace them for you. I've got the paperwork here—"

"I don't really have time for this right now. I'm expecting someone."

"It will only take a minute," Jake said.

"Look, I told you—" Rick paused, and lowered his voice. "I told you—"

"Hi, Jake," the red-haired girl said.

"Uh, hello," Jake said. He was nonplussed. He didn't remember this girl. This very pretty girl.

"It's Riley, Jake. Don't you remember?"

"Oh, yes," Jake said. And he did. "From the pilot class. You passed."

"I did."

"I didn't recognize you in a dress. You always wore coveralls in class."

She twirled around. "I like to be a girl on our ship. Does it make me look pretty?" She smiled.

"Oh, well, yes. It does."

"Excuse me for a moment," Rick said. A man carrying an oddly shaped box approached him. Rick stepped aside and lowered his voice to talk to the man. Jake glanced at them, then looked at them more closely. The man wore a generic skinsuit, but his jacket screamed 'Militia.' Jake couldn't identify his collar flashes, which was odd, but they were the same five colors the Militia used, just in a different order.

"And you switched corps. Are you working as a temp in cargo ops?" Riley asked.

"What?" Jake said.

"Your collar flashes. They are different."

"What? Oh, yeah, sort of." He didn't wear his TGI outfit for this operation. "This is just temp work. My corp loaned me out till my next project." Jake watched Rick out of the corner of his eye. The Militia man handed Rick a chip, then they pulled something out of the box and examined it. Jake recognized the size and shape. And also the part number stenciled on it. What were they doing with twelve of those?

"Did you lose your job?"

"What?"

"Because you failed the course?" Riley asked.

"Yes, kinda."

"That's too bad you failed, Jake. But not everybody is cut out to be a pilot."

"Sure."

"Well, at least you have regular work."

"True."

"You are a salesman now."

"Yes."

"Well, somebody has to do it," she said. Jake didn't know how to reply to that.

Rick stepped over. "I hate to interrupt you kids, but we need to get our cargo loading finished, Riley."

"Sure, sorry, Jake," Riley said.

"Okay, well, nice to see you again, Riley. Hey, Mr. Reece, do you need a hand installing these microwave ovens on board before you leave?"

"Microwave ovens?" Rick asked. "What microwave ovens?"

Jake gestured at the box in front of Rick. "Those microwave ovens. I recognize the shape and the part number. I had to install a bunch of them back at my home station. Those are food tray ovens. It's hard to install with just one person, but with two, it's easy. That's a lot, though. There must be, what, twelve of them?"

Rick looked at Riley. "Oh, these microwave ovens. I'm not installing them. We sell them as replacements to the stations we dock at."

"A dozen is a lot. Most traders only have one. They almost never break." Jake looked at Rick.

Rick looked at the Militia man. "We got a very good price," he said.

"Hope so. You'll have that stock for a long time." Jake turned to the Militia man and extended his hand. "My name is Jake Stewart. I work in cargo ops. We're always looking for a good price on support goods. What corp are you with?" Jake paused. "I don't recognize your flashes."

The Militia man reached for his coat, as if to hide the flashes, then he shook Jake's hand. "I work for Lexi—for Lexi Standard products," he said, naming one of the smaller, more obscure orbital manufacturers.

"Really? I know them well. I grew up on a rim station. Lexi would send a ship twice a year. They specialized in lighting and plumbing hardware as I recall. I'm trying to remember the captain's name—a younger guy, really friendly. Tall. You can't have that many captains, what are their names again?"

The Militia man didn't say anything. The silence stretched.

Rick blinked, then looked at Riley. He made a slight motion with his chin.

Riley coughed. "You know, Jake, you offered to take me for a beer before. I'll bet Dad could finish up while we had a quick one. Right, Dad?"

Rick bobbed his chin once. Then he bobbed it again. "Sure, pumpkin. I'll be finished loading in about two hours. There's a window then. Nice to meet you, Jake."

"Great. See you then, Dad. Let's go, Jake. We don't have

much time to catch up," she said, grabbing him by the arm and steering him around the ring.

Interesting, Jake thought. *She didn't want me talking to that Militia man.* He turned his head to look back at the R&R.

Riley caught the move, draped an arm over his shoulder, and pulled him back toward her. "Let's find somewhere we can sit down and talk. I know a place."

Jake debated going back to talk to the Militia guy, or staying with Riley. In other words, doing his job versus talking to a pretty girl.

Doing his job didn't have a chance.

She led him out of sight of the docks to the less disreputable restaurant on this ring, and stopped in the foyer. She adjusted her dress and twirled once. The twirl made it spin up nicely. She looked Jake over, frowned, pulled his sleeves straight, then buttoned his collar up.

"Hopefully you can get some better clothes after your first paycheck," she said, and led him to a table. Unlike the caf, there was table service here, and this one sold food as well as beer.

"Do you want the straps?" Riley said, gesturing to the belts that could be set up to hold you in your chair.

"Oh, no. I grew up on a station. I'm fine." She had picked a table that put her back to a wall and allowed her a view of the whole room.

"Really? I didn't realize that you were from a station. On the test you were, uh...."

"Incompetent?"

"Well, I don't think you've spent much time as a pilot."

"Not on ships, no. I can handle a launch or a ship's boat, but they move a lot slower. Simpler controls."

"Too much going on too fast on a ship, I guess."

Jake shrugged. He slugged down some basic. Riley hadn't objected when he bought basic for both of them.

"It didn't seem to bother you," Jake said.

"Somebody told me once, 'When they are paying you to make a decision, make a decision.'"

"That's why you passed, I guess."

"You were never a pilot on a ship?" Riley said.

"No, but I've been on ships and stations my whole life. I do a lot of cargo stuff, and some light repairs."

"Was it boring, growing up on a station?"

"It was, sorta," Jake said. He stopped talking, and the silence stretched.

Riley was twirling her hair and looking around. She turned back to Jake and clasped his arm with her hand. "But you must have done something fun. Tell me about it."

Jake began to talk about life on Rim-37, growing up poor, going to school, getting a scholarship, and Belt life in general.

"So then I was contacted by TGI and offered a place in the school," Jake said.

"Wow," Riley said.

"It was quite a big deal for the family."

"Uh-huh."

"I had to do a whole bunch of studying to get ready, of course."

"Of course."

"And it took me almost a year to get there. I had to work passage on a ship."

"A ship?"

Jake began to describe his efforts to get to the academy to claim his scholarship. Riley kept twirling her hair and looking around.

"The first few classes were difficult, but I managed to get through."

"Good."

"My favorite class was dinosaur hunting."

"Great, great— What?" Riley stopped playing with her hair and turned back to Jake. "What class?"

"Cargo handling. I liked cargo handling the best," Jake said. Riley was easy on the eyes, but if all he was going to do was look, he was putting entirely too much effort into this conversation. Time to change tactics.

"But enough about me. Let's talk about you for a while." She brightened up. "That's a pretty dress, where did you get it?"

"You like it? It's so hard to find things in my size. I was looking for weeks for something...." Riley began a narration on orbital shopping issues. It seemed to go on forever, but even shopping stories eventually end.

When she stopped to take a drink of basic, Jake jumped back in. "How do you manage it? Just the two of you?"

"Well, it's hard. Dad does most of the work—he's pilot and navigator, he does the engineering, and hunts for cargo. I do what I can."

"Your dad is certified as a pilot, a navigator, and an engineer," Jake said. "Wowzers, that's amazing."

"Wowzers?"

"Sorry, I mean that's pretty interesting."

"Not really. He's not a very good pilot. I'm much better. He didn't train as one," Riley said. "When he was younger, he wanted to be a dentist, so he joined the Militia to get credit for the university. He got some ship training and provisional certification while he was in. After he did his stint, he tried to go to school, but he failed out of dentistry. He had enough money for one term at Merchant's Academy, and was able to transfer some of his certs, but then he had to go to work. He needed the money. One thing led to another, and now he has a mortgage on the ship. He has to feed us both, and I have a half-sister, from when he was way younger. I've never met her. He sends her money."

"Still, that's pretty impressive. All those certs."

Riley shrugged. "I do all the piloting. Have done for years, just under his license. That class was for me to get my certs so we don't need his anymore. The computer does most of our navigation, and Dad isn't actually an engineer. They don't check the engineer's paperwork all that often. It's only a problem if things break, right?"

"You don't have a licensed engineer on board? That's not safe."

"Jake, we can't afford to hire one. Mom had been the engineer, so we had a go of it when they were both there. But with just him, it's hard. And besides, you know as well as I do that the licensed engineers are just a formality. Like you said, you can fix most things, and if a fusion plant breaks nobody can fix it."

"True. I just like things to be orderly."

"That's no fun. This is way more exciting."

"You like excitement?"

"Very much."

"Being a Free Trader is exciting?"

"Often, but sometimes you have to take what you can get. We spend a lot of time picking up weird cargos that the majors don't want."

"Oh? Anything shady?" Jake asked.

Riley laughed. "As if I'd tell you, Mr. Rule Book. We get by."

"You must have some good stories, at least."

"Well, Dad does the cargo negotiations, but sometimes I talk to the deck guys, about docking fees and so on. I do have one story." She began talking.

The story was long, but Jake kept quiet because he was enjoying looking at her, and she touched his arm from time to time. He liked that.

"So, he was so embarrassed when we left the restaurant that he ended up waiving all the docking fees. Oh, I've kept you too long." She looked at her comm, then rolled the metal foil back onto her food tray, and sealed it up. She had barely touched it. "Dad will eat this. He always eats when he's stressed, and these days he always seems stressed. He eats too much, really, but it's hard for me to complain. He works so hard." She stood up. "You probably need to go. And we're dropping soon."

Jake looked at his comm in surprise. They had been talking for almost two hours. "I'll walk you to the ship," he said, standing up.

"No, no. I have to run. Thanks so much, Jake." She gave him a chaste hug. "Free trades." Riley jumped up. She almost ran out of the restaurant.

"Riley, I can—" Jake called, but she was gone. *What did I say?* Jake wondered. Things were going well and then she was gone. Well, he could at least go down to her ship and see it off. He spent a moment paying for their meal, then strolled out of the restaurant and down to the docks.

Jake sauntered around to the Free Traders' deck, and wandered back to the lock where the R&R was—or should have been. The airlock was empty. Wow, Jake thought. They must have dropped as soon as Riley got back. Jake looked out the viewscreen next to the lock. No return date listed. *Well, I'll look her up next time,* Jake thought. He took a moment to examine the notes on the screen—the gross weight of the R&R before it undocked among them. The station computer used it to correct spin when mass moved. Eighteen containers loaded. Some of the numbers looked familiar. He'd look them up when he went back. He walked back toward the single airlock that opened into the pier.

It's just my job, he thought. He wasn't interested in Riley. Not at all.

Chapter 11

"So, you want to buy a gun?" the Free Trader crewman asked.

"Guns, plural," Nadine said. "What have you got?"

"All sorts," he said.

Liar, Nadine thought. "I want two boarding shotguns, the Old Empire ones, not the locally printed ones. And two full sets of revolvers—four total. Two shoulder holsters, two belt holsters, eight hundred rounds frangible ammunition, one hundred rounds training, and one hundred solid slugs, plus transport cases for all of this."

Nadine looked at him. The crewman couldn't have been more than eighteen. This was obviously his first cruise, and his first attempt at an illegal sale. He began to stutter some sort of reply, which she ignored. She was too busy watching the Militia courier at the next lock.

As far as Nadine was concerned, the Militia was possibly the dumbest quasi-criminal organization ever invented. They had paid her a substantial retainer to be 'on call for emergencies,' and then left her doing almost nothing except dropping between stations on a very irregular basis. She devoted her on-station time to spying on them, and they didn't even seem to notice. She had trailed this one from the shuttle dock directly to the Free Traders' deck with no problem. And did he really think that just re-arranging his collar flashes would fool anybody?

He was carrying an oddly shaped box, and had stopped to talk to two men and a young woman in front of a small Free Trader. Nadine was trying to get a better view of what was going on without being noticed, thus her approach to this idiot.

"I can get that," the crewman said.

"You can?"

"Sure. We have guns in the locker," he said.

"That's a full ship's locker full of gear. You think somebody won't notice when you break in and steal every weapon in the place?" She shifted to get a better view of the Militia guy. Emperor's balls. Jake Stewart was there, talking to the owner. What was he doing there?

"Can I help you?" An older crewman had walked over and confronted the two of them.

"We were just ... making an arrangement, Hamid," the kid said.

Nadine kept her eyes on the Militia guy at the next lock. He was carrying the box into the other ship. She memorized the name—R&R. The older man went with him. Huh. But the girl had just grabbed Jake's arm and was hustling him down the corridor. What was that about? Should she stay and see where the Militia guy went, or follow Jake and his contact?

She made a decision. "He was going to steal your whole ship's locker and sell it to me," Nadine volunteered, leaning back to keep Jake in view as the girl shepherded him away. "Which is pretty stupid, since this station is law level one, and I can buy what I need on the upper rings, but it's always good to know where I can get stuff if I need it. Thanks, boys. Free trades," she said.

She walked away, ignoring the smacking sound as the older crewman hit the younger one on the back of the head. The red-headed girl had a firm grip on Jake's arm, like she had won him at an auction. She wondered what that was about.

Nadine tracked them up another level to where the restaurants were, and watched them step inside. Well, she could use a little lunch herself. But she had to be careful so that Jake didn't see her. And if he did, she had a good reason for being there—lunch.

She stepped inside, breezed past the robotic dispenser, and stopped to look around. Jake and his date had moved farther into the restaurant. And sitting at the bar, right in front of her, was a familiar face.

"Officer Nadine," Pilot-in-Command Officer Third Class Timothy Desmaries said. "What are you doing here?"

Jackpot, Nadine thought. She had not started out well with Pilot-in-Command Officer Third Class Timothy Desmaries, so she decided to hit two moons with one rock.

"Timmy, so glad you are here. I was hoping to see you around." She pushed her shoulders back and squeezed her chest out. His eyes tracked where she wanted them to. "Have you eaten yet? No? Well, I was a little rough the other day, so I think I owe you a dinner." She squeezed her chest together again.

Ten minutes later, she was laughing and smiling at Timmy, while also keeping an eye on Jake and his new friend over Timmy's shoulder.

"So, I said to my uncle, '*Mon ami*, that is not correct,'" Timmy said.

"Wow, Timmy," Nadine said, "you call the chairman of Castle Transport 'ami'? You must be important."

"Well, not in public, of course, but I am his favorite nephew, and he does like to know what is happening out in the field, so he says to me, 'Well, Timothy,'—he calls me Timothy, you see...."

Nadine kept smiling and nodding, but also made sure to keep the couple in sight. That red-headed girl has some moves, she thought. The redhead smiled and nodded with the best of them, and she strategically tapped Jake's arm as she talked. Jake was eating it up, of course. He was an idiot, like most men.

"So, then, of course, we talked about the market a bit, and he told me this," Timmy said. He leaned forward and gestured Nadine closer. Nadine leaned into the table, and automatically squeezed her shoulders together to increase her cleavage. Timmy's eyes dropped and he stopped talking.

Nadine let the silence stretch for a moment. "He said?"

"What?"

"What did he say, Timmy?"

Desmaries tore his eyes up to her face. "Cobalt. He said cobalt."

"Wow," Nadine said. She leaned back in feigned surprise, then sat up straight and stretched her arms behind her, flexing her chest. "Wow. Why cobalt?"

"Well, as I'm sure you know...." He was off again. Nadine kept her posture upright, and her gaze over his shoulder. Jake was smiling again.

Nadine saw the redhead stand up and rush out of the restaurant. Jake looked surprised, and took a moment to sort out the payment chips before the table light flashed green. Afterward, he got up to follow her.

Desmaries was still talking. "But of course, I told him that was not so. Why? I had studied at the academy—"

"Timmy, when is the next shuttle dropping?"

"Shuttle? Very shortly. In fifteen minutes, perhaps."

Okay, Nadine thought. She needed to see this through.

"Timmy," she said, putting her hand on his arm. "Let's walk for a while, okay? I need to go down to the docks and see if there is a package for me at the Free Traders' docks."

"The Free Traders?"

"Yes, I have a friend who said they might be coming up, so I asked her to pick up some new scarves for me."

"But Free Traders? They are disreputable people."

"Oh, they're not all so bad, Timmy, but you have to get to know them. Let's go now," Nadine said, getting up. "I'll see if they're there, and you might learn something." She grabbed his arm again, and smiled until he sputtered and insisted on paying for dinner.

Nadine didn't exactly drag Desmaries along, but she did have to walk fast. She had lost track of the redhead, and she couldn't see Jake either.

"I can just go ahead if you don't want to come to the Free Traders' area," she said.

"No, a little slumming won't kill me. Wow, look at this airlock. Only one for the whole pier. Shocking. Still, what can you expect from these ignorant louts of Free Traders?"

"Pompous ass," Nadine muttered.

"Sorry, what did you say?"

"I said I 'promised assistance' to my friend if she needed it," she lied. "Let's go look for her ship." Nadine steered Desmaries around the Free Trader area. But she didn't see the redhead. It was frustrating.

"What is your friend's ship?"

"I don't know. She hops from ship to ship. But she said she would be up here today, so let's look for her."

"What does she look like?"

"A lot like me." Nadine struck a pose and gave him a big smile. She cocked a hip. "Just look at the girls and see if any of them remind you of me." That would keep him busy, she thought. They began to walk around the dock. Midway, they approached the dock where Jake had been talking to the girl. It was empty, but Jake Stewart was there, reading something on the display.

"Hi, Jakey," Nadine said.

Jake turned from the display. "Nadine. Slumming with the Free Traders today?"

"If I'm seeing you, then yes. Slumming, yes. That's exactly

what I'm doing. I was looking for a girlfriend who had some clothes for me."

"You buy clothes off Free Traders, do you?"

"I take my clothes very seriously, Jakey, and the Free Traders' clothes have a certain *je ne sais quoi* about their styles."

"What does that mean?" Jake said.

"Oh, I don't know. Jakey, this is acting second officer Timothy Desmaries."

Desmaries nodded but didn't stick out his hand for a handshake.

"He is a pilot with Castle Transport."

"I see."

"Timmy's uncle is the chairman of Castle Transport."

"That's nice," Jake said.

"And what do you do for Priority Personnel, Jakey?" Desmaries asked.

"Priority Personnel?" Jake said.

"That's what your collar flashes say," Desmaries said.

"Oh. Right. Well, I'm just short-term with them. I work in sales."

"Of course you do. What do you sell?"

"Jakey sells cleaning supplies, don't you, Jakey?" Nadine piped in.

Jake nodded. Desmaries looked him up and down. "Perhaps you should use some of your own products then. But good day to you, Jakey. I will leave you to your janitors. Let's go, Nadine."

Nadine smiled a thousand-watt smile at Jake as they sauntered away. Interesting, Nadine thought. She needed to know more about that ship, especially if both the Militia and Jake were interested in it.

Chapter 12

Meetings with Nadine were either unpleasant or scary, Jake thought, as he watched her and her new friend walk away. He had never told Nadine what he did, but she somehow knew. She must have looked up where he worked and what he sold. For Jake, that was interesting.

But never mind that—he needed to find out more about the R&R. He thought he should go back to the office and look up when Riley's ship was returning. He'd find out exactly the next time she latched, and invite her out for another drink then—to learn more about the ship and its cargo. Not just about her.

Jake returned to his office and ran back the R&R's cargo history. Several times a year, they landed a big ore shipment, the sale of which seemed to set them up for months. Some small buying and selling, and lots of cleaning supplies. Perhaps they had a deal with groups of prospectors to pick up semi-refined ore every so often.

For the rest of the time, they did a little trading but mostly seemed to ship containers out to different Belt locations. The trans-shipment history was interesting. They had been caught in a full inspection once, where customs inspected the contents of every container on board. They had an interesting variety of goods too. Entire containers of food, for example. Who needed two hundred thousand meal trays? And an entire container of environmental chemicals? That many chemicals would produce O for a very big station. No contraband. What type of Free Trader had no contraband on board at all?

He put a tracking program in his software so he would get a ping whenever Riley's ship was going to latch. They were on some sort of circuit—after loading, they would disappear, with no marked destination, and then return. The last few trips had been shorter and shorter, starting in the hundreds of hours then dropping to less than one hundred. Maybe next time, Riley would be in port long enough for dinner. In the meantime, he had information to gather.

Jake spent a fruitless few more hours searching for stations that were within a twenty-hour round trip under current orbital conditions. Nothing seemed to add up. This was apparently the wrong way to go about it. He decided to go with a different approach. If there were microwave ovens involved, there must be food trays too. Rim-37, his station, had about one thousand people. People ate three meals a day, plus drinks —basic and beer. Food trays cooked in one minute, so the cooking took one thousand person minutes, and the usual rule was, each shift had to be fed in a half hour. So there should be about thirty-three ovens if you wanted to meet that standard.

Huh, he thought. Twelve ovens would cook meals for three or four hundred people at a time. There was definitely no station that big on their route. Still, going by his estimate, three hundred people ate nine hundred meals a day—which would make twenty-seven thousand meals a month. That was almost three full containers of food trays every month. Who was shipping that volume of food every month? It could be the big corps, but they shipped their food up on the mass driver and used their own hulls for their orbital shipments. And Dashi had said somebody might have been stealing food, and had sent a list of serial numbers.

Jake started to research food. According to their manifests, the R&R was shipping a lot of food. But there was no record of them buying it, at least not in any database he could access. Who was selling them that food? Where was it coming from? That food had to come from somewhere. He needed to take a look at it before it got onboard the R&R. But how? Well, he had read the manual. Now he could ask.

"I need to check the contents billing on another container, Ms. Susa," Jake said, getting up from his office chair.

The second-shift boss, another middle-aged lady, looked up from her screen. "What?"

"I need to check another of our containers," Jake said. She didn't look at him, so he looked at her screen. It was another of those soap opera shows, set in the Old Empire. This one seemed to involve a lot of muscular shirtless men running through the woods.

"Ma'am?" Jake asked again.

"So check it. Why are you asking me, Jack?"

"It's Jake. My name is Jake. And I need the senior accountants' shift authorization code."

"Jake, really? But Andrea said—"

"I know my own name. It's Jake. Can I have the code, please? To check the records."

"No."

"Thank you—I mean, what? Why not?"

"I can't give it to you."

"Ma'am, I'm sorry if I was short with you, but it is my name."

"Not that. I mean I don't have it."

"You don't have the shift override code? But you're the shift lead."

"Only first shift has the code. Those codes are only available to the senior shift lead," she said, then returned to watching her screen. One of the shirtless men was now riding a horse through a river.

"But we run twenty-four hours a day."

"No we don't. Cargo loading and unloading is available twenty-four hours, but we charge 50 percent extra on second shift, and double on third. No captain wants to pay that, so if they latch after hours, they just send the crew to the bars, and unload during the next first shift. The bars do run twenty-four hours."

"But that's stupid. Why not staff for twenty-four seven?"

"Money. This way we only need one senior accountant, one senior fire inspector, all those people. We only have to pay one person in those positions, rather than three receptionists, three clerks, three cargo seconds, and so on. Cheaper to force everybody into the same commercial hours."

"What if there is an emergency?"

"A cargo emergency?"

"It could happen," Jake said.

"Station ops wakes people up. We pay double if they have to come in. What do you have to check?"

"I need to check if we loaded a break-bulk container properly," Jake said.

It was much more economical to ship an entire container of anything—food trays, raw ore, finished metal, consumer goods, it didn't matter what. The entire process, from the mass driver to the tugs to the container-based cargo modules on the ships, was all based around standard shipping containers. Shipping containers could be winched on and off ships on stations, in deep space even. Even extra fuel, life support, and power units came loaded in standard-sized containers if needed. The logistics were just too easy.

But sometimes, there was a need to combine shipments or break them up. Jake remembered seeing half a container of food, mixed clothing, life-support supplies, and a new entertainment unit—all in a single container—delivered at Rim-37 once. It only happened the one time, since the cargo crew had stolen a third of the food, three air filters, and all the pants before the shipment got to the station supply store. The station council couldn't pin down exactly who stole what, because the container had been opened multiple times. So, from then on, they only ordered full containers at a time— delivered sealed.

"Can't it wait till first shift?" she asked.

"If it's wrong, we'll end up holding up a whole ship while we repack, and we're on the hook for on-time delivery."

"Why don't you go manually inspect it then?" she said, keeping her eyes on the screen. The shirtless man was now carrying a woman in a white dress in his arms. As he plunged through yet another river, Jake saw that the dress was both completely impractical, and not at all waterproof. And nearly transparent.

"I said, why don't you go manually inspect it?" she repeated.

Jake tore his eyes away from the now transparent dress.

"Manually inspect it?"

"Sure, all our containers stay on the container dock level. They don't get moved up to the ship level till the ship calls for them. If it was being cross-loaded, it's still down there."

"Okay."

"And your inspection code will get you in there after hours. Just use your regular physical inspection code on the ring doors, and on the containers themselves. You can look inside."

"Thanks," Jake said. He looked at the screen again. The shirtless man had just dropped the woman by a campfire. Another woman was hugging him. The two looked similar. Was she a twin of the first one? Or a sister? Jake shook his head. "Thanks. I'll go down and check," he said, and began to walk away.

"The Adventures of Angus McAngus, Laird of Clan McAngus," she said.

"What?"

"That's the name of the series. Just in case you wanted to know."

Jake shook his head again as he walked away. But he did put the title in his comm.

He used his work access code to enter the controlled area, put his music headphones in, and then sauntered along with his hands in his pockets.

Okay, he thought. If he had stolen food, how would he hide it? He paced along the quiet deck, checking the contents of the containers on his comm. He wouldn't hide it at all, he decided. Food was too innocuous to hide. Having a container of food wouldn't be suspicious. Having a container of food labeled as something else would be suspicious. Besides, tariffs on food trays were either low or non-existent. So, the manifest would read "food." But the container's number would be different. Containers got mislabeled or misrouted all the time. And if you picked a container that was supposedly stuck in storage at another station, you just blamed it on data collection errors. The contents were what mattered.

Jake stopped and looked down the container deck. How many of these containers had food in them, he wondered. He checked his records. Three. He decided to look at those first.

Jake found what he was looking for at the first one he checked. It was an old battered container that had probably been around the system a dozen times, but the barcodes and numbers printed on it looked brand new. Jake tried to check its transponder, but he got no response. Usually, that was not a big deal—lots of cargo transponders were broken.

The container wasn't even locked. Jake flipped it open. Inside, he found racks of food trays. Jake picked one tray and scanned the serial number. Not one of Dashi's. Huh, he thought. He stepped back and re-inspected the barcode on the exterior of the container. It appeared to be totally legit. But why was it there, on the break bulk deck? Containers only showed up there if they had to be loaded. He checked the numbers again. All the food trays he could see were legit.

All the food trays he could see.

He pulled out the first box and stacked it clear of the doors. Emperor's balls, this was going to take most of the night, Jake thought. He'd have to unload most of the freaking thing just to see what was inside.

Jake began pulling the rest of the boxes out. All food. All the cheapest food—red-green-blue trays. There was a pallet placed just a few meters away, so he decided to stack them there. He tried to stack them in the same reverse order, so he could put them back exactly how they were when he was done. Hopefully, this way, nobody would notice they had been unloaded.

The first quarter of the container cleared quickly. He broke through a row of boxes and saw different colors behind. There were two different types of food trays there. Interesting, he thought.

He stepped out and onto the deck, walked over to the pallet, and stretched his arms. He bent over to stretch his back.

"What's he doing?" a quiet voice behind him said.

"Looks like he's stealing stuff," a different voice said, just as quietly.

Crap. Station security.

Chapter 13

"Hello, there's an emergency," Nadine said.

"What type of emergency?" the voice said.

"I think I see somebody stealing cargo on the break deck."

"The break deck? What's your name, please?"

"I saw somebody break into the lock. They used a crowbar," Nadine said. Actually, Jake had appeared to have a code. But crowbars sounded better.

"We can't see you, ma'am. Who are you?"

"I'm looking at the camera," Nadine said.

"It appears to be broken, ma'am. It's not displaying."

Of course it isn't, Nadine thought. *I broke it myself yesterday.* "You need to do something," she said. "He's stealing things."

"What's your name, ma'am?"

"I have to go," Nadine said. She flicked the call down. *Good. Let's see Jake explain his way out of this.* She hurried down the hallway and slipped into the back door of the restaurant. There would be no video record of her leaving dinner. She'd entered the restaurant from the front, and selected a table that had a clear view of the cargo-level door. She gave Jake fifteen minutes after he coded himself in before alerting security. Long enough for him to be neck-deep in something.

Jake Stewart wasn't the only one who could search station records, she thought. He was obviously interested in the cargo of the R&R. Finding out where the cargo was stored was easy enough, and she had a drink while she waited for him to show up.

A little guilt crept through her for shopping him to security—he had been so trusting and so naive. But she knew that, when it came to rules and regulations, Jake was as informed as they come, and might probably end up getting them to pay him for unloading their cargo. For the time being, she needed to find out more about that ship. Nadine had her own plan for getting on board, and she didn't need Jake Stewart messing things up.

Jake had started to panic when he heard the voices behind him. *What is security doing here?* Usually, they were lazy enough that they were rarely seen, or corrupt enough that they had been paid not to come down. *Why are they here now?* They never did patrols on this deck at night. If they did, how would the local cargo-loaders steal stuff? On his station, a regular payoff kept security out of the cargo area during the third shift so everybody could organize their smuggling. He'd discreetly checked, and it was the same here. He stood still, with his back to them as they talked.

"Who steals food?" one of the voices said.

"Yeah, that is kind of odd," the second said.

I can handle this, Jake thought. *Don't be a wimp.* He bent over and stretched more, being careful not to look toward the voices' origin. He picked up three boxes and balanced them in his arms. He rocked back and forth, letting the top box slide a bit, and danced sideways until he was in the container. Once inside, he walked to the back and pushed all the loose boxes back, toward the empty front. He cursed loudly and deliberately dropped one box with a thump. Then he stepped out of the container, but kept his face pointed down to his wrist comm, apparently playing with the settings on it.

"Hey, kid, what are you doing?" the first voice asked.

Jake didn't reply, or even acknowledge that he had heard anything. His cousin had been a waiter on Rim-37, and Jake had watched her ignore customers she didn't want to talk to. He had asked her about it, and she had given him some pointers. Don't make eye contact. Move quickly. Face away. He turned his face away from the interlopers and walked over to the pile of boxes. He collected another three, and then slid his way back into the container.

"I said, what are you doing? Hey!" the first voice said.

Jake ignored it and threw the pile of boxes into the front. It was now a big jumble.

He turned around and sauntered out of the container. The two station security officers had moved so that they stood between the container and the pallet. One had his arms crossed, and the other had his hands on a baton at his belt.

Jake reached up and removed the headphones from his ears.

"Help you gentlemen?" Jake asked.

"You're in trouble, kid," baton guy said.

"Trouble? For what?"

"Barratry."

"Huh? Barratry? What's that?" He wondered if Dashi was starting a trend. Did everybody talk with a thesaurus these days?

"Theft of cargo by the crew."

"Theft? I'm not stealing anything."

Baton man removed the baton from his belt and slung it in a circle.

"We had a call. Said you broke in and started stealing things."

A call? That was interesting. "I don't know how you guys would steal stuff, but loading a shipment into a container isn't usually how it's done. Usually, when people steal, they take things out," Jake said.

Baton man looked at his partner, who shrugged. "Makes sense. He was carrying stuff in while we watched him."

"This is official. I work for cargo ops," Jake said.

"Then why are you working third shift? Why not wait till tomorrow?"

"'Cause some idiot in packaging short-shipped some of the shipment, and the second part didn't get here till after they left, so my boss told me to get here and load the rest up, and gave me a lock code."

"Expensive for your boss. Double pay for third shift."

"Not if you send the junior guy, and I'm salary," Jake said.

"Why didn't you answer when we yelled at you earlier?"

"I didn't hear any yells. I had my headphones in."

The guards regarded him for a moment. Jake pulled his comm up and began to type.

"Actually, this works out for me. One of you guys just thumb here that you prohibited loading for security concerns, and I can go home. I didn't want to do this anyway, but I'm the new guy, so I get all the crap jobs."

Jake extended the comm unit toward baton guard and waited. The guards didn't move. Jake coughed. "Uh, if there's a claim on late cargo loading, though, security ends up paying."

His partner turned to baton guy. "For Empire's sake, Raj, let him load it. No skin off our nose."

Raj shrugged. "Okay, whatever. Load up, kid. Next time, keep your headphones off so you can hear us."

Jake nodded. "Of course, officer." He gave them a false grin. Baton man pointed his finger at Jake, and his partner laughed, but they turned and walked away.

Jake watched them for a second. Then he returned to the pile of boxes on the pallet outside the container. Crap, he thought. He'd have to put that entire pallet's worth of boxes back into the container. But before he did, he scanned some of the food trays in the back.

Stolen. Formerly the property of TGI.

And just for fun, he checked the bill of lading for this container. Yup, the R&R, Captain Richard Reece. And now, who had turned him in to security, and why?

"Nadine," Jake said. Why didn't she want him investigating the R&R? He needed to keep a better eye on that girl, and see what was next on her agenda.

Chapter 14

Nadine stuffed her stylish neck and wrist ruffs into a greasy pocket, then hefted a crewman's duffel bag on her shoulder. She'd overpaid for the used coveralls. At least they covered her custom skinsuit. She began to walk toward the docking ring. A thin man in clean, plain blue overalls stepped up beside her.

"Hey, pretty lady, where are you off to?" he asked.

Nadine glanced at him. "I'm signing on a new ship."

"That a fact? A new ship. As what type of crewman?"

"I'm an engineer third class."

"An engineer third class? Well, good for you."

"Yes."

"You got some sort of ID that says that, do you?" he asked, rounding a corner with her. They began climbing a set of stairs. He had long legs. Nadine had to take two steps to his one.

"Not at present," Nadine said.

"Well, missy, it's your lucky day. I happen to have a

complete set of engineering papers here. And 'cause I like your smile, I'll let you have them cheap."

"Thanks. But they're only good if they are in my name."

"Is your name Nadine?"

"It is."

He spread his arms wide. "What a coincidence, sweetheart. I happen to have a set of papers in that exact name."

Nadine laughed. "You're an ass, Tommy. Thanks for the rush job."

"Pleasure is all mine. Given the price." He handed her a chip, which she slipped into a pocket.

"Did you make that call I paid for?"

"Sure did. See, my cousin has a friend, and his friend's sister is sleeping with the district manager, and the manager goes to this gym, and well, you meet other people at a gym—"

"I don't really care about the details."

"That's a shame. Getting that fixed up was a work of art. But rest assured, your requested discussion is going on right now."

"Right now?"

"As we speak. You get to that lock, and you'll be able to hear for yourself. I gotta run. Need to see a man about a dog," Tommy said. He then peeled off toward a side corridor.

"Thanks, Tommy," Nadine called out, after which she continued forward. She walked down to the Free Traders' area.

The R&R was latched on to the shared truss—the scheduled departure time was indicated, but the outbound traffic slot wasn't. Riley and her dad stood next to the ship's loading hatch, alongside a pile of boxes. She wore a regular skinsuit, with a bright yellow dress over it. Nadine wanted that dress. It looked like sunshine. Rick wore crumpled coveralls over his skinsuit, and seemed very chubby standing next to her slim frame. The two of them were arguing with a short black-haired woman in a Castle Transport uniform. Her overalls had the words "Stellen" and "Station Operations" printed on it. Nadine walked toward the group. She wanted to hear the conversation before they noticed her.

"Look, that's more than fair," Stellen said. "You are supposed to have a licensed engineer onboard. We're fining you just starting today, and you have to clear the paperwork with us before you go."

"I told you, we have an engineer," Rick said.

"The paperwork says otherwise. The license number you gave us is registered to a ship permanently Docked at Militia-3."

"That's their fault, not ours. They must have made a mistake with the attachment."

"If they did, they made this mistake twenty-seven years ago when they went into a permanent docking orbit. And this engineer, Angelina Misou, is ninety-two years old. A little old to be on a Free Trader, don't you think?"

"She's very spry for her age," Riley said.

Stellen stepped back and swung her hand in an expansive gesture. "Well, let's see her old bones come hopping down the dock here and climb on board, and I'll forget the whole thing."

"Engineers are expensive," Rick said.

"So are new docking trusses when you crash into them

because your thrusters pack up at the last second—which, by the way, wouldn't have happened had you been maintaining them."

"Look, we'll be dropping today. Can't you give us a break?"

"I've already given you a break by not backdating the charges. What happened to that nice lady who was your engineer last time we inspected?"

"My wife. She died."

"Oh." Stellen frowned. "I'm sorry. Look, I gotta do my job here. I can say that you have an engineer reporting on board today, but you gotta have the paperwork cleared up by tomorrow."

"What if we don't? What if we do our business and just drop?" Riley asked.

"That will solve my problems, but not yours. The computer will just flag you in violation, and if you try to dock here again, instead of me, a security crew would be meeting you, and we won't be selling you any supplies. Probably same with the other corps. You can try the Free Trader stations then, but you're not going to be coming back here, or to any corporate station for that matter," Stellen said.

Nadine loitered at the next lock, pretending to read the shipping schedule. Perfect, she thought. All she needed was for them to get a little louder, and she could say she had overheard that they needed an engineer. She had an engineer's paperwork, and she needed a berth.

Considering the departure time listed on the board, they should be moving through their launch window right now.

She had been observing the argument out of the corner of her eye when somebody addressed her.

"Good morning, Nadine. You're up early," Jake said, striding by.

"Good morning, Jake," she said automatically. Wait. "Jake? Jake, what are you doing here?"

Jake winked at her, joined the group on the loading hatch and introduced himself.

"Mr. Reece, Jake Stewart, engineering technician second class, reporting." Jake smiled at Stellen. "Officer Stellen, I think that will clear the paperwork."

Rick blinked. Riley looked surprised.

Stellen scowled. "Who are you? Did you say you were a technician second class? Not a full engineer?"

"Yes. I have a TGI license. I'll give you my license number." Jake did.

"They need a full engineer."

"Actually, the regs say that for vessels this size, they only need to be inspected by a full engineer at least once every three months if they have an allied corp technician assigned. If I'm assigned, then they have three months until they need a full engineer to inspect."

"You are part of the crew? You're shipping with them?"

"I don't have to ship with them. I just have to assign my license to them."

"That's not true. Regs state that you have to be on board."

"Station regs for Castle Transport employees say that I have to be on board," Jake said, "but, the thing is, I'm not a

CT employee. I have a TGI license, and the inter-corporate ruleset applies here." Jake began talking.

Nadine listened. Give it to Jake, he knew his rulebooks. It helped that Stellen didn't really care, as long as she got a clearance on her computer. Jake talked her through the screens on her program.

"Just click here, then here, put my license number here—and click 'not assigned as crew,' accept that, and it will submit it to your computer. Then wait."

Her screen turned green. "Approved," Jake said.

"Approved," Stellen agreed. "You have conditional approval for ninety days, captain. Enjoy your visit. I'm off." She went on to the next ship.

Rick turned to Jake. "Um, that was great. Thank you. Ah, how much is that going to cost me."

"Nothing," Jake said. "Happy to help." He looked at the floor. "I was, uh, just coming down to see if Riley wanted to go to lunch with me."

"You wanted to ask me to lunch?" Riley said.

"Well, not if you were busy or anything, or if you had something going on. But that's okay if you did. I understand."

There was silence for a moment. Rick looked at Jake. "But Jake, I have to ask, why help us out with that engineer thing?"

"Oh, I heard the argument. About the license. I grew up on a small station. I feel for you with all this corporate stuff. I know a lot about regulations and paperwork, so I decided to help you out."

Riley looked uncertain. "Jake, that was sweet, but Dad and I have a launch window. We can't stay."

"Oh," Jake said. His voice dropped and he faked a smile. "Well, maybe next time. You will be back soon?"

"Not for a while, Jake, sorry," Riley said.

Rick coughed. "We'll be back in about a hundred hours, Jake. You two can go out then."

Riley looked at her dad. "I think I've got plans then."

"Cancel them," Rick said. "We owe Jake a favor."

For a moment, Riley glared at her dad, who glared back at her. She grimaced and then turned to Jake, flashing a smile. "Dad's right. We need to do something nice for you. When we get back, I'll get reservations at Max's— It's a bistro. You'll like it. See you then."

Jake exchanged a few pleasantries, assured her he'd be there, and walked away, smiling.

"Well, thanks for your time. Delivery will be next week. We'll see you later. Free trades," Rick said. He released the radio channel, then drew a long breath and exhaled in a whoosh. He shook his head and picked another channel.

"R&R, requesting drop slot."

"Drop when ready, R&R," the radio voice said.

"Understood. R&R out," Rick said.

Riley watched her father from the other seat in the control room, then she turned and surveyed her screen. Rick began to shovel food into his mouth.

"That went well, sweetie. We can drop off that container on our way—pick up a transport fee. Then do our special run and be back at the station," Rick said.

"Dad, do we have to keep doing these special runs?"

"I don't like them either, sweetie. But we need the cash."

"But shipping stolen goods is illegal."

"We don't know that it's stolen."

"Who else sells fifty thousand red-green-blue trays? It's got to be stolen."

"We don't know that, sweetie."

"Dad. And that ship, and those people—why do they need so much food every month? And they always have weapons."

"They pay well, sweetie. And after your mom died, we need a place where our paperwork isn't investigated too closely. They've never asked about us being short an engineer. It's a good thing that your friend signed for us here. You should keep being nice to him."

"Do I have to?"

"Well, yes, actually," Rick said. He turned to his daughter. "I need time to fix this engineer thing. When we're back, take him out to dinner, talk to him. That's all."

"Dad, are you pimping me out?"

"No, just treat him like a regular cargo contact. Make it like a business dinner."

Riley flicked a switch, then frowned. "I guess I can do that."

"Besides, you might find yourself liking him once you get to know him."

"He's not my type."

"You mean he has a steady, regular job, works hard at it, and doesn't make you pay for his meals?"

"Dad."

"Oh, and I don't think he slept with your best friend, or has he?"

"Dad, shut up."

"Sorry. I never liked Jean-Marc."

"As you have told me many times. And fine, you were right, and I was wrong. Happy now? Jake is nice, but that's all."

"Nice? Uh-oh. That's the kiss of death. Even I know that. Why is he just 'nice'?"

"Dad, he went to a merchant's academy, for the Emperor's sake."

"Do you know I met your mother at a merchant's academy?"

"You did?"

"Yes. She was on a Free Trader scholarship."

"Well, he's not a Free Trader. He's from the Belt."

"So?"

"Dad. He's a clerk. He sells cleaning supplies. He checks shipping paperwork. He's boring. Girls don't like boring. They don't even like to talk to boring guys."

"Huh," Rick said, pointing at a screen with a view of the loading dock. "Appears at least one girl disagrees with you."

Nadine had watched the whole thing with her mouth open. Jake waited till the docking hatch spun closed and the R&R dropped before walking back to her.

"Nadine."

"Jake."

"Sorry your plan to get onboard the R&R as crew didn't work."

"I have no idea what you are talking about, Jake," Nadine said.

Jake started to speak, but he stopped and cocked his head. "You normally call me Jakey."

"What?"

"You normally call me Jakey. Why are you calling me Jake now?"

"I still have no idea what you are talking about, Jake—Jakey."

"I had a tracker on the ship in the system. I saw them pop up on the ops crew inspection list today. They weren't due for inspection for another seven months. It had to be a setup. Rick would have had some plan for the regular inspection—paid somebody off or something—but this would be a surprise to him. And since the station directory listed our newest engineering technician as one 'Nadine,' I figured it was you. Not to mention the crewman's duffel you are carrying."

"Jake, you have quite an imagination."

"I do. I imagined somebody had called security on me last night. Only one person knew what ship's cargo I was interested in, and where I was. It wasn't too hard to connect the dots."

"Jakey, you are sounding ridiculous."

"That's possible. But I know why I'm interested in this ship. Now, I'm curious as to why you are. I'm having dinner with Riley in a few days. She should be able to fill me in if I ask the right questions."

"Jakey, you sound like you've been drinking. I'll talk to you tomorrow."

"Sounds good to me. And don't forget to tell your boss how Jake Stewart messed up your plans."

Nadine gritted her teeth. She'd had plans go awry before. But not because of a paper-pusher like Jake Stewart—him and his red-headed tramp.

Chapter 15

"It's not stalking," Jake said to himself. "It's work." He watched the counter on his screen. Riley and the R&R had been docked for one hour and forty-seven minutes, and still no call. His tracker program had pinged him when she latched.

But she did call eventually, and she had booked a restaurant. He headed down and waited in the lobby until Riley arrived. She was twenty-five minutes late. "You look great," Jake said. "Is that dress custom-made?"

"I got it altered to fit me," Riley said. "Some of the smaller stations are happy to trade services like sewing for cargo. Dad has a set of custom shirts. He can never get standard ones to fit him in the collar."

"Because he's a big guy," Jake said.

"No, because he's fat," Riley said. "But he's my dad, and I love him."

She seemed happy to see him and chatted genially. They sat down and looked at the menu. The special was buffalo, at a very good price. Riley had not eaten it before, and she seemed to enjoy the taste. She had more stories about things that happened on a Free Trader. They were mostly mundane, but she made an effort to make them sound funny or exciting. She was friendly, but not encouraging. It wasn't the best date Jake had ever had, if it even was a date. Riley seemed to be treating him more like a passenger being entertained than a potential boyfriend. But she did pay more attention to him than before, asking him about his skills.

"Can you repair a fusion drive?"

"Funny, Riley, only the Old Empire can do that. I can fix controls, a little, and do most of the environmental and electrical stuff."

"We hired a guy once who said he could fix a fusion drive, so Dad decided to test him."

Riley began a story about how her dad had put a prospective crew member through his paces. She was quite the raconteur when she put her mind to it.

Riley waved her arms. "So then, Dad said, 'Okay, just hold this wire for a second,' and of course, it was live, so the shock bounced him over the bench, and he knocked the coupler down. And then Dad said, 'I hope you don't think I'm paying for that.'"

Jake laughed. "What happened to the guy?"

"Oh, I dated him for a few months. He was a horrible mechanic, but he had lots of other skills."

Jake kept smiling. "So as a Free Trader, do you have a guy in every port?"

"Two."

"Two ports?"

"Two guys per port. That way, if one is busy, the other is usually available."

"Oh. Do you have them fill out an application form or something?"

"Usually. I have standards."

"Really?"

"Sure. He has to be two inches taller than me."

Jake sat up straight in his chair. He was taller than her, but he didn't know by how much.

"What else?"

"Good job. He has to pay for dinner and drinks if we go out."

"I see," Jake said. So much for his bonus. Shouldn't have ordered dessert either.

"And he has to like to do fun things. When I was at Orbital-42, there was a guy there. We got a set of those wing things, and went to the zero-g area."

She started talking about flying with him. "He thought he'd impress me with his skills, but I've been on ships my whole life, so he was having problems keeping up. And when I dove down the core to the next level, he tried to follow."

She really was pretty, Jake thought. Just a light dusting of freckles and red hair, and she seemed so alive.

"I picked him up from the medical clinic after. Three broken fingers, a sprained ankle, and forty-two stitches. He's been too embarrassed to comm me since."

Jake laughed. "It sounds like life on a Free Trader can be pretty interesting."

"It can sometimes. It's fun most of the time. But it can be a bit dangerous. That's how we lost Mom. She didn't pay enough attention to the radiation guidelines. This was her dress," Riley said, flaring her arms.

"I'm sorry," Jake said. "I know how you feel. All I have left of my dad are his boots, really." Jake stuck a foot out.

"Great quality. Those are very expensive boots for a Belter. More like what the high-end corporate crews use."

"He spent a lot of money on them. They will last forever," Jake agreed. "I always think about him when I look at these."

"What happened to him?"

"He died in an accident. He cut some fuel lines to free some people in a transport. There was an explosion, and a blowout. Three others were killed, and the station was damaged by flying debris."

"Oh, I'm sorry."

"It was tough for a long time on the station. A lot of people blamed Dad for it, and the families of the three who died took it out on me. Their kids did, anyway."

"That's sad, Jake," she said. She put her hand on his arm. "I'm sorry."

That doesn't feel bad at all, he thought.

"So, how did your microwave oven sale go?" Jake asked.

"Microwaves?"

"The ones your father bought from that guy. Did you sell them all?"

"I think we did. Why?"

"I know somebody who wants to buy a few. If he has any left, I'll give him a good price."

"They're all gone."

"All of them? Where did you sell them?"

Riley shrugged. "Dad handles all that cargo stuff. I find it boring. Why are you so interested?"

"No reason," Jake said. "Tell me more about being a pilot."

"Well, look who's here!" said a voice to Jake's right. They had moved to the bar after dinner. Riley had walked to the other end to buy an after-dinner drink.

"Hello, Nadine," Jake said. He sighed. He'd tried to minimize contact until he could get this work over with, but the station wasn't that big.

"Timmy, you remember our mop-salesman friend?" Nadine said, turning to the man next to her.

Timmy just nodded. Jake nodded back.

"How is the cleaning supply market doing, Jake?"

Jake had learned that when he was asked questions that were designed to embarrass him, it was best just to flood people with data. It didn't take the sting away, but it did make them stop talking to him.

"Not too bad, Nadine. Bleach products are up by 3 percent over last quarter, but that's only for the bulk liquids, of course. The water pellets have gone up a bit more. It really depends on how you categorize them. The bulk ones are doing best, but I think there are opportunities in other packaging models."

Timmy looked very confused. "Water pellets?"

"Yes, they go in the environmental system for scrubbing the water. After you run the re-circulator, you add them."

Jake had begun to describe, in detail, the operations of a water-reclamation system, when Riley returned.

"Who are your friends, Jake?" she asked.

"Uh, this is Nadine. She was a colleague on a different job. We were on a trading mission, sort of, but she worked for a competitor."

"I did most of the big work. Jake just followed along and cleaned up afterwards," Nadine said. "He's very good that way. I'd just give him a smile, and he'd do the grunt work for me. I didn't trust him with anything important, of course." Nadine gave Riley a long glance.

Riley handed Jake the drink in her left hand. Then, she leaned into Jake, and put her left hand on his shoulder. He wasn't sure exactly how she did it, but somehow, she seemed to glue the entire side of her body to him, from his ankle all the way up to his shoulder. She took a drink from her glass.

"Oh really? That's too bad. My family owns some Free Traders. He's been helping us with our work here at the station." She began to caress Jake's shoulder. "He's handling all of our engineering issues right now. And he's doing an excellent job."

Jake wasn't sure how good a job he was doing, but he'd be willing to do a lot more engineering if she kept running her hands over his shoulder like that.

"Engineering? Jake's got an engineering license? I don't think so," Nadine said.

If anything, Riley melted more into Jake's side. "The station says he does."

"Oh," Nadine said, turning to Jake. "I'm impressed. If I had known that I might have given you different work."

"It is impressive. Jake has been very impressive with all the tasks I've given him," Riley said. She smiled up at Jake, who blushed. "Drink your Calvados, dear." Riley turned to Nadine. "It's an apple brandy, distilled in the foothills north of Landing. Very smooth. Do you like brandy?"

Timmy coughed. "We have it sometimes in my family."

Riley turned to him with a bright smile. "Perhaps Nadine will get some for you. If you are a good boy."

Nadine smiled back at Riley. Jake winced. For a moment, he was reminded of a video he saw in which a very angry animal was snarling and baring its teeth. Riley smiled back. Ow, Jake thought. Make that two angry animals snarling and baring their teeth at each other.

Riley tossed her glass off. "Well, it was nice meeting you. Goodnight. Drink up, Jake, and let's go. We've got things to do," she said, and half-dragged Jake toward the door.

Riley stayed glued to Jake's side until they left. Then she laughed. "Oh, that was fun. Who was that bitch?"

"A work colleague. From a competing company."

"Is she a former somebody?"

"A former somebody? You mean...? No. No."

"But you like her."

"She's very attractive, but she's never been very interested in me."

"You think so? She acted pretty interested in you."

"How?"

"She stopped to talk with you while she had a man with her."

"I don't think that's the case."

"Girls know."

"Um, okay. Will your dad be upset if I come back to the ship with you?"

"No, because you're not going there. I am. That was just to irritate your friend. But I will give you a kiss goodnight here." She kissed him chastely on the cheek.

"Ah, thank you. Will I see you again when you come back?"

Riley shook her head. "Perhaps, Jake. But I'm usually pretty busy. Two guys in every port, you know."

"Right, sure. Well, that's okay. I'll probably be busy as well."

"Doing what?" Riley smiled.

"Maybe I'll ask Nadine out," Jake said.

Riley laughed out loud. "Of course you will, of course you will."

"You don't think I'll ask her out?"

Riley grabbed his shoulder. "Jake, tell you what. If you ask Nadine out for a date, and she agrees, look me up when we're latched again. Jake Stewart, mop salesman, out for the evening. I want to hear that story."

"How long will you be gone?"

"Twenty-two hours out to drop some stuff at a station, twenty-nine hours back, and depends how long we stay there. So, fifty-five hours minimum."

"I'll be here," Jake said. *And I'll be looking to see what stations are twenty-two hours away, and why they need so many microwave ovens,* he thought.

Chapter 16

"Way to go, tiger," the bartender said.

"What?" Jake said. Jake had nowhere to go after Nadine and Riley left, so he had returned to the bar and ordered another beer.

"Good job with the ladies. You are an inspiration to single men everywhere." He shoved a beer toward Jake. Jake took a drink and grimaced. "Belter beer?" Jake said.

"You didn't specify, and frankly...."

"I know. I look like a Belter. I'm dressed like a Belter. I have Belter boots on. I am a Belter. Fine," Jake said. He drained his glass in one long swallow. "Give me another of these crappy Belter beers."

"Heard your conversations earlier. Saw the girls. And now you are back here alone. Which one do you like?"

"I like both of them, but not that way."

"The way they look, I sure like them that way."

"Okay, exactly that way. But one is crazy and dangerous, and all she likes to do is tease me and yank my chain. And the other is smart and energetic, but she just likes to get my hopes up and then dash them."

"Which is which?"

"I'm not sure. Does it matter?"

"Not at all. So they both yank your chain."

"Well, yeah, sort of."

"Do each of them do this when the other is around?"

Jake thought for a moment. "They do seem to react to the other's presence."

"You, my friend, are the backup guy." He leaned forward. "Let me explain something to you about women."

"And you know all about women?"

"Yes, because A, I'm a bartender, and B, you don't seem to be much of an expert, and C, you are sitting here by yourself, so I'm bound to know more about it than you," the bartender said, and topped up Jake's beer. "Every woman has four guys. Guy A, Guy B, Guy C, and Guy D." He held up four fingers and counted them down. "The main guy she has, the main guy she wants, her side guy, and her backup guy."

"Four guys?"

"Yes. First, the guy she wants. She has fun with him. She likes spending time with him, might marry him someday. She'll introduce him to her friends, her mom. This is her main guy—Guy A."

"Okay."

"But her main guy is not perfect. He's got a job, but not the best. She wants him to spend more money on her. Maybe he doesn't dress well. To keep him on his toes, she brings in a little competition. Guy B. And she makes sure Guy A knows it. The two are similar, but there are some things that Guy B does better. He's taller, or has a better job. There is real competition there between A and B. Sometimes, she dumps one for the other. Got it so far?"

"I guess."

"Good. Then there's Guy C, her side guy. He's very good looking. Fun, kind of wild. But bad news. He has no job, or too many ex-girlfriends. When she breaks up with one of her main guys, she does a detour with her side guy. But only for a little while."

"What does this have to do with me?"

"You're the fourth guy, Guy D—the backup guy."

"What does that mean?"

"Women are planners. The side guy, Guy C, is for fun. Guy A and B are long-term. But what if Guy A gets tired of her and dumps her, and Guy B is busy with somebody else?"

"I'm confused."

"Both main guys are taken. She doesn't want side guy. What does she do now?"

"Wastes her time hanging around a bar listening to confusing bartender stories?"

"Guy D. Backup guy. That's you. Solid. Reliable. Always available. You are both of those girls' backup guy."

"I'm a backup?"

"Right. To use an analogy, you probably have a couple good pairs of socks to wear with your skinsuit. Rotate them and clean them. But in the back of your locker...." The bartender stopped to take a drink from a glass of water.

"What's in the back of my locker?"

"A worn out pair of socks. Stretched. Stained. Not much use. But you keep them there, just in case. In case you lose your other socks. 'Cause you always need socks."

"So, I'm an old pair of stained socks."

"You got it."

"That is the stupidest thing I've heard in a while. I don't believe you."

"Fine with me. Will both of these girls spend some time with you? Talk to you?"

"Well, yeah."

"And they talk about their other boyfriends. Or bring them along?"

"Yes."

"So, they aren't interested in you, unless the other girl is there, and then they get all touchy, grab your arm, that sort of stuff."

"Yeeeessss."

"And snipe at each other?"

"Yesssss."

"There you go. They are like dogs, guarding a bone. They don't want the bone right now. But they might later. You're the bone."

"Now I'm a chewed dog bone?"

"You probably don't get chewed much from the looks of it. I think a bit of friendly chewing might improve your mood."

Jake took another drink, then spat it back into his glass. "Do you have anything other than Belter beer?"

"You don't like the taste? I thought all Belters loved it?" He shoved a different beer in front of Jake.

"We don't love it. We're just used to it out in the Belt."

"Oh. What's it like?"

"The beer? It tastes like the water left after you wash clothes in a sink."

"Never washed clothes in a sink. No, I meant living in the Belt. Being by yourself, dependent on your own resources, the chance to strike it rich. It sounds great."

"It isn't. Belters are poor. For five years, I only owned two shirts. Belters don't strike it rich. You have a better chance than me."

"Yeah? Ever met some rich guy who said, 'I wanted to make my fortune, so I became a bartender'? I don't think so. Hang on," the bartender said, sliding down the bar to serve another customer. He came back. "I'd rather be a Belter. Here I work twelve hours a day at this crappy job, six days a week. I'm going nowhere."

Jake shrugged. "Why don't you go out to the Belt and seek your fortune—whatever that means."

"Because I'm scared of the Belt. I'm scared of change. I'm waiting for somebody else to fix it up for me." He pulled a glass down and polished it. "Why don't you ask one of those girls out?"

"They might say no. As long as I don't push it, there's always the chance that things will get better with them. They might ask me out."

"That will never happen. We're both scared of asking for what we want. Neither of us is making things happen. We're just waiting for things to happen to us." Another customer called, and the bartender walked away.

Jake thought about this for a while. He had made some things happen—school, some jobs. But a lot of the time he just collected information and waited. What if he asked for what he wanted?

He pondered that, then drank his beer down. He waved at the bartender and pointed at the vodka bottle. When the shot arrived, he drank it down.

"I need a test—a trial run," he said. He turned around and surveyed the bar.

"So, it's a bird?" Ulrike asked, propping the comm screen up against her beer.

"Yes, it's called a parrot," Gwen said. "Old Earth stock. But hardy and long-lived. The specialist store on Orbital-16 has a bunch. They don't mind low-g. They can fly around the ship, and they don't eat much. No human-transmittable diseases, so they can come into any station." She took a drink from a green glass beer bottle.

"Well, they look pretty small, so no mass issues. I guess if you want a pet it's a good one."

"And they can talk."

"The shop owner says they can talk. I'm dubious. But if it's true, you can get it to say to you 'Oh, Hans, Hans, kiss me again,'" Ulrike said.

Gwen blushed. "It's over with Hans, and it has nothing to do with him anyway."

"Gwen, you don't need a pet. You need a man."

"Uli, I don't want a man. Not now. I was with Hans for a long time. I don't need a new steady."

"Gwen, treat getting a man like looking for a new ship. You don't have to buy him. Just take him for a test drive. That's all. You should have slept with his best friend after he dumped you."

Gwen stared at her beer and spun the glass in her hand. "Helmut was just being nice."

"He's a pig. They are both pigs. Look, Gwen, we need to find you somebody new. Somebody with a sense of humor, which Hans didn't have. What about those two over at that table?"

"They look good. Nice hair. But they're a little short for me, Uli," Gwen said.

"Why do I have to have such tall friends? Fine. What about over there?" Ulrike gestured.

"That's a possibility."

"And those three over there. They look like they would be up for something."

"They're good too."

"And that guy at the bar who was talking to those stuck-up bitches earlier." Ulrike pointed.

"Yes. He's tall enough."

"Lots of options then. We just need to figure out how to get them to come over here."

Gwen blew out her breath with a *bleesh* sound. "I don't know how to do that. When I try to look alluring, I just look like I have gas."

"Not attractive."

"And when I try to talk, I sound like an idiot."

"Tell them work stories. Talk about engines. Guys like engines."

"I'm pilot on a cargo tug. Second pilot. On a rusty tug."

"Your tug isn't rusty, Gwen."

"Thanks."

"No O in space, so no rust. But lots of micro-meteorite damage. And do you have to crash into the containers every time? It looks like somebody took a giant hammer to your cage."

"Thanks for the piloting advice, Uli. But that won't help me to meet anybody."

"You could try to smile once in a while. Then again, you might not have to. Look." Ulrike jerked her head.

Gwen turned around and saw the man from the bar walking toward them. "Well," she said. The man reached their table and pulled out a chair and sat down.

"Hello, ladies. Is this chair taken?" Jake said.

"Could be."

"Could be? Could be me, I guess, then. My name is Jake. I need to sit where I can see the door, and you two pretty ladies looked like you had room. So, here I am."

"Why do you need to see the door?" Gwen asked.

"I'm a spy and a criminal. I'm expecting somebody to drop off a bribe, so I have to watch a table."

"Really? That sounds entertaining. We could use some entertainment."

"Entertainment? Sure. How about I tell you some jokes. Say, is that a parrot you have on-screen there?"

"Yes."

"Okay, so there is this guy who bought a parrot. He brought him home and said, 'Hey parrot, do you talk?' And the parrot said, 'I sure do talk, and let me tell you something, you stupid ugly...,'"

Chapter 17

Jake was late for work the next day—at least for him, but not for the rest of the office. Not only did nobody pass any comments, nobody noticed. His search parameters for finding stations within a twenty-two-hour round trip were not producing much. Lots of stations came within range, but only briefly, and none matched up for more than one trip. He now had data of three of Riley and Rick's trips. He'd need more data to decide where they went.

"Round the corner, he's in there," Jake heard from out front. A familiar figure appeared in front of him.

"Hello, Nadine. What's up?"

"I didn't see you at breakfast this morning, Jake."

"I slept in."

"With that girl?"

"No, not with that girl." Jake smiled. "Regardless, none of your business. What do you want?"

"I'm surprised at you, Jake."

"Why—because I have an engineering technician's license?"

"I am surprised about that, too. That's a side of you I didn't know about. But mostly, I'm surprised that you were out with that wench."

"Wench? Why? You think I have bad taste?"

"It's not that. It is unusual for you."

"Well, it will be more usual in the future. Are you here to talk about my dating life?"

"No, actually, I have some information to share with you. I've known it for a while, but I figured it wasn't important enough to share with you till now."

"Okay." Jake waited.

Nadine looked at him. "Jake, aren't you mad that I didn't tell you before?"

"Nope."

"What about our sharing rules?"

"I never believed you'd follow them."

"You used to be so big about rules, Jake."

"Nadine, tell me what you want to tell me, or don't. I have work to do."

"So aggressive. Jake, are you going to be like this all the time? It's actually kind of attractive."

"The information, Nadine."

"Two things. I got a notice from my boss that the Militia is stealing food from TGI."

"I already knew that. What else?"

Nadine blinked. "You did? You must be lying. But Jake Stewart doesn't lie." Jake spread his hands and said nothing.

She continued. "The Militia is paying me to wait here. At some point they want me to pick up a ship and fly it back."

"Okay. When and which one?"

"Don't know yet. They said they will tell me. Oh, and they said they wanted me specifically, because in addition to being smoking hot, and an exceptional pilot and all-around awesome person, they needed a glider pilot."

"They said all that?"

"They sure did."

"I guess they forgot to mention your modesty."

"That was assumed."

"I'll have to study up on space gliders. I don't know much about them." Jake waited.

"Do you have anything to tell me about that ship?" Nadine asked.

"Which ship?"

"The one with the red-headed wench?"

"The same one you tried to sneak onto as crew?"

"I never did."

"Nadine. What's so interesting about that ship?"

"Other than the girl?" Nadine smiled. "Fine. A package was delivered there by the Militia. I'm curious about what it was."

"Microwave ovens."

"What?"

"There were microwave ovens in those boxes. I checked them. And the person who delivered them was in the Militia." Jake paused. He had a thought. "That must have been your

Militia contact who delivered them. That's why you were trying to get onto that ship."

"Maybe. Why are you interested in them, Jake?"

"Because of the pretty girl."

"Jake, don't be ridiculous. She's way out of your league. You're too shy to make any progress there," Nadine said. She looked at Jake for a moment. "It must have something to do with the food. Is that what you were tracking—stolen food?"

"Why do you think she's out of my league?"

"She is, Jake. Jokes aside, you just aren't aggressive enough to ask her out. Are they stealing the food?"

"What would you say if I told you I was supposed to see her again when she came back?"

"I'd say you are lying. But we need to find out where that ship is going on its cruises."

"I agree," Jake said.

Nadine looked at Jake. Jake looked at Nadine.

"We agree?" Nadine said.

"Appears so," said Jake.

"Kind of creepy if you ask me," Nadine said. "Hm. Okay, I have a new plan. I know how to get on board that ship."

"Tell me."

"Sorry, Jakey." Nadine smiled. "You'll just get in the way. I'll let you know what I find out."

"Of course you will," Jake said.

"If you make it into work on time. Well, I'm off to buy another expensive breakfast. Ta-ta for now, Jakey," Nadine said, flouncing out.

Jake watcher her go. An idea was forming in his head, but

he'd need to do some more research about microwave ovens—and gliders.

Jake yawned as he stepped through the lock on the cargo deck. He'd been up half the night organizing things for this morning. Instead of a skinsuit, he had on his full Belter semi-hard suit, work belt, full gauntlets, and boots. His helmet was clipped onto his belt. He stopped in front of an office and dialed his shift boss on his comm.

"Cargo ops."

"Hi, it's Jake. I'm down on the Free Traders deck to cross-check the outgoing shipment reports with the on-duty cargo ops guys."

"More reports?"

"Yes. I sent you an email. Can you just approve it?"

"You want to do inspections? Today? It's quarter end."

"Well, I like to be sure that everything works out, you know," Jake said. He turned to look down the deck. Lock thirty-five was still red. "And I submitted all my quarter-end reports yesterday."

"I got all those. Did you have to send so many? Okay, I see it, inspection of cargo. This is a freaking long email."

"Yeah, it's got the list of all the ships I want to check, and the contents of the possible cargo containers."

"There must be two hundred containers on this list," she said.

"Three hundred thirty-six. Twenty-one Free Traders. Sixteen containers each, full loads."

"Wow."

"Do you want me to go over each one with you? I've got details for all of them," Jake said.

"No, no, that's fine. No need for all those details. No. Okay, I approved it in the system. Hey, I put you in for a bonus."

"You did?"

"Yup. One-quarter percent of your monthly pay."

"Uh, wow," Jake said. "I don't know what to say."

"It's your monthly base pay, of course, not any extra you get for taking those other shifts."

"Right, of course." Jake kept his eyes on lock thirty-five. It had just turned yellow. Ship inbound but no hard seal yet.

"And each shift is only eight hours—even if you work fourteen or so, it only counts as eight."

"Ah, yeah. Thanks, I know that."

"So you have to deduct those off your hours worked, of course, for the bonus. But hey, it's still extra money."

"Uh, thanks for your help. I appreciate it."

"No problem, Jack, see you later," his boss said.

"It's Jake," Jake said, but she had already hung up.

Jake sighed and looked back. The lock had turned green. Somebody had latched. He slid between the cargo office and the next truss, holding his comm to his ear like he was listening to a phone call. He saw the lock cycle, and Riley stepped out and headed into the station. He expected them to be on station to take on two containers—a load of food and a half load of cleaning supplies. Riley was probably going to drop off some payments, then run back to the ship.

Rick stood in front of the ship and checked his comm. He

looked like he was waiting for somebody. A woman obscured Jake's vision. Over her skinsuit, she wore an elegant corporate jacket and pant set in charcoal gray. Rick turned to greet her and nodded his head a couple of times. Jake saw some motion that must have been her handing him a message chip. Rick put the chip into his comm unit and looked at it for a moment, spoke once or twice, nodded and then made a 'follow me' gesture and walked onto the ship. The woman followed him, and Jake got a good look at her face as she went by.

It was Nadine.

Rick followed Nadine through the airlock but left it unlatched. "Sorry, had to get off the open deck there before we had a chat," he said, then stepped into the common area on the habitation deck. "What was your name again?"

"Call me Nadine."

"Okay. This note says I'm supposed to take you somewhere."

"Yes."

"Where is that?"

"I don't know. But you do."

"What do you mean?"

"Look, Ricky—"

"Richard, actually, but you can call me Rick."

Nadine beamed one of her thousand-watt smiles at Rick. "We have mutual friends. They pay me to stand by and do some drop-ship runs till they need me. Apparently they need me now to drive a different ship. They told me to go see you, that you'd take me there."

Rick shook his head. "I don't think so. I don't know what

you are talking about. This sounds like some sort of fishy entrapment thing. I think you need to go."

"Fine with me, I'll go," Nadine said. But she didn't move. "What do you want me to tell the Militia guy who gave me my travel chip? That you didn't want to take me? I'm sure that will go over well with your friends." She continued to stand there.

Rick stared at her but didn't say anything. "I don't know anything about this."

"Don't you have somebody to call?"

"Not usually."

"This isn't usual. Make a call."

"Maybe I'll do that," Rick said. "Why don't you wait in a stateroom till we figure this out?"

"And have you lock me in? Nope," Nadine said.

"I won't lock you in. I just don't want you roaming around my ship."

"I don't roam. Especially if I'm not being paid. I'll wait here while you make a call."

"I want to look in your bag."

"Nope."

"Why?" Rick asked. "What's in there? Weapons?"

"Sure," Nadine said. "Weaponized tampons. But they're no good for guys."

A snapping noise sounded behind Nadine's left ear. She turned and saw the barrel of a shotgun pointing at her face."

"That's okay," Riley said. "I can use them. I was a little short. Step away from the bag."

Jake walked into the deck office and waited. After a minute, he was called over by a clerk. Jake explained what he wanted and handed him a message chip. The clerk disappeared into an office for a moment, then reappeared and motioned Jake to follow him. Jake went around the desk and into an office labeled 'CARGO MANAGEMENT.'

"You want to what?" the cargo boss asked. She was a very small, very dainty-looking woman. Her skinsuit was colorful and custom, and she looked very feminine in it. She even had wrist and neck scarves on. Jake would have taken her for a dilettante playing at being cargo boss, except she had full magnetic boots on, a pair of hard gauntlets connected to her belt, and a double-size atmo pack. The cargo hand next to her was much more what Jake was used to. He had a semi-hard suit on, an obviously broken nose, and a mean look.

"I need to go outside and visually inspect cargo markings and lockings, and ship gear for these shipments."

"Not going to happen. First, there are a ton of shipments here on this list, and we have to notify every ship captain, or you have to meet them in person. They are all going to be pissed. Second, we only get ship gear requests for high-value cargo, not the crap on this list. It's not worth checking. If it falls off, they won't even slow down. Third, you need to be a cargo-hand three to go outside when we're doing loading operations. Fourth, this is a two-person job, and I'm not going to loan you a crewman to assist for the whole shift it will take to do a quarter of this. Whose stupid idea is this?"

"Well, my boss told me to come down here. She's in accounting. I don't think she had much real ops time."

"Empire damned accountants," the cargo boss said as she

scanned the list. "You want to inspect the connections for fourteen containers of structural aluminum? What are you going to find there? I should call this lady and sort this out."

The cargo crew beside her spoke up. "Want me to go up there and bang heads, boss?"

She put down her comm and shot the crewman a glare. For such a small woman she had a very mean look. The crewman gulped. "Shutting up, boss," he said.

She looked back at Jake. "Look, I don't want to start a war with accounting. Nobody wins that. And this is crap work for you. Why are they doing this? And why now?"

"I think it's something to do with bonuses. My boss promised me one if I could get this done by quarter end."

"Ahhhh." The cargo boss's face cleared. She handed the comm back. "Got it. Okay, kid, want some advice?"

"Sure," Jake said. This was what he had hoped for.

"This is what they call a checkbox item. They just need to hit their metrics on inspections. Any outside inspections are worth points for their bonuses. You don't need to do a hundred, you only need to do three. That's the magic number for bonus points. As long as you do three, your boss won't be really mad."

Jake already knew this, but plastered a fake look of relief on his face. "Oh, good. That shouldn't take so long." He pretended to study the comm unit. "There are three in a row down there that only have a couple of containers. One is the highest value on the list. I could do those three really quickly, and get out of your hair."

"That would work."

"And I've got a station cargo-hand three license."

"This station?"

"No, a Rim station. But it's on the station's approved list." *It is now,* Jake thought. He had put it on there last night—right after creating his 'license.'

"We don't take Rim station credentials."

"Accounting does. I checked, and you take mine for some reason. Here's my code—put it in and see."

Jake gave her the number, and she put it in. He talked her through the additional screens for Rim stations, and waited till she got an approved screen.

"How did you get a Rim station license?" she asked.

"I grew up on one. I've been moving cargo my whole life. That's pretty standard on a Rim station."

"Too true. I should have guessed. You have all Belter gear on. Those are nice boots. Old ones."

"They were my dad's."

"Those are old imperial navy boots."

"They are? But he wasn't in the imperial navy."

"Well, he got them off somebody who was then. The Belters copied them off the navy. The navy ones have that extra ridge there, that flange, and they have a beacon in the compartment in the soles," she said, pointing.

"A beacon? A compartment?" Jake asked.

"Yup, mess around with the bottom when you have time. Okay, that helps me with the license issue, but we got other work to do, and I can't spare a crewman."

"Are there any one-person jobs you need done? I could go out with one of your guys as overwatch, then when they finish their thing, we could just overfly those three ships. You get some maintenance done, I get my inspection, and maybe my boss will put me in for that bonus."

"Outstanding. Great idea. Murphy," she said, turning to the crewman.

"Yes, boss?"

"Suit up, go outside with that kid, and fix that antenna repeater that got knocked off last time that idiot commander drove his trader into the truss. That will take you, what, thirty minutes."

"Less, boss."

"Good. Be careful and watch yourself. Stay hooked, and act like you are alone. I don't trust this kid, license or no, but I need the antenna back online. And if this saves me waiting till the repair crews get around to it, great. And with the two of you out there, it meets station regs."

"Got it, boss."

"Keep him close while you do the repair, then overfly those three ships, and let him touch the winches if he wants. But keep an eye on him until you see what's what. He says he's a Belter, and he dresses like one, but you can never be sure."

"Got it. Let's go, kid."

Chapter 18

Jake and Murphy stepped out onto the surface of the truss. Murphy leaned toward Jake and touched helmets.

"Okay, kid, we're going to slide down here really slow and easy until we're over dock forty-three. Once there, we'll lock on, and you'll stay tied on while I reset that antenna."

Jake looked down the truss. He could see the vertical bars by each dock and located the one labeled forty-three, then he turned back to Murphy.

"If that's the way you want to do it, fine. But I'll meet you there."

Jake leaned back and unclipped his tether from Murphy. He flexed his feet, disengaged his magnets with his chin button, and pushed off in one smooth motion. He tucked himself forward so that he began to spin. He rotated, staying within reach of the grab bars on the surface. He sailed along, passing truss after truss. Not long after, truss forty-three began to draw closer. Grasping a grab bar, he corrected his spin and engaged his magnets just before clunking onto the truss.

His magnetized boots held him there, and he looked over his shoulder. Murphy still remained at the exact same spot Jake had left him outside the airlock. Seeing Jake attached, he exercised a duplicate of Jake's flight, except he landed a meter higher and clanked on there. Murphy leaned his helmet toward Jake.

"I guess you have been outside a time or two," Murphy said.

"Since I was four," Jake said.

"Okay, you pass. You want to help with this antenna?"

"Sure. I'll pass tools and you do what you need to. Then we can do my overflight."

"Good enough."

The antenna took longer than the thirty minutes anticipated, but not so much longer. Jake saw the radio light flicker on Murphy's collar from time to time. He was in communication with inside.

"Okay, done," Murphy said. "Let's get this overflight over with. Ha! I made a joke. Over the overflight. Get it?"

"Sure. The first one is there," Jake said, pointing.

Jake made sure that the overflights were more than cursory, but not long enough to be obviously delaying. He looked at each winch, flashed lights on it, inspected the couplings, and made notes on his comm unit. Thorough, but not irritatingly so. But time-consuming.

They finished up the last coupling, and Jake stepped over toward the nearest airlock. It was a single-person manual model—slow to enter and exit. Jake decided to implement his plan. He leaned back and touched helmets. "Hey, are you in radio contact with your boss?"

"Yes."

"You can radio her that you saw me inside this airlock, and then flip yourself back to cargo main and join your crew there. They can vouch for your arrival. Save you clearing in and out again, and meets regs."

"That's great. Thanks. Free trades, kid," Murphy said.

Jake broke the helmet connection, gave him a thumbs up, and began to spin the locking wheel on the airlock. He didn't take his eyes from the lock until he swung the door open, then he looked around. Murphy was nowhere in sight. Jake closed the lock and spun the wheel closed. He turned off his regular beacon. To the station tracking systems, the disappearance of his beacon meant he had entered the airlock.

Jake climbed down a truss away from the docking ring and toward the container ring. Partway down, he stopped and turned off both his emergency beacon and his emergency light. Now, even a radio query wouldn't trip a beacon. He spun 180 degrees and looked below him. The container ring rotated slower than the docking ring. The ships on the docking ring needed gravity. The containers on the next docking ring needed less. All he needed to do now was watch the container ring until the right container came into view.

Jake watched the numbered container docks. Most had containers attached. Jake saw one labeled '57' appear. He needed the container in dock sixty-three. He continued watching and counting, and soon saw a container with blue lettering on its side. He pushed himself off in a gentle launch, and floated down, landing on the truss not more than five meters from the container. He swung alongside it and edged hand over hand to the outer edge. The doors on the opposite end from the station lock were closed and latched, but they opened when Jake pulled them out. The container was already depressurized. Inside was a large blocky backpack, to which a huge pile of balled-up netting was attached. Jake towed them out of the container, closed the door, and climbed his way to the top. He shouldered the backpack—nets and all—and looked up at the docking ring. Now, he waited for a particular ship to slide by. As soon as he saw it, he launched himself into space.

He moved smoothly, but not for long. The net had unpacked behind him and began to spool out, and he started to tumble. The roll was slow at first, but intensified as more net streamed out behind him. The tumble started to unbalance him, and the net was tangling his arm. He couldn't quite adjust the spin, and began to roll a bit from side to side. Jake struggled to stretch his arms out to counteract the roll, but he could only get them partway. He was spinning too fast and adrift. If he didn't correct it soon, he'd smash into the truss.

And with no beacon on and no record of him being outside, he'd drift in space forever. And die when his air ran out.

Jake continued to struggle with the net, pulling harder at his hands. They were entangled in the net. He was still rolling, and he was going to hit hard. Struggling wasn't working. Jake stopped pulling. *Don't panic. Relax,* he thought. He watched his spin. He couldn't stop it, but could he correct it? Jake pulled himself into a tight ball, as tight as he could. Momentum must be conserved, so he began to spin faster. More of the net came out and wrapped around his arm. Then more.

The last of the net came out and hung up on his backpack. Jake was still spinning hard, but at least now it was steady. He saw the truss flash through his vision, disappear, and then flash again. "Easy, Jake," he said to himself. "You've done this thousands of times."

He was spinning very rapidly, and careening toward the truss. At the last possible minute, he fully uncurled his body. This slowed him down considerably, but he was still moving. He managed to stick his boots out in front of him and engaged the magnets. He banged into the truss, feet first. The magnets gripped, but didn't hold for long. He had slowed down, but his momentum was too great for him to completely stop. He bounced off the first truss and approached the second behind it. His pace was slow enough that he was able to slap his hand down and push himself sideways, missing a bruising impact with the metal flange. He sailed along the side of the truss now, snatched the next grab bar with one hand, and snapped to a halt.

It took a few minutes for his breathing to return to normal. He didn't move. He just hung there, breathing. His hands started to tremble, so he hung there even longer. Eventually, it passed, and he began to unwind himself from the net and stow it on the backpack. This time, he triple-checked the straps before starting toward the R&R.

Nadine felt the acceleration as the engines fired up. She punched the comm button in her cube, but nobody answered, so she pushed it again. And again. After the third try, Riley's voice answered.

"What?" Riley said.

"I'm bored," Nadine said.

"And I care why?"

"You guys need me. You don't want me to be unhappy."

"I kinda like that you are unhappy. I'm not sure we need you."

"Yes, you do. If you didn't, you would have left me on the station, or put me out an airlock. But we're under thrust right now, so that means we are going somewhere. And you wouldn't be taking me somewhere if the people you called, but said you didn't, hadn't said it was okay."

"What if these non-called people said to keep you locked up?" Riley asked.

"They wouldn't say that."

"Guess again."

"They wouldn't. They need me too. That's why they hired me."

"You have eight cubic meters of space all to yourself, your own bunk and head—not even a roommate. Be grateful. My dad owns this boat, and I still have to share a room with him sometimes."

"Really? Must be a problem with overnight guests."

"You have no idea."

"The people who hired you don't want me unhappy. This is making me unhappy."

"You'll get over it."

Nadine rolled her eyes. Riley sounded like the admiral. "Okay, you have to keep me away from the bridge, I get that. But why not let me roam around the habitation module? It's only one deck, and you can lock down the bridge and the engineering tunnel hatches. And I can drink some basic, use the lounge, heat a tray. Why not? You took the guns in my bag."

"Because we can't lock down the airlock, and you're wearing a skinsuit. All you need is a helmet and gloves, which we also can't lock down. And you can climb out on the deck and explore, and unlatch the containers—see where we're going —and climb down to engineering, and shut off the fuel, or disconnect the power."

Nadine cursed before pushing the comm button again.

"I was just going to unplug the control cables. Easier to do, harder to find and fix, and no possibility of damage, or of accidentally destroying a ship I happen to be living on."

Riley laughed. "I should have thought of that one. Thanks."

"No charge," Nadine said. "What happens now? You can't be too much of a bitch to me. It sounds like we might be working together. What have I ever done to you?"

"I don't actually need a reason to be a bitch to you. I might just like the practice," Riley said. Another voice sounded in the background, and the comm went dead. Nadine waited. The new voice came on the comm.

"Nadine, this is Rick. Riley's going to come down and escort you to the lounge. You can eat and fill up on basic. We have a couple ship chores that need two people. If you promise to behave yourself, you can hang out with her. But no trouble."

Nadine pressed the comm. "That's fine. I want you to

get where you need to get so I can get my job started. Come on down."

"Riley's on the way."

"Is she going to give me back my bag?"

"No, we're not giving you any guns," Rick said. "Just wait for Riley."

Nadine stepped back and smiled. She reached down to her ankle and pulled the hidden Gauss pistol out of its holster. Riley might be good at running a ship, but she didn't know shit about searching people. The Gauss pistol showed that it was fully charged, so she returned it to the holster.

"I don't need your stinking guns," Nadine said to herself. "Not yet, anyway."

Riley was begrudgingly as good as her word. Nadine filled up on basic, which she hated, but a girl needed her electro-lytes, right? They each heated a tray and chatted a bit. The chat went on for a long time. From the sounds of it, Riley was a pretty good pilot, at least as good as she could be outside of formal training. Somebody had to fly this thing, and it was big enough Rick couldn't do it all on his own. Riley exuded competence, and Nadine liked that. Riley knew a lot about cargo and ship economics. She also seemed to know her way around most of the ship systems, and had some idea which end of a shotgun was the dangerous part. All good skills to have on a Free Trader. And she was pretty, with that red hair and freckles. No wonder Jake Stewart perked up when she was around.

Nadine would feel sad if she had to shoot her.

Riley, for her part, found Nadine's insouciance refreshing

after having to deal with her dad's boring trader colleagues. Her dad was a great guy, but he was, well, her dad. He was always stressed, rarely smiled, and was very steady. She loved him, but he wasn't much fun. Nadine seemed much edgier, as if anything could suddenly happen around her. An evening in a bar with her was bound to turn into an epic story. She was obviously a skilled pilot and had a lot of interesting things to say about the corporations and politics, and what was driving the trading market, and the Free Traders. She'd had a full set of revolvers and a long dagger in her bag, and she didn't look like the type of girl to carry those if she couldn't use them. Good plan if you were going to be a shady pilot-for-hire. And that long blonde hair—no wonder Jake Stewart smiled that goofy smile at her.

Riley would feel sorry if she had to dump her out an airlock.

Nadine kept her pistol hidden as she helped Riley out. It was true that she had been bored, and a malfunctioning life-support system would kill everybody, so she made sure that her help was useful.

"What's left?" Nadine asked as she helped tighten a bolt on an access panel. Visible inspections of air filters sounded stupid, but after you'd nearly died because of a problem with air recirculation, you tended to take them seriously.

"We need to go down the access tunnel. Two of the emptier container hookups are showing abnormalities. Drawing too much power. Could be a short," Riley said, leading the way to the airlock and unlocking it with a code. Nadine stood right behind her and memorized the code. Maybe it would work on the bridge.

"Why do you even bother with that? You have power to spare while you're boosting."

"True. We've seen it on a couple of trips. They are just outside of normal, but not much. But this is the first time we've ever had two at once."

"Whatever. I said I'd help, so I'm helping."

"Thanks," Riley said. She closed the second door, and they proceeded away from the airlock. "And it's a one-time code."

"What?"

"That code you just memorized. It only works once. All the internal locks are set up for single-use codes. The ship computer will accept it the first time, then ignore it from then on."

"I have no idea what you are talking about," Nadine said. Emperor's balls, she thought. The girl was good.

"And my dad and I have codes. Duress codes. Trying to convince me to tell him something won't work. Hold this light."

Nadine took the light from her as they moved down the access way to the container headspace.

Riley climbed up a short ladder to see the head end of the container. This container had been mated to a collar so that the doors could be opened from inside the ship.

"Here's the first container. See the power draw? Not much extra. Could be a small short, but we'll just look inside to see if there is a problem."

Nadine looked at the display next to it. "It's supposed to be empty."

"Yup. Supposed to be," Riley agreed. "It's stuck. Hang on." She picked up a wrench and slid it onto the locking wheel. "Duress codes. Location codes, time codes—all sorts. If I'm talking to my dad, he and I can exchange a lot of information without people knowing. So don't even think about hijacking the ship."

"That's a lot of codes," Nadine said. "And why would I do that? You're taking me where I want to go." Though she might say that, Nadine didn't like that she wasn't in control of things. Damn, she'd have to shoot the girl first to prove she was serious. Just a small shooting. She reached down and pulled the Gauss pistol out of her holster and pointed it at Riley's head. Riley didn't notice as she was struggling to get the hatch open.

"There," Riley said, leaning on the wrench. She still hadn't seen the gun. "It was stuck hard." She yanked the bar, and the hatch flew open.

"Empress's vulva," Riley said.

Nadine stepped behind her to see what was going on.

"Hi, ladies," Jake Stewart said. He was relaxing in a cargo net, carefully draped from corner to corner of the container. His comm unit was open on his lap. A portable O generator was bolted to the floor, along with an electric heater. The comm unit was playing a video.

"Good to see you two. I figured you'd find me eventually. Nadine, why are you pointing a gun at Riley?"

Riley looked around at Nadine, then back at Jake. Her mouth worked, but she didn't say anything.

Nadine was equally surprised, but she didn't lower the gun. "Jake, what are you doing here? How did you get here? What's going on?" She looked at his screen. "Is that the Adventures of Angus McAngus you're watching?"

Things were a little confused for the next few minutes. There was a lot of shouting. Nadine kept flipping her gun back and forth between Jake and Riley, threatening to shoot them both. Riley threatened them both with the wrench, and promised they would be spaced. Jake talked about partial pressure of gasses.

"Containers are a perfectly safe way to travel. It's the amount of O that's important, Nadine, not the pressure per se. As long as I get enough O, I will survive. I have to watch the CO2 buildup, of course, but this unit freezes it out. As long as I connect to the circulation pipes, the CO2 goes away. And the electrolysis splits O out of water vapor I breathe out as well. It just vents the H outside. And if you calculate the internal volume of the container—"

"We don't need to hear any more calculations, Jake," Nadine said, still holding her gun, but now pointing it at the deck. "I get why you haven't suffocated, fine. But why didn't the acceleration mush you against the walls? I'm sure I felt nearly 3 g for about two minutes before."

Riley had dropped her hands to her sides, but she still held the wrench. "Yes, Jake. Dad tweaked the engines a bit. We have to be in our couches when he drops."

"The nets are flexible—they stretch. So, as the acceleration starts up, they have enough give that I don't get bruised. Well, not too badly bruised, and then when you are under sustained thrust, I just hang there. I don't get banged up against the walls. It takes a while to set up, but it's just a cargo net."

The two girls looked at each other. "Jake, why are you here?" Riley asked.

"Well, I knew you needed an engineering type person, so I figured I'd just invite my way into your crew. You need somebody like me."

"We need you?" Riley said. "Why would we hire you? We wanted a more experienced, regular engineer."

"You can't afford that. I don't mean money. I mean, you can't have somebody finding out what you're doing."

"What we're doing? We're a Free Trader. We're not doing anything strange."

"Well, I'm in cargo ops, Riley. And I'm not stupid. I'm not sure what you are doing, but it's something a little sketchy. Your cargo mixes don't add up, and your trip profiles are falsified. It sounds interesting. I want in," Jake said.

"What about your job on the station?"

"I didn't like it. It was pretty boring. I've decided to turn over a new leaf. I don't want to be bored anymore. Do some more exciting things."

"Exciting? Dying of suffocation in a container doesn't sound exciting to me," Nadine said.

"I told you, Nadine, if you calculate the volume of air in there and then check the partial pressure—"

"Enough of your volumes, Jake. Enough," Nadine said. She turned to Riley. "I'll tell you something about our friend,

Jake, here. He's useless with a gun, can't hit a subsidized merchant from a loading dock, but give him a rule book, or a calculation, or a volume, and he's right there," Nadine said. She shook her head. "The question is, can we trust him?"

"What do you mean, 'we'?" Riley said. "When did it become 'we'? You pointed a gun at me. Jake didn't do that."

"I walked in and introduced myself. He stowed away. You can't exactly trust Jake either," Nadine said.

"That's not true—" Jake said.

"*Shut up*, Jake," both girls said. Jake held up his hands and backed down the container headspace.

"Yes, but the point remains. He hasn't done anything to me."

"Sneaking onto your ship isn't 'doing something to you,' is that what you mean?"

"He didn't point a gun at me."

"Well, you shouldn't have taken my guns away. And I'm supposed to be on this ship, unlike him. I'm a valued passenger, remember? And I don't feel very valued right now."

"Passengers don't need to be armed, and they're not supposed to pirate the ship partway."

"I didn't pirate anything, you stupid bitch. I just wanted my clothes back. And my knives. But you started it."

"I started it? Look, bimbo brains, I didn't start anything."

"You pointed a gun at me when I got on board."

"You were snooping. And if you want to start something right now, blondie—"

CLANG! Everybody stopped talking.

"What was that?" Riley asked, looking around.

Nadine turned toward Jake. "I think it came from that container next to Jake," she said.

Jake had stepped back from the argument and had been leaning against a container watching the girls yell at each other. The noise had startled him upright. He looked at the container.

CLANG! The noise came again. He raised his eyebrows and reached for the handle.

"Jake, maybe you should wait for us," Nadine said.

Jake ignored her and pulled the handle. Unlike the container he'd holed up in, this one swung open easily. He stared inside, and stepped back. A babble of voices started up. Jake looked back at Riley, very puzzled.

"Riley, why are there two dozen guys in GG colors in this container of office supplies?"

Chapter 19

"Dad, they've been kidnapped or something. This is horrible. We're people slavers."

"We are not."

"Dad, what in the Emperor's name is going on?" Riley said, watching the crowd line up for a drink of basic.

"Easy, sweetie. Just easy," Rick said.

"What's happening then? Who kidnapped these people?"

"I'm not sure. This is as much a surprise to me as it is to you," Rick said.

Jake looked at Rick. "What did you think the fifty thousand food trays were for?"

"Jake. How did you get here?"

Riley explained Jake's presence. The twenty or so workers in the container had streamed out after Jake had opened the doors and began yelling at Jake. Unfortunately, they were yelling in Spanish, which Jake did not understand.

Nadine did and spoke with them. Afterward, she led them up the cargo tunnel to the lounge. They were all very thirsty, and very much wanted to use a toilet. Two lines formed—one at the head, and one at the basic tap. They were orderly and quieted down after they lined up. After using the head, they sat and talked to Nadine until Rick came down.

"Dad, what are we going to do?" Riley asked. "Why are they here? Where are they going? What are we going to do when we meet the transfer ship?"

"Aha, that's how it worked," Jake said.

"How what worked?" Riley asked.

"You only loaded two containers at a time—always food. I couldn't figure out which station was within twenty-two hours' round-trip flight. But there isn't one. You are meeting a ship in the dark. You swap containers, and then it goes to a higher orbit. To an outer station."

"You were tracking when we dropped?" Rick asked.

"Sort of," Jake said. "Mostly I wanted to know when you latched."

Rick reached down and took the wrench from Riley's hand. "Why did you want to know when my ship latched, Jake?" Rick said. He slapped his palm with the wrench.

Jake looked at the wrench. Uh-oh. He squared his shoulders and looked Rick in the eye.

"I didn't care about your ship, Rick. I wanted to make sure that I had a spare night when your daughter was around so I could take her out to dinner, or drinks, or something."

Rick stopped slapping the wrench in his palm and looked at his daughter. Riley reddened slightly, then her eyes narrowed. "What do you mean by a 'spare' night, Jake?" she asked.

"Some nights I wouldn't be able to take you to dinner. I would be busy."

"With who?" Riley asked.

"Doing what? Something?" Rick asked. He slapped the wrench in his hand again.

Jake opened his mouth but was saved by Nadine putting her hand on his shoulder. "You can talk later, Jakey. Everyone, this is Jorge, Jorge, this is everyone."

"Hello. Thank you for the basic and the facilities," Jorge said. He was a stocky dark-haired man with a weathered face. "It was very crowded in the container. May we please stay in the lounge until we reach the station?"

"You speak standard English," Jake said.

"Of course I do," Jorge said. "What sort of idiot doesn't speak standard?"

"But you spoke Spanish to me," Jake said.

"We thought this was a Castle Transport ship. They all speak Spanish. Look, it can't be much longer to the station, right? Can we just stay in the lounge? We won't be any trouble, and we'll go back in the container for the station drop-off."

"What station drop-off?" Rick asked.

"Where you put us down at the station so we can get to our jobs," Jorge said.

"Put you at the station? No, no, you don't have to do that," Riley said. "We can take you back to the orbital. You'll be free there."

"Take us back to the orbitals? Why would you do that? We don't want to go there," Jorge said.

"You don't?"

"Absolutely not. We paid a great deal of money to be brought out here. And I'm sure you were paid as well. We want to go to the station."

"Which station?" Jake asked.

"I'm not sure. Don't you know?" Jorge said.

"You want us to put you back in the container?" Riley said.

"When you are ready. Look, this is all arranged. We have jobs waiting."

"Jobs out here? Why not dirtside? Why come all the way out here?" Jake asked.

Jorge shrugged. "Some of us, perhaps, have some credit issues with the GG company store, or perhaps some minor legal issues. But that is past, on the surface. We are in orbit now. Groundside issues do not matter here. We will be workers on a station and earn a decent wage."

"But you won't be safe in the containers," Riley said.

"We won't? Haven't you done this before?" Jorge looked at them. "Didn't you know we were in there?"

Rick looked nonplussed. Jake looked bland. Riley looked at Nadine's hand on Jake's shoulder. Jorge looked confused. Nadine saw the look on Riley's face and leaned into Jake more, then she smirked at Riley.

"You didn't know we were in the containers?" Jorge asked.

Rick coughed. "Uh, no. We didn't."

"You weren't monitoring the container life support?"

"No."

"What if something happened to us?"

"We wouldn't know. Look, we usually just move a few

containers of cut-rate food trays. I don't know anything about people."

"How many times have you done this, Rick?" Jake asked.

"Not now, Jake. Look, Jorge, you guys can wait in the lounge. There's no problems. I mean, there won't be, right? It's the Militia that's picking you up."

"The Militia? No, we were approached by somebody working for Castle Transport. That is where my cousin worked. When he came back, he said the work was hard but paid well. We expected to be on a Castle Transport station for a year, then come back to the surface like my cousin."

"Dad, are we working for the Militia?" Riley asked.

"Of course you are," Nadine said. "That's who sent me to be a shuttle pilot. I got notifications from them. And your dad meets with them all the time."

"That's not true. The people we meet aren't Militia," Riley said.

Rick cleared his throat. "Well, they aren't, no. But our contact back at the station is Militia," Rick said.

"As is mine," Nadine said. "They confirmed that to Rick."

Everyone looked at Rick. He didn't say anything. "You did contact your buyers about me, didn't you, Rick?" Nadine said.

"I didn't really have time. We had a window to make. You wanted to be on the ship, so I put you on the ship. I figured I'd bring you back to the station when we are done."

"So, is Jake with the Militia?" Riley asked.

They all looked at Jake.

"I don't know anything about the Militia. I just wanted to

get in on this smuggling thing. I could use a little more cash. You know what a clerk four makes on-station? And, well, Riley was here, and you needed an engineer, so I thought maybe something could be worked out."

"You stowed away to be with my daughter?" Rick asked. He started to thwack the wrench again.

"Dad, stop that." Riley grabbed the wrench from him. "I'm a grown woman. I can take care of myself." Riley turned. "Is that true, Jake?"

"That was part of it, yes. And you do need an engineer. This would make it easier to talk to you. You were always so busy before."

Jorge raised his eyebrows. "*Un asunto del corazón*. Well, well."

Riley colored. "That was sweet, Jake. Thank you. But you didn't need to."

Nadine slapped Jake's shoulder. "Jakey! What a surprise. Who would have thought you had such a romantic soul. Not like you at all. You're always so shy around girls."

"Some girls," Jake said. He tried to squirm away from Nadine's hand, but she was doing that feminine vice thing again.

"That was sweet, Jake, but it was a surprise. Your timing isn't that great," Riley said.

Rick looked glum. "Well, we do need an engineer. And you are here now, so welcome to the crew. At least for this trip. We'll talk more later. Jorge, you guys can stay in the lounge as long as you want. We have lots of trays and basic. Have as much as you want. Riley, put Jake in one of those spare cubes. Nadine, you don't have to stay in your cube. And Jake, since you're here, can you come out with me and take a look at the thrusters? Two of them are offline, and I think it's the control lines. Riley, go to the control room and check our course to the rendezvous. Our ETA should be about three hours." Rick beckoned Jake and stalked toward the airlock. Nadine patted Jake's shoulder and smirked at Riley again. Jorge looked back and forth at the two women and smiled a private smile.

Jake followed Rick into the airlock. He had his bag, with helmet, gloves, and boots.

"Rick, you really didn't know those people were in there?"

"Nope."

"You sell these guys food, environmentals, and consumables, right?"

"Yes."

"What do you bring back?"

"Processed ore and empty containers."

"You never bring back people?"

Rick shook his head and dropped his helmet. He punched the airlock controls, and the air was sucked into the tanks. He leaned forward till his helmet touched Jake's.

"Not even once, Jake. Not a single person."

"Jake, move over so I can key the radio," Riley said, sliding into the control room.

"Shouldn't we scan them first?" Jake asked. They had arrived at the rendezvous. He moved to the second console and reconfigured it as a sensor station, then began to study the readings. "Do you have any sensors at all?"

"Telescope and basic radar. The radar isn't that great."

"That's all? No infrared? No radar receivers?"

"Jake, we're a Free Trader. Sensors cost money. We have what the ship came with."

"Are you sure that's your contact for the containers? It's not a freighter?" Jake asked.

"Yes," Riley said. "It's a passenger launch. Big passenger cabin. Space for two containers, single engine, short range." She switched her radio to the lowest setting. "Sidecar, this is R&R, over."

"Sidecar here. Awaiting two container swap, over," a man's voice said.

"Sidecar, one container swap. Ring Alpha, container five. And we have, uh, passengers for you, over."

"Only one container. And passengers? We don't get passengers."

"We are pretty sure they are yours. There are twenty-one of them."

"Twenty-one? We're not expecting any passengers. Where from?"

"One of the containers broke open in transit. There were twenty workers inside."

"Twenty workers? Inside the container? Wait one." The man's voice paused for about a minute. "We're okay with twenty, but you said twenty-one."

"We also have a shuttle pilot for you."

"A shuttle pilot? Why would we need a shuttle pilot?" the man asked.

"To fly a shuttle. I don't know. She says you sent for her. You can ask her. We'll be happy to get her off our hands." Riley smiled at that, then began to type on her board.

"That's an odd ship to have out in the dark," Jake said. "With its range and all. Riley, are you sure this is all legit?"

Riley shrugged. "You should have thought of that before you signed up, Jake." She began to maneuver toward the other ship. Jake noticed how precise she was with the thrusters.

"You have a very delicate touch on the thrusters," Jake said.

"Fuel costs money," Riley said. The radio squawked, and Riley switched back. "Sorry, just fixing up the approach. How do you want to transfer the passengers?"

"We'll come alongside and rig a tube. Stand by for a party coming over. We'll pick up the shuttle pilot then."

"Standing by."

Rick and Nadine crowded into the control room. "What's the plan, sweetie?" Rick asked Riley.

"They're going to send a team over to rig a tube for the passengers, and take Nadine off our hands," Riley said.

Nadine looked at the sensor screen. "Hey, that's a launch. What's it doing way out here?" She frowned. "Something is strange. Why do they need all these workers? Why an old launch?" She shook her head and turned to Rick. "Don't do it, Rick. Don't let them on your ship. Something is wrong."

"Why shouldn't I? We meet up with them every trip. This is the same. They put a crew out, we release the chains, and they swap containers."

"Rick, I've been talking with these GG guys—they expected to be working at a station. They have relatives who did it too. But the relatives came back."

"So?"

"Jake told me you've never brought anybody back. This doesn't sound right."

"Why do you care? I mean you're going with them, right? You shouldn't be worried about them. Are you worried about going with them?"

"No, but—" Nadine said.

"Unless you're not supposed to be here. Then you should be worried."

"Rick, don't even let them near your airlock," Jake said. "This could be bad. They could sabotage the ship."

"Oh, come on," Rick said. "What can they do to my ship?"

"Set off a breaching charge—like a sandcaster round—and breach the lock," Nadine said, glaring at Jake.

"Shoot out your control runs with a rifle, and cut off maneuvering and commo," Jake said, glaring back.

"Break into your storage and steal all your cash, and stuff it in a suitcase and jump back," Nadine said.

"Bring a horrible disease on board and kill you all with it."

"Shoot you in the chest, chain you to a desk, and force you to steal from your friends."

"Get your friends killed and steal your ship."

Rick looked back and forth between the two and cleared his throat. "That's an interesting conversation. I think you two know each other better than you let on. But we've been doing business with these guys for a while. We'll just swap a container, set up the tube, send all these people over, and we'll be on our way."

"Rick, this isn't a good idea. Do you have a ship's locker?" Jake asked.

"Yes, but it's locked. And it's going to stay locked. We don't need guns. Look, just give us some space here. Riley and I will meet up with these guys. We'll swap containers, get these people—and you, Nadine—off my ship, and on the way back to the station, we'll talk about your employment, Jake. Don't worry, I think we can work something out. Now, shoo. I need your console." Rick waved Jake away from the control station.

Jake climbed out and caught Nadine's eye. He jerked his head toward the hatch in a gesture. She climbed out ahead of him and waited in silence as he locked the hatch.

"Well?" she said.

"This isn't right. I didn't expect people in the containers. My boss didn't say anything about this," Jake said.

"Neither did mine. This could be trouble. I should have stayed at Downport and brushed up on my glider skills."

"Where did you learn to fly a glider?"

"I learned at cadet school. These Militia guys asked about that when they hired me—said I had to be able to fly a glider."

"Wow, that's amazing."

"That I can fly a glider?"

"No, that you were in cadet school. It's kind of hard to think of you in those uniforms. Did they have those little pleated-skirt things?"

Nadine hit him hard on the shoulder. "Focus, Jake. We have potentially hostile people coming here. Are we together on this?"

Jake rubbed his arm. "Yup. Truce?"

"Truce. I'll find the ship's locker," Nadine said.

"And I'll find a crowbar and bolt cutters," Jake said.

"Oh, and, Jake?"

"Yes?"

"I looked awesome in those pleated skirts."

While Rick and Riley organized the ship rendezvous, Jake and Nadine organized some other things. Nadine chivvied the workers into getting their bags, drinking basic, using the head, and generally getting prepared to leave. She also made sure that they were strapped into something and told them not to move until Jake or she let them up. Jake couldn't find bolt cutters, but he did find a toolbox. He used the screwdrivers he found to unscrew the locks from the locker doors, then began to loot it for useful items.

Nadine took a holster belt and strapped two of the biggest revolvers on around her waist. Next, she pushed a smaller revolver into her waistband at the small of her back. Then she produced a tiny pistol that fit in her hand. The barrel looked odd. It was an open coil. There was no trigger, just a button on the top of the grip.

"What's that?" Jake asked.

"Gauss gun," Nadine said. She pulled at the gun. The coil clicked off the top, and the grip split into two pieces. She reached down and pushed on the heels of her magnetic boots. Two small panels clicked open, exposing compartments. She slid the coil into her left boot, and the magazine and control into her right. Then she put a fourth revolver in an outer pocket of her traveling bag.

"Is all that really necessary?" Jake asked.

"Yes. They'll expect me to have a hidden gun, so after they

pull off the holster, they'll search me, and find the backup gun on my back. They'll laugh and be full of themselves and won't bother to search anymore, so they won't find the Gauss gun. That, I want to keep. If they search the bag, they'll find another revolver, so they'll miss the knives. I want to keep those, too."

"Oh," Jake said. He thought for a minute and dove into his cabin. A few minutes later, he came out wearing his Belter semi-hard suit and his personal tool kit. He filled up all the pockets with various tools, clipped several more to his belt, and also clipped on a small revolver. Then he stashed a revolver in the tool kit.

"Only two guns? What if they find them both?"

"Nadine, have you ever seen me shoot?"

"Not exactly, but I've talked to people who have, and they say you are only dangerous to yourself."

"That's true, so having a gun doesn't help me. But if they take the gun, they might leave the tools, and I'm much better with those."

Nadine looked at him. "That's actually pretty smart, Jake. You're getting better at this. You might even be mildly good at it someday."

"I was good enough to clean you out of cash once. How many people have done that to you?"

Nadine laughed. "Not very many. I was pretty angry when that happened. But I have to admit, it was well played. Okay, to each their own. I'll shoot things, and you unbolt things. Let's go."

The two ships were within visual distance by the time Jake

and Nadine returned to the control room, and the airlock next to it. Rick and Riley had coordinated so that the R&R's airlock was aligned with the Sidecar's. Riley was adjusting the thrust to keep the two ships in sync.

"Whoever is driving over there has no idea what they are doing," Nadine said. "Look, he's still rolling."

"They're always like this. We tell them to sit tight, and we conform to them. Their cargo guy isn't any good either. If we weren't feeding him directions, then we'd never get the containers moved. But they've sent over their A-team to help set up the tube," Riley said. "Dad, they just opened the lock. Somebody is floating across."

"I'll go see them," Rick said. "Nadine, is that a gun on your belt?"

"I'm just happy to see you, Rick," Nadine said.

"I told you there's no need for that. You too, Jake? The Emperor's balls. Don't either of you two do anything stupid," Rick said, stepping through the bridge hatch behind them, then turning and facing the lock.

The airlock swung open, and two suited figures stepped out. Both had on semi-hard suits, like Jake's, with full helmet and gauntlets—and both had shotguns.

And both pointed the shotguns at the group and cocked them with a clacking sound.

Nadine didn't even need to be told, she just raised her hands. "Guess they're happy to see us too, Rick."

Chapter 20

Jake looked around the cabin he was locked into, and he reflected that, for still being young, he was a bit of a connoisseur of cells. This one wasn't bad. He had a toilet, a bunk, and a basic tap. The door was locked shut, but not jammed. He knew this because he had taken the faceplate off and tested the circuits. His tool smuggling had been successful. If there were a fire or loss of pressure, it would open automatically, so he wouldn't burn to death by accident. They could still do it on purpose, of course. He still had his own environmental control, and even though he didn't have comms, he could still tap into the ship's network. And he wasn't handcuffed to a bunk.

He had strapped himself into his bunk after banging into a wall while the ships were maneuvering. He went from being pressed into the bunk to almost rolling off the side, to crashing up against the straps. What were these idiots doing?

He flipped on the comm, and the footage from the video cameras told the story. The two ships were spinning and weaving relative to each other. Whoever was at the controls had no idea what they were doing. There was no tube connection between the two ships. Thrusters fired at random. Jake stayed strapped into his bunk and watched the chaos unfold. After about two hours, the door slid open. Two scowling men in skinsuits with shotguns looked at him. "You're Rick's new guy, Jake?" one asked.

"That's me."

"Mack wants to talk to you."

"Is Mack the one in charge?"

"Yup."

"Good," Jake said. He unbelted from the bunk, slid to the floor, and engaged the magnets in his boots. "Then I want to see Mack."

The gunmen slid out into the corridor and stumbled toward the lounge. They were so clumsy that Jake was afraid they would inadvertently shoot him. The thug in front swung the lounge door open and motioned Jake through. Jake entered the lounge and faced the tables against the far wall. The two men flanked him on either side. A man with dirty blond hair sat belted into a chair. He was big and muscular. His skinsuit was tailored so tightly that you could actually see veins bulging out of his upper arms.

"You're Jake?" he said.

"Yes, I am."

"You are the new engineering guy?"

"I do cargo too."

"How come you had revolvers?"

"Space is dangerous. How come you guys came on board with shotguns?"

"We weren't expecting passengers."

"You must have been. The container was consigned to you. This looks like a regular thing."

Mack put his comm down and stood up. He stepped close to Jake and glared. "That sounds disapproving," he said. "I don't like disapproving people."

"It's not my business," Jake said. The ship spun as another thruster fired. It fired again, followed by a crashing sound this time. The ship swayed to one side, then back, then forward. One shotgun guy stumbled into Mack, knocking him over, and the two of them rolled around. The other rocked back and fell down. He discharged the gun with an earsplitting boom as he fell backward. An overhead light shattered, and broken plastic showered all of them.

"Idiots!" Mack snarled. He rolled over, grabbed the shotgun, and smacked the man on the floor. He swung the shotgun several times, then stopped and looked at the butt of the shotgun. He had bent it. Mack threw the gun down the corridor, then hauled himself up and walked to an intercom.

"What was that?" The intercom squawked back, but Mack screamed over it. "Don't do that again or I'll push you out a lock."

The first man, the one who had bumped into Mack, had hauled himself up. Mack walked over to him and got in his face. "By the Emperor's balls, can't you handle acceleration?"

"Sorry, boss, just not used to it," he said.

"Your collar," Jake said. He'd swayed a bit, but a single arm rested against the wall had kept him upright.

"What?" the shotgun man said. He looked at Jake.

"The button is on your collar," Jake repeated.

"What button?" the shotgun man said.

"You have magnetic boots on. Don't you know?"

"This isn't my regular gear."

"I can see that. Mr. Mack, I don't want to get shot by accident. Please, take his gun while I fix this."

Mack looked at Jake for a moment, then nodded. He held out his hand, and the swaying crewman handed him the gun. Jake walked over and pushed the collar button that engaged the magnetic boots. He showed the crewman how to engage and disengage it.

"Push to unlock, step, push to lock, push the other side to unlock, step, push to lock, back again," Jake said. He showed both of them how to push the button with their chin.

"Watch me. I use my chin as part of the walking so I can slide along," Jake said. Clipping his collar button with his chin was second nature to Jake. The gunmen were a bit awkward, but they started to get it.

"And lock yourself down when you stop walking. That way, you won't drop the gun when the maneuvering thrusters fire," Jake said. He stepped back.

"You've done this for a while, Jake?" Mack asked.

"I grew up on a station. Why are the two ships banging around so much? And why isn't there a tube set up?"

"Our pilots are having some problems keeping velocity constant."

"Your pilots? You mean Rick?"

"Rick is relegating at his leisure in his cabin while we sort things out."

"Relegating? Do you mean relaxing at his leisure? Never mind. How come you don't have cargo lines out?" Jake asked.

"Cargo lines?" Mack cocked an eyebrow.

"How come you aren't just lashing the ships together and using the winches to haul them in?"

"I don't know. I'm ground operations. I've got people for that." Mack turned and punched the intercom. "People, why don't we have cargo lines out?"

There was a long pause. "We've never used them," the intercom said. "We've got tugs or an auto-docking. Only the Free Traders use lines."

"They would seem to be the optimal arrangement. Why not use them here?" Mack asked.

"Uh, I've never done it. I don't think we know how," the intercom said.

Jake coughed. "Uh, Mr. Mack. I don't want to be out here forever. I can rig lines. But I need a pilot who has done this before, and I need a partner on the other ship to help me out."

Mack flipped the intercom off and turned to Jake. "We don't need your help. We can take care of things ourselves. What are you doing on this ship? You're not part of the regular crew." Another banging sound rang out. Everybody swayed and looked up. There was a long pause, then a long screech that made Jake's hair stand on end.

"Yeah, that probably took off a complete set of control lines." Jake looked back at Mack. "My job was lousy. I was up for a promotion—if I worked hard for an entire year they would give me a raise. One percent. Who wants that? Rick needed somebody with the right license who knew his way around a ship. They couldn't afford to hire me legit, so I just invited myself aboard."

There was a whining sound, and then a loud scratch that continued for a few seconds. "That was one of the transversal bracing wires parting," Jake said. "Break enough of those and the trusses break apart. Is Nadine one of your pilots?"

"The new girl? Not yet. We're not sure why she's here, either. And we took four revolvers and two knives off her."

"She's not a very trusting sort," Jake said. Four revolvers, no mention of Gauss guns. Good. "But she has done cargo docking before, as has Riley. And Rick and I have been on the hull together, so I have a suggestion. Let us take over as pilots, and put us out on the hull to rig some lines."

"On the hull? Why should I trust you?" Mack said.

"No reason. But we'll do better than these guys. And if I don't, you can just leave me out there. Or shoot me later." There was another bang, and the ship shook again.

"I'd rather shoot you later," Mack said. "I always like to have something to look forward to."

An hour later, Jake stood on the hull of the Sidecar and ratcheted a winch. He could see Riley on the hull of the R&R doing the same thing. Rick was at the controls of the R&R, while Nadine was driving the Sidecar. They were communicating via the common channel. Four lines ran between the ships—the bow of one to the stern of the other—both ventral and dorsal, forming two large X shapes connecting the two ships top and bottom. The two pilots made delicate thrust movements that rolled the ships away from each other, but then the lines tightened and kept them equidistant, counteracting the movement. As long as they tried to roll or yaw away, the lines stayed taut, and the ships stayed still in relation to each other. Nadine continually fired the Sidecar's thrusters in short bursts, keeping the ship steady, but burning lots of fuel. Rick was more conservative on the R&R. He would accept much more roll before firing a very short burst. Nadine was obviously used to somebody else paying for things. Two of the Sidecar's crew had unspooled a boarding tube and were just fixing it to the R&R's lock.

"Rick and I can hold from here, Jake," Nadine said over the common channel. She was in the pilot's chair of the Sidecar. "But you and Riley need to stand by on the hull till they get this sorted. Rick, everything good over there?"

"The ship is holding fine. I don't like the guy with the shotgun behind me though," Rick said.

"I've got one of those here, too," Nadine said.

Jake watched the boarding tube pressurize, and saw people begin swimming over it.

"Nadine, they're finally moving. Should be maybe fifteen minutes to get across. Then maybe fifteen minutes to disengage the lines."

"That's if we do it, Jake. If these useless Militia shuttle pilots do it, we'll be here for a whole orbit."

"How do you know they're Militia shuttle pilots?" Jake asked.

"They need a tug to bring them in. Their shuttles have big

main engines, but lousy thrusters. These guys were trained by the Militia—they don't know how to do small maneuvers. None of the Militia can do them."

"Even the commanders?"

"Most of the ship commanders have bought their commissions. They suck."

"This is not a really interesting conversation," Mack's voice said. He had been monitoring the channel. "Keep this channel for necessary coordination only. You two stay out there and get us uncoupled when the tube is rolled up."

"And do it quickly, Jake, so we can get out of here," Rick said.

"About that, Rick. When we're done, Jake and Riley are going to go on the Sidecar, and we'll put a few more people in with you. You'll follow us. We'll give you a vector when we're ready to leave," Mack said.

"We're not going with you. That's not part of our deal. I deliver containers, you pay me, I go back for more. That's what we do here," Rick said.

"And we appreciate all your good work, Rick. In fact, there will be a bonus in it for you. But this passenger thing has thrown us for a loop. We can't have you running around right now. So, what we're going to do is take your delivery fee and double it, and we're going to pay it to you every week while you are with us. You just have to bring your ship along with us for a while."

"How long is a while?"

"A while. Rick, we pay well. It will be easy work. Why not take the easy way?" Mack said.

"I don't like that option. Is there another way?"

"That was the easy way. There's a hard way too."

"What's that?"

"Ask the guy with the shotgun behind you."

Rick stayed on the R&R. Nadine was locking down the board. The GG workers were locked in the back section of the launch. Jake and Riley sat together in the Sidecar's lounge eating a tray.

"Jake, we need to do something," Riley said.

"What?" Jake asked.

"What? What do you mean, 'what'?"

"Well, we're being fed, we've got air, Rick has a contract for his ship. From people he knows. You've been doing business with these guys for a while, right?"

"Well, yes. But they didn't kidnap us before. Or point guns at us."

"Did they pay on time?"

"Yes."

"They're not hurting us. They are not hurting the workers. We don't know where we're going, true, but I've had a lot of jobs like that. Lots of contracts run for a year or longer, so it's not that much different."

"We can take control of my ship back."

"The two of us with revolvers against a bunch of thugs with shotguns?"

"Exactly."

"Well, first of all, we don't have any revolvers. And second, I'm not a very good shot. In fact, I'm a horribly bad shot."

"How bad?"

"Once, a group of three of us were held up by robbers. I pulled my gun and tried to shoot them. I missed, and shot my boss instead."

"You shot your boss?"

"It was an accident."

"Well, these thugs don't know that."

"Nadine is probably telling them right now."

Riley narrowed her eyes. "I figured you would be no use at all, Jake."

"Well, I can't shoot, that's for sure," Jake agreed.

"You're not much for getting things done, are you?"

"Well, I got you released from that engineering hold on-station."

"That's true."

"And I did figure out that you were smuggling stolen food to some sort of secret place."

"It's not stolen," Riley said.

"Yes it is. I have the records in my comm. And don't bother to deny it. You knew something was wrong with this whole deal."

"Okay, I did think there was something wrong with that. But Dad kept denying it. What was I supposed to do?"

"And I figured out how to get onto your ship without you knowing."

"True. But what about these guys with guns now?"

"I'm a bit scared of them. But I'm mostly angry. But I have learned that when somebody points a gun at you, the best thing is to be patient. I just waited, and then when I met Mack, I convinced him to let us fix the docking."

"Wait, you convinced Mack to let us help? I thought he came up with that himself," Riley said.

"No, I talked him into it. He wanted to talk to me about something, but I told him what needed to be done, and convinced him to let us do it," Jake said.

"I didn't know that. He never said. He just asked us to help. You didn't say anything till now."

"Well, I am now. I'm useful. I'm not good with guns, or fighting. But I can figure things out. And I figure now that these guys don't want to kill us. Or even bother us. They were surprised that we saw the workers, so they had to do something different. I think they're regretting it now."

"I see."

"In fact, I predict that, if we wait, they'll offer us jobs. Good jobs, well paid. Spacer jobs."

"You do, huh? Interesting."

"We just have to be patient."

"How long do we have to wait?"

"Just until their guys nearly kill us again."

Chapter 21

"Cheers! Let's toast this suspicious meeting," Mack said, holding his glass forward. Mack, Jake, Nadine, Rick, Riley, and one of Mack's guys sat at the lounge table. Mack had just poured shots from a metal flask.

Rick had raised his glass, but paused, then looked at Mack. "Suspicious meeting?"

"It is a word meaning 'conducive to success,'" Mack said.

Rick looked at the others. They all looked puzzled except for Jake. "Auspicious," he said.

Mack glared at him. "Suspicious, like I said."

Jake held his glass up. "We toast differently in the Belt, Mack. We say, 'Free trades,' or 'Lucky strikes.'"

The four spacers pushed their glasses together, and the metal clanked. "Lucky strikes," they chorused, and then Mack followed suit.

Rick, Jake, Riley, and Nadine sat at one side of the lounge table. Mack and one of his guys, the biggest one—Jack, or Jim, or something like that—sat on the other. He had said

'Call me JJ,' so Jake had stuck with that. The six of them were eating dinner. Jake poked at his food. It was just trays, but at least some of the more interesting ones. This one had sliced radish in one foil packet.

"I have been told all you Belters did talk different. Now I know some Belter lingo." He took a drink from his glass. "I think you'll all like this. It's triple-distilled vodka. Very expensive stuff. The extra distilling makes it much smoother than normal vodka. I'll bet you've never tasted anything like this."

Nadine swallowed hers in one shot and held out her glass for more. "This is very smooth. How do they do it?"

"It's very pure. They have to concentrate the potatoes over three times. That's why it becomes so expensive. All the extra power. Jake, I'll bet you've never had vodka this pure in the crap-hole station you come from."

Jake sipped the vodka. He'd had problems with drinking too much before. "No, we had no problem purifying it. We'd get 100 percent pure vodka all the time, easy. Distillation wasn't the expensive part."

Mack mouthed Jake's last sentence before responding. "The distillerification wasn't expensive?"

Jake blinked, then nodded. "Not at all. We vacuum-distilled. Plenty of vacuum out there. We could purify all we wanted—just set up a rig, bring it outside, and bleed off atmo till the boiling point of the liquid dropped where you wanted. That was easy. What was hard was getting the potatoes way out there."

Nadine smiled at Jake. "Mack, Jake's very good at that sort of thing. All sorts of useless knowledge."

"Not that useless," Riley said. "Not if you want good vodka." She drank her shot down and held out her glass hand for more. Mack unscrewed the metal cap and refilled everyone's glasses.

"I never would have thought of that. Using vacuum to distillerate something," Mack said.

"It's pretty common knowledge if you spend a lot of time in orbit, Mack," Riley said.

"I am not an orbital person," Mack said. "My expertise lies within elsewhere."

"So, Mack, why are we here?" Nadine asked.

Mack turned to the big man to his right. "JJ, time to go and watch on the bridge."

JJ had been silently spooning his tray clean. "Not my watch right now, Mack."

Mack stopped smiling. He blinked once, then held JJ's gaze and spoke slowly. "I say, 'JJ, it's time to go on the bridge.' You say, 'Right away, boss.' That is all what I expect to hear. Go now. Go right now." He kept his stare on JJ, and JJ nodded.

"Right away, boss," he said and slid back from the table and scampered off.

Mack turned back to the group. He smiled again. "They forget who is in charge sometimes. I remind them. Now, Jake, maybe that sort of space thing is commonly known where you come from, but that's not my area of things. I've got a good crew here, good people. Tough. Hard people. You don't want to mess with them, and they don't want to mess with me, so that means that nobody messes with me."

He smiled again and tossed his vodka down. Then he poured himself another shot.

"But the thing is, peoples, that we lack certain skills. Jake knows about vacuum, and can fix mechanical things, like his door. Yes, Jake, I found out about that. And the two of you," Mack pointed at Nadine and Riley, "you two can pilot ships. Pilot them without the computers. And you know about things like cargo winches, and lines, and magnetic boots and things like that. Most of my people do not know of those things."

"What do your people know, Mack?" Nadine asked.

"They are good with guns. And hurting people. Very good at that. I have some small skill in that area as well."

"Then why are we having dinner with you?" Nadine asked.

Mack smiled at her. "You are a direct one, aren't you?"

Nadine smiled back. "Ms. Direct, that's me. In fact, I'm the queen of mis-direction."

Mack dropped his smile and hunched forward. "Well, I'll be frank, peoples. Let me irradiate the problem. I have a contract to run a mining asteroid. I've been told it is pretty rich in ore, at least the people who hire me say so, and from what I've been able to make work, it seems to be true. But we have all sorts of things breaking—we don't have enough people to run the systems on the stations, and fixing things that break is a problem. It stops us from making money. I don't like that. My employers don't like that. I need some special workers. And I think you four could help me out with that."

Mack took another sip of vodka and smiled at the group.

"Doing what, exactly?" Nadine asked.

"I need maintenance and production bosses, people who understand station systems like electrical, life support, and such like. Somebody who can monitor a fusion plant. I've been told that ship systems and station systems are the same, is that true?"

The four spacers nodded.

"Good. I need that, and I also need folks who understand cargo and containers, and people who can dock a ship. I don't need them every day, but we need to move more cargo and more ore out. You four seem like you know these things. Now, we may have had a somewhat irregular introduction, but I am in a hiring mode. You could be my asphyxiates."

The four looked at each other. Nadine got it first. "We could be your associates? What does that pay?"

He named a pay rate that was about triple what an experienced spacer could make, and a bonus system that was even more lucrative. All they had to do was help him run a station.

Nadine didn't need to be convinced. "Mack, for that much money, I'm happy to be your asphyxiate. I'm in."

Jake cleared his throat. "Mack, how long will we have to do this for?"

"Until we're finished."

"How long will that be?"

"At least six months. Possibly longer. Possibly a year."

"What type of off-station breaks do we get?"

Mack smiled, and it wasn't a nice smile. "Sorry, Jake, no rest for our peoples. Full steam till the end."

"Where is it?"

"That's not important. We're taking you there. As you have

already figured, our pilots are not great at some maneuvers, but they can punch a course into a computer and get us to the outer Belt. You don't need to know where we are going."

"What about those other guys—the ones from the container?" Riley asked.

"They agreed to work at a different station for a year. We're keeping the year, just changing the destination."

"Do they know that?"

Mack shrugged and gave a kind of 'what can you do?' shoulder roll. "We'll pay them the same. Why do they care?"

"Can they help you with this?" Jake asked.

"Nope." Mack took a swig of his drink. "They can work the mining equipment and do some basic work, but none of them have any advanced electrical or mechanical knowledge. They were all field hands for GG—worked where the robot harvesters couldn't reach."

"What if we don't want to do this, Mack?" Jake asked.

"Well, if I cannot subsidize your skills, I will have to use my own modest skills."

Mack regarded the metal bottle in his hand, and then banged it savagely against the table. Everybody jumped. Mack lifted the bottle up, and showed the large dent in the side. "I only do a few things, but I do them very well."

Jake relaxed in his couch as the Sidecar ran under thrust. He, Nadine, Riley, and twenty indentured workers—or 'indents,' as Mack called them—filled up the passenger sections of the shuttle. The R&R followed behind, with a full load of freight. Rick had just slaved his board to the Sidecar and gone for a nap.

Jake had a room to himself, as the usual occupants were over babysitting Rick. After signing on with Mack, they all had full computer access, including comm, but Mack had warned he would shoot anybody who caused trouble. He might have been joking. He probably wasn't. Jake was supposed to report to Dashi on a regular basis, but he didn't see the need to send a message right now. So, it wasn't a problem.

There was a security lock between him and the bridge, and he needed a code for that, which he didn't have. But otherwise, he ranged freely around the ship, even to engineering. "Make yourself useful," Mack had said. "If there is anything that needs to be fixed, let me know, then go fix it." Jake had fixed an electrical panel and a storage tank. The regular crew seemed clueless on repairs, and Mack either didn't know or didn't care how much trouble Jake could cause him with a few minutes in the environmental plant.

The door bonged.

"Come in," Jake said.

Nadine stepped through the door. "Hi, Jakey."

"Hello, Nadine. What do you want?"

"Always so direct."

"I have to be. I need to make sure I don't irritate you or you'll shoot me."

"They took all my guns, Jake."

"Not all of them," Jake said.

Nadine looked at him. "No, not all of them. Did you tell them?"

"Nope," Jake said.

Nadine twirled her fingers in her long blonde hair. "Now,

why wouldn't you do that? I thought you were trying to suck up to them."

"A little. But I don't entirely trust them."

"And you trust me more than them."

Jake thought about that for a moment. "I do, yes."

"Why?"

"The interests of our employers—mine and whoever yours are this week—appear to be aligned on this. They asked me to find out a few things about these food shipments."

"They asked you to stow away on the R&R?"

"Not exactly. I decided to use my initiative. It seems to have worked out."

"Jake Stewart, are you saying you didn't follow orders? Did you break the rules?"

"A little. But I wanted to find out more about what was going on."

"And that pretty redheaded girl had nothing to do with it?"

"She is very pretty," Jake said.

"You rebel, you." Nadine sauntered over and flopped onto the end of his couch. Her hips just touched Jake's leg. "This is a new Jake Stewart. I think I like him better than the old Jake Stewart."

"Thanks, but I'm still the same guy."

"No, you seem much more fun now." She leaned over and draped herself over his legs, and smiled at him. "So, tell me, Jake, what's going on here. Why these people, and why all this food? Why the bad gangster routine?"

Jake cleared his throat. She was close enough that he could smell her.

"You smell good. What is it?"

"Perfume. Orange. Do you like it?" Nadine sat up and leaned closer. "It's in my shampoo as well." She dangled her hair over his face.

Jake did smell it. "It smells great." She smelled great. She felt very hot on his legs, and the hair tickled.

"It makes my hair very soft. Where do you think we are going?"

"A high station. Something with a very eccentric orbit. A big mine. Not on the regular routes. They have only a short window to meet the lower stations and trade goods, then they're too far away."

"That's interesting, Jake. Do you like it when I do this?" She waved her hair over him again.

"Um, hmmm."

"So, why did they make us come with them?"

"They are heading away from Delta. The orbit will take them high for a few weeks or months. They're loading as much cargo as they can, 'cause they won't be able to for a while."

"That's interesting. Why the indentured workers?" She brushed her hair across his face again.

"Regular workers won't sign on for that long a passage without a break. And the high-eccentricity stations are dangerous—if something goes wrong, they're too fast and too far for rescue. That's why they have to offer bonuses, or take on people who are more desperate. Um. Nadine?"

"Yes, Jake?" Nadine said. She began to run her fingernails up and down his arm.

"Can I ask you to do something for me?"

"Of course, Jake, what would you like me to do?" Nadine ran her fingernails along him again.

"Tell me why you are here."

"In your cabin? Isn't it obvious?"

Jake laughed out loud. "Not really, Nadine. You haven't shown any interest in me before. I know you want something. I'm just not sure what. But I'm enjoying the effort a lot."

"Maybe I just want to see you?"

"Maybe you are collecting information to send back to your bosses."

The door dinged.

"Nadine," Jake said. "Did you lock the door behind you?"

"No, why?" Nadine asked.

The door slipped open and Riley walked in. She was looking down at a bottle in her hands.

"Hi, Jake, I've been thinking. I wanted to tell you how sweet I thought it was that you stowed away and— Oh." Riley stopped. "Am I interrupting?"

Jake took a good look at her. Tight skinsuit. Collar and wrist ruffles. Stylish headband. She had dressed up.

"No, no," Jake said, sitting up and pushing Nadine off him. "Nadine and I were just talking about stuff, that's all."

Nadine smiled brightly at Riley. "Yes, talking. About. Stuff." She grabbed Jake's arm again.

Riley looked at Nadine, then Jake. "Jake, I thought ... oh." Riley reddened. Redheads really did blush a lot.

"Riley, it's not what you think. Thanks for coming. Nadine was just leaving."

"I was?" Nadine asked. "I didn't know that. We still have some 'stuff' to talk about, right, Jakey?" She smiled at Riley. "Don't worry, Riley, it won't take long. Jake is always concise in thought and deed. Finishes things quickly."

Riley reddened even more. She put the bottle on the desk. "Jake this is from me— From Dad— From Dad and I, to welcome you to the crew, and thanks for helping out. We're— We're looking forward to working together. Goodbye." She turned around and walked out. The door slid shut behind her.

Jake glared at Nadine. She started to laugh. "Bitch," Jake said, but without much heat.

Nadine laughed even harder. "Agreed. But you knew that anyway."

"What do you really want, Nadine?"

"Where are we going, who are these people, and what are they doing?"

"Well, we'll find out in about fifty hours, if I read the course plot right. We'll be where we're going then. I guess you'll have to wait till then."

"I'm not very patient, Jake."

"That's all I know. Why did they pick you? Why do they need you as a pilot?"

Nadine sobered for a moment. "I don't know. They said they needed somebody who could fly a glider."

"You said that. But why a glider?"

"No idea. Well, thanks for the info about the stations, Jake. I'll think about that."

Nadine got up and strode to the door.

"Nadine, you didn't need to do this fake seduction to ask me questions. I would have told you without it."

Nadine stopped in the doorway and smiled at him. "I know that, Jake. But I kind of liked it."

Chapter 22

"Riley," Jake said to her in the lounge. She was sitting, drinking basic.

"Jake," she said.

"Do you mind if I sit here?"

"Free trades, Jake. Sit where you want."

"Thanks," Jake said. "How's your dad coming with that new fuel utilization program?"

Jake had talked to Rick about the ships. Rick knew a lot about engines, probably more than Jake, but Jake was much stronger on cargo, comm, and other ancillary systems. Stations didn't have engines, but they did have thrusters and life support—and they had bills to pay. Jake showed Rick how to run a variety of cargo loading programs in the navigation computer that would reduce fuel consumption by about 10 percent and loading time by up to 15 percent. Not big savings, but Rick was a businessman who understood that a dollar of costs saved was a dollar of profit. Rick taught Jake a few things about financing a ship and dealing with banks and loans that were very interesting. He also gave Jake a few hints about Riley. Project Rick had been a success.

"Fine. Where's your girlfriend today?"

"You mean Nadine?"

"Yes."

"First, she's your roommate, so you know better than me. Second, she's not my girlfriend."

"She sure looked like it."

"She's a little pushy and manipulative when she wants something. She's hard to resist."

"You didn't seem to be resisting all that hard."

"Riley, why did you bring that bottle to my room?"

"Dad and I wanted to welcome you on board."

"Uh-huh," Jake took a drink of his basic. "I don't know Rick all that well, but I don't think he'd say, 'Riley, put on some nice clothes and give this bottle to Jake when he is alone in his cabin.' Of course, I could be wrong."

"You think I came there just to see you?"

"Yes."

"Jake Stewart, I wouldn't date you—unless you were the last man in the universe, and stranded with me on an asteroid."

Aha, Jake thought. *I've got a chance.*

"Look, Riley, part of the reason I'm here is that I wanted to see more of you. If you don't want that, I understand. But I am interested."

"What about Nadine?"

"What about her?"

"She's interested in you."

"She's an attractive lady. She's kind of aggressive sometimes."

"You weren't exactly complaining."

"Riley. I am interested in you. But unless I missed an email, we haven't even gone out on a proper date yet. I'm not sure why that is your business right now."

Riley glared at Jake for a moment, then bit her lip. "I suppose. We're not dating, so I can't complain."

"But I'm still interested. We'll be at that station place soon. Let's see what happens there, and maybe we can get a drink that isn't basic."

Riley nodded.

Jake decided he needed to do some public relations work with Mack, so he cornered him at the basic spout.

"You're telling me we don't need these constant thrust changes?" Mack asked.

"No, we don't. Just do one change at the midpoint of the voyage, and one correction near the end. It will save some fuel, cut down wear on the systems, we won't have to stop what we're doing ten times a shift to strap in, and we can get more maintenance done," Jake said.

"My people tell me we need to do small changes every hour, otherwise things will worsen."

"Your people would be correct if we were in close orbit and with an atmosphere. Atmo slows us down, which drops us lower, which means thicker atmo, which means more drag, which slows us down more, which means bigger thrust corrections, so things get worse if they are not fixed quickly."

"So?"

"We're too far away. There is no atmosphere here. If we are off-course, the drag won't get worse. It's just gravity out here, and as long as we're headed in the right direction, it's much more effective to do a couple of big corrections once, rather than small ones over time. They work out to be the same. Out here, a vector is a vector is a vector."

"A vector is a vector is a vector," Mack repeated. "I like that."

"Uh, sure, good," Jake said.

"Why didn't my people know this?"

"Because they are has-been Militia orbital shuttle pilots who don't understand ring operations."

"How did you know that?"

Jake ran another mug of basic. "First, the constant vector changes are how the Militia does things. They don't have cargo, and they don't do maintenance underway unless in an emergency, so they don't understand how disruptive it is. Second, the militia is notorious for having bad pilots."

"Why?"

"They have to buy their ranks."

"What does buying their ranks have to do with it?"

"Because the commissions are so expensive. The senior Militia officers are either rich, taking up a corporate-owned slot, or very, very good at their jobs. And there are not many of the latter. Sure, they take about 5 percent of the very best enlisted people and make them officers, free of charge. But only the very best. And once you become an officer, you stay in the Militia for the perks, the tax advantages, and the pres- tige. These guys wouldn't have quit if they were real officers, or competent enlisted crew. Take a look at this." Jake handed Mack a navigation chip.

"What's this?"

"A course to our destination that will shave off time and cut fuel consumption. And a list of cargo maintenance we can do while they are drifting."

"Good job. Why are you doing this?"

"I get the impression that this trip is a long job interview for Riley, Rick, Nadine, and me. I want a good job, not just some crap one that you assign me. One that pays well. I can be very useful to you."

"How so?"

"I know cargo. I know stations. I'm used to the Belt. I can be your operations manager."

"I'm my operations manager."

"You are a manager, that's for sure. You know how to be in charge of people, and you are used to being in charge. And you know a lot of things. I figure you ran a shift at a processing plant or a mine or a factory. A big one. But you don't know space."

"I did something like that. But I have other skills as well. Skills to keep people in line."

"That's fine. You can do that. But I can handle your operations for you. I think you're getting bad advice. I'll bet if you take mine, you'll do better."

"Well, young Mr. Stewart. We'll see about that in a little while, won't we?"

"Confirm the CO2 line is shut off," Jake said.

"Shut off," Riley said.

Jake twisted a valve.

"Stuck, like everything else on this ship. This is, what, the fifth one today?"

"Sixth."

"I hate doing life-support maintenance."

"Stop your whining. We have nothing else to do until we get to that station, so you might as well make yourself useful."

Jake put a wrench in and used it to twist the valve. It creaked open. He levered a fitting off the end of the pipe and shined a light inside. He and Riley were inspecting filters in the life-support system.

"Looks marginal," Jake said.

"How marginal? We've only got three spares."

"Not that marginal. It will do for another week or so." Jake popped it back in and began to rewind the valve.

"I can't believe these guys have so few spares. It's a wonder they aren't all dead."

"They're not big on maintenance, that's for sure. I hope this station is in better shape, or at least has more spares."

A loud CRACK sounded, then somebody screamed.

"What was that?" Riley said.

"Don't know," Jake said. "But it came from the passengers' cabin." He closed the valve. "Let's go see."

Strange noises in a ship under thrust could be deadly. They needed to find out what they were. Riley and Jake pulled themselves hand-over-hand toward the main passenger cabin, and popped up into the couch area. Nadine dropped in from farther toward the bow.

"What's happening?" Riley asked.

"Board was green when I looked," Nadine said. "What about you?"

"We were working on the CO2 scrubber. It's fine. We didn't have any other alarms," she said.

They all sniffed the air. Sweat, food, and a vague latrine smell. But no smoke, burning plastic, or ozone. No dangerous smells. A noise behind them led them to the lounge.

Mack and two of his men were facing down a group of about ten of the indentured workers in the lounge. Another one was sitting on the floor, cradling what looked like a broken arm. Mack was swinging a wrench in a circle with his hand.

"I said that I won't tolerate any type of immunity, and I will deal with it strongly," Mack said, pointing his finger at the group.

"Mack, what's going on?" Nadine asked.

Mack turned. "Oh, Miss Direction, how are you? Nothing important, just an immunity that I had to deal with. How is the maintenance going, Jake?" He looked at Jake.

"Uh, fine," Jake said. "We're short on CO2 filter spares, but we'll last another week or so. I'll give you an order," Jake said.

"An order for CO2 spares. That's a great idea. We should have spares. You do that," Mack said. The man on the floor holding his arm groaned and said something. Mack looked down.

"You. I told you that this discussion was over. Keep quiet."

"Mack, what happened? We heard a crack, then a scream," Nadine said.

"Yes, you did."

"But what happened?"

"This gentleman here and his friends said that they didn't want to go to our station. They were talking about taking over the ship. I told them that was immunity, and I wouldn't tolerate it."

"Mutiny— They tried to mutiny?" Jake asked.

"Immunity, like I said. But I stopped them."

"How?"

"This gentleman here was most insistent, and he kept yelling at me, so I broke his arm, with this wrench here." Mack hefted the wrench.

"You broke his arm with that wrench?" Jake asked.

"Yes," Mack said. Everybody was silent, so he continued. "Really, a wrench is a most excellent tool for breaking arms. Easy to carry, easy to swing, packs a good punch, and doesn't break." Mack paused to swing it around again.

"I may not know much about CO2 lines, but I do know my wrenches. In fact, Jake," Mack continued, "since you have awakened me to the importance of having spares, I'll have you put another of these wrenches on your spares list. I think we should have two." He spun the wrench again.

The man on the floor spoke up, but it was in Spanish.

"I told you to keep quiet," Mack said. "Or at least if you said anything, say it in a language I understand."

Nadine spoke up. "He says his arm hurts and he wants to go home."

"He wants to go home, does he?" Mack said. "Well, I don't

want any unwilling workers here. We'll get him started. Boys, help him out."

The two men with Mack picked up the man and dragged him to the airlock. He whimpered as they shoved him in and closed the door.

"Mack," Jake said, "what are you doing?"

"Giving him what he wanted," Mack replied. He nodded toward the man at the lock. "Send him home."

The lock man punched the 'Evacuate' button, and they heard the fans evacuate the lock, then the whoosh as he hit the outer door release. Mack stepped over toward the door and looked out the viewport.

Everybody else stood frozen in shock.

Mack turned back to the group. "He's on his way. Anybody else want to go home?"

"We should shoot him," Nadine said, "and take control of the ship." They were standing in a corridor near engineering. Jake was removing an air vent.

"Not you too," Jake said. "Riley said the same thing."

"Then we're in agreement. Good," Nadine said. The three of them had retired to fix another vent.

"No, we're not. First, there is more than just him. He has, what, eight guys here? We can't get them all. Give me that wrench."

Nadine handed him a wrench. "Sure we can. We'll take 'em by surprise. I've got a gun."

"Not that wrench. The other one. You've got one gun, but they will have more. I don't know how many they have in the ship's locker, but it's more than one."

"I'll go into the engine room and say I'll blow the ship up if they don't go back," Riley said, handing him the other wrench.

"He won't believe you. I don't believe you," Jake said.

"You don't think I'll blow up the ship?"

Jake put his wrench down and looked at her. "No. No, I do not."

"I'll just shut off the air then," Riley said.

"So Nadine and I can die as well?"

"You two get into the bridge and stay there. It has its own air supply."

"Yes, it does. Of course, you'll have to kill all those indents as well. Poor bastards." Jake yanked the vent off the wall and dumped it on the ground with a clatter.

"Oh, right. Okay ... we'll all rush them then. Us and all the indents," Riley said.

"That will be hard to keep as a surprise, and if they get any warning at all, they'll beat us to death with wrenches. These guys are tough. Give me that filter."

Riley handed him the filter, and Jake began to screw it in. He continued. "Mack didn't even blink at putting that guy out the lock. This will get us all killed. It would only work if we could shoot them all at once. In the back. While they sleep."

"I can do that," Nadine said, bouncing up on her toes. "I want to do that. Let's do that."

"It won't work," Jake said.

"Don't be such a wimp, Jake. Be a man for once," Nadine said.

Jake gritted his teeth. "I'm not being a wimp, I'm being practical." He grabbed the vent and began to re-attach it.

"Sounds the same as being a wimp to me," Riley said.

"No, it's not. And there is one other problem."

"Of course, there is, Jakey, you can always find another problem," Nadine said.

"Rick. He's alone on the R&R, and he doesn't have any weapons."

Both girls paused. Riley looked worried. "They won't hurt Dad. They need him to pilot the ship," Riley said.

"He can still pilot the ship with a broken leg, or two broken legs," Jake said. "And even if we seized this ship, Mack's guys would be happy to break his bones one at a time, until we gave up," Jake said. He tightened another bolt.

"We have to do something," Riley said.

"No. We. Do. Not." Jake said. He had to grit his teeth again. "We have to wait and see what happens. We're not under threat right now. We're not sure where we're going or how to get away from here. And we're outnumbered by very violent people."

"You are such a coward, Jake Stewart," Riley said. She dropped her wrench and stomped off.

"I'm with your girlfriend on this, Jake," Nadine said. "You need to grow a pair."

"She's not my girlfriend, and I'm not a coward, Nadine. I'm just being practical."

"As she said before, sounds the same to me. Bye, Jakey. And don't worry, us girls will figure something out to save you from the nasty men." She sauntered off after Riley.

Jake watched her go, then turned toward the vent. The last bolt would not quite fit. Jake wrestled with it for a moment, then leaned back and hammered on it as hard as he could until it was firmly jammed in.

Chapter 23

"What's that smell?" Nadine asked. They had just entered Mack's station from the Sidecar.

"The smell? Oh, that's just mold. It started a couple weeks ago. Don't worry about it," Mack said.

"Mold? All over? That's bad," Nadine said.

"Don't be a wuss. It's just a smell. You can put up with it."

"There's a problem with your life-support system. It's not removing the water vapor the way it's supposed to," Nadine said.

"You can tell that from just the smell, can you?" Mack stopped and turned around.

"Yes. Mold needs humidity to grow. Too much humidity means life-support problems."

"I didn't know that. But it's just water, right? No big deal."

The four spacers looked at each other.

"Well," Jake said, "water can short out electrical equipment, which is bad. And cause things to rust. And mold makes some people sick."

"Is that why we have headaches all the time?" Mack said.

"What type of headaches?" Rick asked.

"We get a bit sleepy sometimes, get a headache. Some of the guys say they get tired easily. They are just being lazy," Mack said.

"When did this start happening?" Jake asked.

"A few weeks ago. Why do you care?"

"Uh, Mack, did you get more workers a few weeks ago?"

"A bunch of guys. And let me tell you, they are the laziest of the bunch. They are pretty slow and spend most of their time sleeping."

Jake looked at the other spacers. "Carbon dioxide." They all nodded. Rick looked pale.

Mack shrugged. "Well, whatever. We need to get you guys introduced and settled in, then—"

"Mack, we don't have time for this. We need to fix it now."

Mack bristled. "We'll fix it when I'm good and ready. First, you folks follow me—"

"Mack, don't be an ass. We need to fix it now. Where's the air exchanger? We need to go there now," Nadine said. "Everybody, follow me."

Mack stepped forward and grabbed Nadine by the shoulders. He lifted her right off the floor and brought her to his eye level. Jake was impressed. Nadine wasn't small.

"I said we'll go there when I'm ready," he snarled and glared at her.

Jake hurried up next to them. "Mack, she's right. This is a major emergency. The life support may already have failed. We need to fix this before we have to suit up and use backup air."

That got Mack's attention. He dropped Nadine. She recovered, but looked surprised.

"Suit up?"

"Mack, too much carbon dioxide can kill us in minutes once it gets above a certain percentage."

"How do you know that's it?"

"Those are standard symptoms of carbon dioxide poisoning. And combined with the extra water vapor, it means the life-support system is being overrun. We need to see it. Now."

Mack looked at Jake for a moment, then at the others. They all nodded. He shrugged. "Okay," he said, turning to a corridor. "Follow me."

Mack led them out of the docking area past two more ship locks and then through an airlock. The asteroid was rotating, so 'up' was actually toward the surface. They approached a ladder. Mack went first, followed by Nadine, Jake, Rick, and Riley. Through the viewports, Jake could see a full mining mill—grinder, solar mirrors, evaporators, condenser, and storage. The equipment showed a lot of wear from use, and lots of micro-meteorite damage. He could see a fuel plant that could crack H and O from water, and a water-ice asteroid parked within visual distance.

"Look at all those ships chained to the surface," Nadine said, gesturing at the viewport. "That's a Militia cutter, but with no engines or power plant. What are those three wrecks next to it?"

"Tugs," Jake said. "Or at least they used to be tugs. They're missing a lot of stuff. No cages or control rooms. No engines either."

"That's a freighter chained down on the far side. The one with all the cables. Mack, what are the cables on that freighter for?" Nadine said.

Mack stopped climbing and looked out the viewport. "We use its fusion plant. My people said it's better than the in-station one." He resumed his climb.

Jake kept looking at the ships. Three derelict tugs, a busted cutter, a grounded freighter, and another grounded freighter at the end. It looked like a shuttle without wings. He stopped and used his comm to take a picture. Rick bumped into him.

"Jake?"

"Sorry, Rick, just checking something I need to look at later," Jake said. He checked that the picture was clear enough, and continued climbing.

They entered a control room. Inside, two people were staring at screens. It had a military look about it. The console operators wore revolvers, and there were shotguns chained in a cabinet. Mack stepped into a bunk room visible on one side, and spoke to the people in there. He returned and gestured the four spacers into another airlock. Mack staged them through and they entered another corridor. Each side was lined with standard habitat modules. Jake did a quick count and figured there was room for perhaps sixty people. That was a reasonable crew for the mining equipment that he had seen, especially if they ran three shifts. They walked to the end of the corridor, and entered the life-support area.

The life-support system had four cryogenic distillers that were supposed to freeze water, carbon monoxide, and carbon dioxide out of the air. One was disconnected, two had tripped their breakers and gone into emergency shutoff, and the remaining one was operating at only 20 percent efficiency. Also, both heating systems in the vents were offline. Jake ran through the control screens, assessed the issues, and took charge.

"Rick, you and Riley suit up, get some crowbars and heaters. Go outside. Some of the vents are frozen shut. The system can't push the air through, so crack them open. Nadine, get a heater, come back here and find the pipes on the inside, melt the dry ice out of them. See if there is any frozen nitrogen there as well. Suit up first and seal the compartment. There might be methane in there as well. In fact, if you can, vent the whole compartment to space first. Mack, show Rick and Riley the lock, then go with Nadine and help her get an electric heater, then meet Riley and Rick at the lock and help them get outside. I'm going to trace the electrical line and see why those other systems tripped the breakers, and I need to trace why the heating system is offline. Mack, do you have an emergency O cracking system on your fusion reactor?"

Everybody except Mack nodded and moved off. Mack looked at Jake. "Cracking system? Nitrogen? Methane? You sound like a chemistry professor."

"Mack, this is really serious. Stations expose their air to near-vacuum for very precisely calculated times. The vacuum cools the air so much that the water, the carbon dioxide, and some other gases freeze out. The gases condense on these heating elements—look here in this diagram." He showed Mack a screen. "Then, they take the cold air and reheat it so that we can breathe it again. And then they turn the heating elements back on, which re-gasifies the precipitants and vents them to space. That's not happening here. The heating system is off-line. The pipes are blocked with frozen gases. If we can't get them heated up, the whole system will fail, then we'll all die once the air in our suits runs out."

"Oh," Mack said, holding up his hands. "Okay, professor, you are in charge on this one. What do we need to do?"

The team worked a full day without stopping. At first Mack was bemused, but he began to respond to everybody's serious-as-a-heart-attack mien. The four of them were so concerned that he began to doubt his former insouciance. Except he'd said he was 'doubting his former insurance.' Either way, when Jake showed him some of the pipes that were almost totally blocked with frozen precipitants, he looked troubled.

"This could have caused me all sorts of troubling things."

"Indeed," Jake said. "But we're okay now. We just need to make sure that we have a regular maintenance and flushing schedule. The four of us can do it, and we'll teach some of the other workers to do the regular stuff. Should we include some of your guys in the training?"

"No, no. My guys have other things to do," Mack said. He looked at Jake. "You did a good job, professor. I'm happy. I think I will make you that operations manager after all."

"What does that mean, exactly?"

"You'll be in charge of all the maintenance on the station, your three friends, and the indents that you need."

"That's fine, Mack, but I'll need to give your guys some instructions from time to time. There are a few things that need doing in the security office, and other places, and I'll need free rein there."

Mack looked at him for a moment. "I'll consider that, professor. For now, you are in charge of just the maintenance."

Jake coughed. "Uh, Mack, I worked on a mining station. I can do things there too."

Mack laughed. "Already looking for a promotion. Okay, give me the ideas on the mining part, and we'll see what happens there. Congratulations on your promotion."

Jake proved to be a decent administrator. He came up with a list of things that needed fixing, divided them up by skillset, and put the station staff to work. They were in so much danger that they dropped their previous talk of rebellion for a few days to get things done.

On the third day after their arrival, the group sat together, each drinking a cup of basic and discussing the day's tasks.

"What is this place?" Nadine asked

"How do you mean?" Rick asked. "It's a station. A mine."

"But who built it? It's so different. Look at the styles. The basic spouts are different—oval rather than round. The furniture and fittings are all legos, but not any type I've seen before. They are Empire standard—these chairs would bolt onto the deck of any station I've ever been on—but they have a metal mesh at the back, not spindles."

Everybody twisted and looked at their chairs. The station, ship, and furniture was standard. Chairs, tables, lockers, beds, and all fittings were standardized. Everything was designed to be fitted to a ten-centimeter-by-ten-centimeter grid. A chair's floor space could be forty by forty centimeters, or sixty by sixty centimeters, but always on the grid. Floors, walls, and ceilings were all one-meter or two-meter square panels, with standard bolt holes. Every station or ship had a bag of hundreds of standard nuts and bolts to attach items. The whole system was called legos for some unknown reason.

"And look at the colors. They're more formal," Riley said.

"More formal? Colors can't be formal," Nadine said. "They can be blue or bright, or something like that. Not formal."

"They can. They can be whatever they want," Riley said. "The colors on our ship are happy. Regular station colors are businesslike. TGI corporate colors are thoughtful. Castle Transport is staid. These colors are formal."

"Okay, merchant girl, you mean they are gray and brown," Nadine said. "That's formal, is it?" She frowned and looked around. "But you know, merchie, you are on to something. These colors are different than anything I've seen before."

"More formal," insisted Riley.

"It's old," Rick said, "at least this side. The frames of those exterior floodlights I repaired yesterday had actually started to oxidize from the air that leaked out of the lock. Imagine how long it takes for that little bit of air to actually oxidize something."

"Imperial Scout Service," Jake said.

"Who is?" Rick said.

"This is an old Imperial Scout Service station," Jake said. "Look at the way it was designed. A secure loading dock for the scout ships, and secure station area for the scouts. It has its own dock and fusion reactor, completely self-contained.

I've seen pictures in the vids. The scouts built them by the hundreds to handle communication and survey ships. It was usually the first station in a system. This could be the original scout station built here hundreds of years ago. Before the Abandonment."

"But why up here?" Nadine asked. "All the resources are in the lower belts, and this station goes very high. You'll need to dump a lot of velocity to get off this and down low."

"That's what they wanted. This wasn't set up to service anything on Delta. It was set up to service passing jump ships. When the jump ships stopped coming, after the Abandonment, it wasn't worth keeping up. I'll bet it was abandoned years ago, and only reactivated recently. I'll bet the Militia had it in their records, and secretly opened it up," Jake said.

They all contemplated that.

"But why would the Militia do that? They don't need a mine. There are lots of better mines lower. The corps will sell them all they need," Rick said.

"And why the secrecy?" Riley asked.

"They don't want anybody to know they have a source of metals," Jake said. "An independent source. Separate from the corps. The emergency charter of the Delta corporation says the corps keep their own resources and control their own stations and settlements, and they have their own internal police forces. They own the monorail in common, but the Militia owns the shuttles, the mass driver, and the maintenance stations. It provides the policing for shared settlements, like Landing. But the corps didn't want the Militia to get too much power, so it's prohibited from owning any sort of factory or resource-producing station."

Everybody looked at Jake. "What does that have to do with the price of oxygen, then?" Nadine asked.

"Well, if the Militia can get its own source of metals, fuels, water, etcetera., it doesn't need to listen to the corps. They could do what they want. They could stage a coup."

"How would that work?" Nadine asked.

"The Militia controls ground-to-space access. They could interdict that. The space-based corps would run out of food, and the ground-based corps would lose access to resources. If the Militia could keep an embargo going for a while, the corporations would be forced to let them take control."

"But won't the Militia be affected as well?" Rick asked. "Won't they run out of stuff?"

"Well, this is a mine, and they'll have access to at least some materials here. Metals for parts for sure. And there is fuel, H, and O right here. They don't have a tanker, but they could jury-rig one."

"What about food?" Rick asked.

"It's in the warehouse," Jake said. "First thing I looked for when I got here. They've been stockpiling it here. There are about fifty containers full of food. That's not a lot for a busy station like TGI Main, but it will keep the whole Militia going for a while."

"Where did it come from?" Riley asked.

"The Militia stole it. Some of it was marked as lost during orbital boost by the source corps, but it's here now. The

Militia control the mass driver. They must have arranged to steal it."

"But there are no Militia people here. There is Mack and his guys, but they are, like, contractors or something. Why not use Militia people?" Rick asked.

"Because almost all of the Militia people have a secondary job with one corp or another. The number of purely Militia people is very small. If you sent any Militia person here, somebody corporate would notice. They would notice that somebody had been transferred, and this wouldn't stay secret for long," Jake said.

"It's the Empire Rising people," Nadine said. "Those weirdos who want to return to Old Empire values."

"Those strange ones who braid their hair, and don't drink," Rick said.

"They say they don't drink on duty, and they're always on duty till the old Emperor says otherwise. And since the old Emperor isn't around to let them go home, they just hang around and make pests of themselves," Nadine said.

"There isn't enough of them. You think they set up all this?" Rick said.

"Somebody did," Nadine said. "And we've been kidnapped to here in a secret mining station that's been hidden for hundreds of years, crewed by slaves, controlled by criminals —hired by rogue Militia elements—that have been receiving stolen goods. Have a better explanation?"

Chapter 24

"You can't help yourself, can you?" Nadine asked Jake during breakfast the next morning. The four of them were alone in the lounge. They had their own lounge, separate from the others.

"What?" Jake said.

"You can't help yourself from fixing things. You see something that isn't being done the way you want, and you tweak a schedule or suggest a maintenance change. Whether it's your job or not."

"I lived on a station for most of my life. Maintenance is important. People get hurt when you neglect it."

"That's true," Riley said. "But you gave suggestions about the mining as well. Those suggestions about tuning the mirrors have helped them out."

"Why not give them suggestions that help them out? I gave your dad suggestions that helped him out."

"He did," Rick agreed. He munched on his low-calorie breakfast tray. Since they were stuck there, he had implemented a regime of gym work and tried to cut down on the number of trays he was eating. And he'd actually lost a kilo.

"Yes, but my dad isn't walking around with a gun on his hip and throwing people out an airlock like Mack is," Riley said.

"It didn't bother you when you were selling them stolen goods before," Nadine said.

"We didn't know about the workers. I thought it was just a scam. I'm sorry I got you into this, sweetie," Rick said, looking at Riley.

"What about me?" Nadine asked.

"You brought yourself along," Riley said. "As did Jake. Jake, why are you helping Mack so much?"

"Mack's lazy. If I have a suggestion that involved work for Mack, he turns it down. But if I'm willing to do the work, or better yet, just do the work, Mack usually approves. So, I make efficiencies."

"You make efficiencies? Did you take the same language course Mack did?" Nadine said. "But why help him, Jake? He kills people. These folks are slaves. I'm a slave. I don't like that. We need to get out of here."

"Nadine's right," Riley said. "We need to get out of here."

"They let me back on the R&R a few times," Rick said. "For tools and clothes and things like that. They always keep an eye on me, but they do let me go there. I think I could get us back on."

"Great—the four of us get on the R&R, fire it up, and I'll fly us out of here," Nadine said.

"Won't they be able to catch us with their ship?" Riley asked.

"It's a passenger launch. It's fast but short-ranged. We can't outrun them from a standing start, but if we get some time, we can get far enough away that they can't catch us before they run out of fuel," Nadine said.

"Does it have weapons?" Rick asked.

"Probably not. Launches don't usually. It's too small for a mass driver. They could have a laser mounted somewhere, but I didn't see one."

"They didn't empty the ship's locker," Rick said. "They took the keys from me, but the guns are still there."

"Good," Riley said.

"Why is that good?" Nadine said.

"You don't keep a spare master set of keys hidden somewhere secret on your ship? That's not very smart," Riley said.

"Bite me," Nadine said.

"Girls," Rick said. "I could get them to let me on board the R&R again. I can get the keys without them seeing, no problem. A few hours of messy environmental maintenance and they are bound to leave me alone long enough for me to grab a few guns. When I come back with the tools, I'll hand them out, we could grab the guards, force our way back onto the ship, and get out of here," Rick said.

"Won't they check your tools?" Nadine asked.

"They never have before," Rick said.

"When?" Riley asked.

"No time like the present," Nadine said. "I've got access to one gun they missed. It's hidden in the tool closet. I'll grab that. You get on board. The three of us will wait in the lounge. When you come back with the rest of the guns, we'll shoot our way through and take off. What do you think?"

"I think it sounds great," Riley said. "Let's do it. Dad?"

Rick took a deep breath. "I want you out of here as soon as possible. You can pilot the ship without me if need be. I'll go last, and hold them off, and you three can go."

"Dad," Riley said.

"Don't worry, merchie, it won't come to that. Your dad gets the guns, a bit of yelling, and we're on our way. We'll be fine." Nadine stood up. "Let's go."

Rick and Riley got to their feet and began to move toward the door. All three of them stopped when they realized that Jake hadn't moved. He sat with his eyes closed and his head on his cupped hands.

"Jake?" Rick said.

"Rick, did they reinforce the magnetic grapples after we latched?" Jake asked.

"Well, yes, we're chained in now. But we can pop the chains."

"We'll have to have somebody on the hull when we do that."

"Riley or Nadine can do it. They both understand cargo equipment," Rick said.

"Nadine has never used cargo gear. It will have to be Riley," Jake said. Rick shuffled uncomfortably and looked at his daughter.

"I'll be in a skinsuit, Dad, no problem," Riley said.

"Have you ever shot a person, Rick?" Jake asked.

"No."

"It's harder than it looks. Are you a good marksman?"

"I don't know. But I don't have to be. I'll just shoot a lot of bullets at them. They'll duck."

"Those are six-shot revolvers. Even Mack's people can count. After six, they'll rush you."

"I'll bring two," Rick said.

"Or I can shoot them," Nadine said. "Try telling me I'm a bad shot. I'll demonstrate on you first."

"Where would we go from here, Rick? What type of orbit are we in? Can you navigate a course for us?" Jake said.

Rick looked at his daughter and coughed. "We're pretty high. I'm not sure what's up here. Riley does our navigation."

Riley looked at Jake. "Jake, we can't just stay here forever."

"I'm not saying stay here forever, but I don't see the point in firing out of here and ending up drifting, then getting picked up by Mack's Militia buddies. He definitely has friends in the Militia. I want to collect more information."

"That's our Jake. Wants more information," Nadine said. "You know, Jake, for a while I thought you were going to man up, but it seems like you're back to your old ways."

Jake ignored her. "And, Rick, what about all those workers that are here? The workers you brought out here? Are you just going to abandon them here?"

"We'll tell somebody when we get back," Rick said.

"Mack will space them before anybody gets here and claim you were raving," Jake said.

Rick leaned toward Jake. "I don't care. It's my fault my

daughter is here. I want her off this rock. Are you going to help us or not?"

All three of them looked at him. Jake shook his head and stood up. "Let's go," he said.

They suited up in semi-hard suits to get some protection from gunfire. Rick left for the R&R. The three others commandeered an office near the lock. In case somebody asked what they were doing, Jake put up a diagram of the heating system on the wall, complete with red outlined failures and a parts list. They were there only half an hour before a sweating Rick returned carrying a big toolbox.

"Well?" Nadine said.

"Got everything. They left me alone on the bridge for few minutes, and I was able to check the fuel. Still about half—plenty to get far away."

"And the guns?" Riley said.

"Three of them, one each for the rest of us. Some bad news: They cleaned most of the ammunition out of the locker, but there was enough for these guns and an extra half-dozen for each of us," Rick said. He pulled the guns out of his tool bag and handed them around. Nadine pulled her Gauss pistol out and held it by her leg. Riley and Rick both loaded their revolvers and put them in holsters attached to their belts.

"You're sweating a lot, Rick," Jake said.

"It's this Empire-damned semi-hard suit," Rick said. "They've turned the heat up on the ship."

Jake looked at Rick's suit. "Did they ask any questions about the suit?"

"No, why would they?"

"You've never worn one on board before," Jake said.

Rick shrugged. "They didn't say anything. Ready?"

"Ready," Nadine said.

"Ready," Riley said.

"Riley, stay behind me. Jake?" Rick said.

Jake just nodded.

Nadine took the lead. They trooped down the hall, turned the corner, and walked into the airlock to the truss.

Nadine whipped her hand over her head and fired at the ceiling. "I'll shoot the first person who moves," she said. She stepped back and swung her pistol from side to side. Dust floated from where her last shot had impacted the ceiling.

Mack was there, along with two of his guys. They were sitting at a table across the room, talking.

"What is this?" Mack said.

"Give us your guns, Mack," Nadine said. "We're getting out of here. We'll shoot you if you stop us."

"Really? You can't shoot all of us with that little pistol," Mack said. "A pistol that small, it can have only a single shot, and you already fired that up there...."

Mack's group started to stand up from the table.

"That's an Old Empire Gauss pistol," Rick said. He stepped up toward Mack, pointing his gun with his right hand. He used his left to push Riley behind him. "It shoots micro-needles, not shells. Her magazine will have hundreds of them."

"I'm not afraid of some tiny little needles, old man," Mack said. He continued to rise.

"You should be," Jake said. "It's physics. Momentum is

mass times velocity squared. The needles are very, very little, true. But they are moving ten, maybe twenty kilometers a second. They'll just leave a little hole in the front, but the energy liberated will blow your lungs out through your backbone. Plus, since it's magnetic, the rate of fire is hundreds of needles per second if she puts it on automatic. It will look kind of like she fed you through one of those metal cutting saws."

"Well, thank you, professor," said Mack. He sat down and waved off his guys.

"Here," Mack said. He pulled a pistol out of his belt with two fingers, and slid it across the floor to Nadine. "You guys too," he said to his companions, and they did likewise.

Nadine faced them and brandished the pistol. "We're getting out of here. Mack, just let us go, otherwise I'll fill you full of holes. Tiny holes, but thousands of them."

"Okay, go ahead," Mack said, and leaned back and crossed his arms.

"Okay?" Nadine said.

"Sure, go," Mack said. "You've got the guns. How can I stop you?" He smiled at them, and gestured to the airlock.

Rick and Riley stepped toward the airlock and began to spin the locking wheel. It stuck. Nadine kept her gun trained on Mack and his guys.

Mack kept smiling. His eyes drifted up and focused above Jake's shoulder. Jake turned around. Mack had been looking at a video monitor. It showed an empty airlock. But there was a flash of motion in one corner. Somebody was in the airlock.

"Nadine," Jake said.

"What, Jake?" Nadine asked.

"I don't think—"

"Shut up, Jake," Riley said. "The door is stuck. Help us with it."

"Riley, I don't think—" Jake began.

"Shut up, Jake," Nadine said. "Now is not the time. You either help us leave, or stay here and stay with Mack."

Jake looked at Riley and Rick struggling with the lock. It was stuck. He looked back at Mack. Mack was smiling and winked at Jake.

Jake sighed and flipped open his revolver. He then dumped the bullets in the cylinder into his hand, and reloaded it with green-banded bullets he'd pulled from the pouch in his backpack.

"I have a plan, Nadine," Jake said.

"Of course, you do, Jake. What's your call?"

Jake clicked the gun shut and tried to spin the cylinder. It jammed. He pulled it out and reseated it. It spun this time.

"I'm glad that worked. You know I'm not good with guns, Nadine," Jake said. He pushed the revolver toward Nadine's arm.

She glanced at him. "Jake, I'm busy here. Just put it in your pocket or something so that you don't hurt anybody. Chances are you'll shoot yourself. Now, what's your plan to get out of here?"

"It's complicated," Jake said.

He paused and rolled his hand to the side to check it. He reached down and held the pistol in both hands, and squeezed the trigger.

Nadine screamed as the bullet broke her arm. She immediately dropped her Gauss pistol.

Rick turned from the airlock. He was too shocked to speak, so he didn't cringe at all when Jake turned toward him and shot him in the chest of his semi-hard suit, twice. The first shot jerked him backward, the second one knocked him down, and he collapsed in a heap on the floor.

Riley screamed as her father fell down in front of her and looked up at Jake. Jake made a kind of 'oops' motion with his shoulder. Riley froze for a second, then turned to run away. Jake shot her in the leg. It took three shots. She fell, holding her leg.

Mack blinked for a moment, but then slid out from behind the chair and reached down to grab Nadine's dropped pistol. He had reached his fingers forward when Jake's foot came down on his hand, trapping it on top of the pistol. Mack started to draw backward but stopped when he looked up and saw Jake pointing the revolver directly into his left eye.

Jake stood over him and increased the pressure on the trigger. Mack saw the trigger move back very slowly. Jake held his finger pressure and spoke. "I'm not very good with guns, Mack, and I don't want to shoot you by accident. I'm going to move my foot, and I want you to scoot backwards. You should do this quickly. I can't hold that pressure forever, and if I have to do something with my finger, it's going to clench it, not relax it. Understand?"

"Got it," Mack whispered, eyes on the trigger finger. Jake lifted his foot but kept his heel on the ground, and Mack leaned back on his haunches and began to slide backward.

Jake kept the revolver pointed at his head until Mack was seated back on the chair, then Jake stooped and recovered the Gauss pistol with his left hand, and fumbled it into a pouch on his belt.

Nadine groaned and rolled a bit. Jake stepped toward her and pointed the pistol at her chest and fired one round. Her chest banged against the ground, and there was a whoosh of her breath rolling out. Jake pulled the trigger again but only had a click. He tried a second time and got another click.

"Right," Jake said. It's a six-shooter. I forgot. They always yelled at me in training. I never counted my shots right."

Mack nodded at Jake but didn't move. Jake nodded at him.

"I know. It's kind of like your favorite house cat just grew fangs and slashed his neighbor's throat."

Mack smiled. "And was eating chunks of his face."

Jake looked at the revolver and frowned. He pocketed it and sat down at the next table over. Then he pulled the Gauss gun out of his belt pouch with his left hand and transferred it to his right hand. He looked at the gun in his hand. "A little small for me, I think, but I can see why Nadine liked it. Now, Mack." Jake spun the gun in his hand once, then twice. "Huh. That's more fun than it looks. Now, Mack, earlier we talked about a job—a promotion. I've decided I will be your deputy. I feel you have a good operation here, but it could be a great operation with modern accounting practices. We need better inventory, logistics, allowances for wastage, and we need a system to smooth out production. I have a number of ideas, but frankly, rather than trying to explain them all, I really think you should just let me start implementing them myself. It will be my responsibility if they don't work out, but if they do, I expect to be well compensated. Very well compensated. I think in this exploratory period, it's best if you just give me a free hand to implement the changes I want. What do you say?"

Mack had regained a bit of his composure, but his attention was captured by Jake's random spinning of the Gauss pistol in his right hand. He looked up at Jake and gestured down with his chin.

"What? Oh, sorry," Jake said. He stopped spinning the loaded pistol and put it in his pocket. "Sorry. What do you say? Can we discuss this now?"

Mack nodded. "Sure, Jake, why not."

"Good, good. Okay." Jake turned around. "You folks in the lock can come out. Don't shoot anybody. The emergency's over. Mack and I are talking."

There was a long silence. Finally, Mack yelled, "Okay, show's over, come out—Everything's fine."

The lock's door spun open, and three of Mack's guys came out. They carried strange-looking weapons with a long metal box below them.

"Are those machine guns? I've never seen one for real, only in pictures," Jake said.

"They're called sub-machine guns," Mack said. "Don't shoot as rapidly as your friend's Gauss guns, but we've got lots of them." He sounded proud.

"Where did you get them— Oh, the Militia gave them to you?"

"Right," Mack said.

"Huh. What was the tip-off? The semi-hard suit?"

Mack nodded. "He never wore that before."

"And you left the guns there but monitored somehow, so that you could see if we were planning something."

"Yes."

"And the ammo was fake, or blank, or something."

"Training."

"Smart. I knew it would never work. But there was no talking to them. I like to be on the winning team. I believe that this establishes my bona fides, then."

"Bona fides?"

"Proof I'm on your side. Shooting my friends proved I'm with you."

"I guess it did," Mack said.

"Good. Now, the first issue is inventory and storage. We need a full inventory of what's been produced so far, so I need to talk to whatshisname, the red-headed guy, and we need to make changes right away. Oh, and Mack, I think you need to call somebody to put those three in a medical unit. Next, the staffing of the shifts. We're not getting the production that we could, and I have a plan."

Jake continued to talk, even when the medic took his friends away.

Chapter 25

"If we lie to these people, they might kill us," Mack said.

"Only if they figure it out, and they won't," Jake said.

"I'm not sure about this, Mr. Professor," Mack said.

It was a few weeks after Jake's surprise defection. Mack had put Jake in charge of production, telling him to 'prove his loyalty.' And Jake had. While his initial changes had caused an immediate rise in production, his more complex ones had caused it to soar. Now, Jake was proposing even more ambitious and complex changes.

"If we are going to cheat, we're going to cheat in detail," Jake explained, sitting at his desk. "Mining returns should vary, as the quality of ore and the density of secondary metals change. By being variable, we won't have to worry about an audit uncovering any shortages."

"I don't understand why you asked for that radar equipment."

"This has been a poorly yielding claim. Your bosses figure that you're siphoning off some. Everybody does."

"Nobody better siphon off me, or I'll shoot 'em," Mack said.

"Mack, we can't have a sudden surge in production. If we do, they'll get suspicious. They'll think you've been holding back till now. We need a reason. That radar is the reason."

"We'll just report the same amount as we do now."

"Then you won't get any more money."

"Will a radar get us more money?"

"It won't. But the changes I've made in production will. We're processing more than double the ore we did just two weeks ago. We're producing twice as much aluminum and nickel, which is worth a lot of money. But only if we sell it or ship it to your bosses. How do you get your cut out of that?"

"We ship it to them?"

"And our numbers increase. Then they think you could have done this before, and maybe you were stealing from them. With the radar, we have a reason—we can say we found richer deposits, and that's why they are getting more cargo."

"We just tell them we are processing more ore."

"They will expect to receive more gold and platinum, because the percentages should remain the same in the same ore field."

"They can't have my gold!"

"Exactly. We process double the ore than we admit to. That inflates our returns, so we look above-average. Getting a little bit better won't trigger any alarms. Then, we just make sure that the amount of base and precious metals we report is within industry norms for our reported processing, rather than our actual processing, and we can pocket the difference."

"Won't they suspect we are doing this?"

"That's why we have the radar equipment. The radar mapping equipment is used to find the direction and density of a mineral seam. Any miner looking at our reports will see a steady improvement after we started using it. The gains in efficiency will make sense to them."

"I'm glad it makes sense to you. It's a little confusing for me." Mack got up and walked around the table and stretched. They were in Jake's office. Jake had been using it for meetings for several days. He had invited some of the indents and asked for suggestions. They discussed production changes and schedules. There were even slides and spreadsheets.

"Mr. Professor, you've surprised the hell out of me. I never thought you'd turn pirate. I didn't think you had the guts," Mack said.

"Well, there is the old saying, 'If you can't beat 'em, join 'em.' And I got tired of being lectured by do-gooders about what I could and couldn't do. Besides, it's a very interesting technical problem. By under-reporting the base metals production, we can hide the changes in trace metal amounts. Even if they get miners to look at our reports, we'll be in line for normal operations."

"What you said," Mack said. "I have to admit, giving the indents more food and some cash for more production was a masterstroke."

"Before, they would work just enough not to get beaten up. Now they get something. Rewarding them for good behavior is much more effective than just punishing them for bad behavior."

"But punishing them is fun."

"We're not here for fun. We're here to make money," Jake said.

"I still think we should have killed that starship crew, and your friend, Nadine."

"I didn't know they were frangibles. I'm not very good with guns. I didn't shoot to kill them, just to stop them from messing up my plans. The killing would have been a side effect. Once the threat was neutralized, there was no need to kill them."

"You scared the crap out of me, for sure."

"That wasn't the idea either. I just saw a problem and moved to fix it. It was just business."

Mack regarded him for a moment. "You are a cold-blooded bastard, aren't you. Killing people is just business?"

"For me. You think I should get angry or excited about it?"

Mack was quiet for a moment. "I'm not sure. I've only killed people who made me angry."

"Anger is a poor servant. There should be a reason."

"I had a reason—they disrespected me."

"Yes, but did that disrespect impact your business?"

Mack shook his head. "I always kill hot. You kill cold, don't you?"

"I'm an accountant, Mack. Numbers don't lie, and they don't have emotions either."

"I guess so." Mack shrugged. "You are not what I'm used to, Jake. But I can't fault your methods."

"No, you can't. I'm going to make you rich. And me too, of course."

"Huh. How do I know that you won't kill me and take my share? Maybe I should kill you first?"

"You could, I suppose. But that would also kill the extra money you're making. How much more are you making now, every month? Double? Triple?"

"Double at least," Mack agreed.

"Triple. If you killed me, you would get what I've got put by. Which is only a few weeks. Or we could keep doing this forever—you handle the day-to-day, and I do the paperwork and administration, and you make twice as much, forever."

Mack nodded. "You are clever. I'll give you that. Clever is good. It works for me."

"Good, then no problems."

"You're still a bit squeamish. Do you want me to kill those trader people—Riley and Rick?"

Jake shook his head. "No. How do we get that radar here?"

"I don't know," Mack said.

"I want Rick to go do it."

"Rick? Why?"

Jake began to tick off points on his fingers. "He's a trained crewman, we have a freighter, we need a radar and also an extra generator, and we need to move out a load of our heavy metal production. He can do that. We can bypass your contacts for the extra ore and just take cash. He is perfect to transport our production and bring back supplies."

"I guess it was luck that you had those frangibles in your gun and not solid shot."

"Good luck for him, I guess. But we need to take advantage of it. I'm going to talk to him today and see how he feels.

If he gives me the right answers, we'll give them a full load to take back."

"I don't think you can trust him."

"I have a plan for that too."

"He'll steal everything," Mack insisted.

"You would steal everything, Mack. He's not you."

"If it was me, I'd come back with an army of mercs in the ship."

"You know where to hire an army, but does he?"

"Well, probably not."

"And if he did hire them, would he be able to buy weapons?"

"Some."

"As good as your guys'? As many?"

Mack shook his head. "Nope."

Jake stretched his hands over his head and continued rearranging the schedule on his computer. Mack had the same worries every shift. He was worried about letting Rick take metals back to low orbit for sale. He was worried Rick would turn them in. And every shift, Jake made the same arguments. Mack's greed always won. Rick's ship was going to be stuffed as full of metal as Jake could make it.

"If it was you doing it, Mack, how would you get the guys and the guns to take us over?"

Mack began with his theory, which involved a lot of fighting, stealing, and some torture. Jake interjected with a question from time to time to keep Mack talking.

"Mack, I need to keep both shifts on full bore till a day after R&R drops. We can't stop just because he's gone. We'll have too much in process at the time, and we'll risk long-term issues on the evaporators if we don't empty the pipeline we created."

"Okay, whatever you say, Jake."

"And I want the refined potassium and phosphorous compounds separated out from this shipment. I think the market isn't ready right now. We can do much better later."

"Why wait?"

"We're bringing in a lot of tungsten that might depress prices in the future, so we need to sell that while the selling is good. We'll store the potassium and phosphorus here. There's an empty container in that derelict orbital shuttle you have. I'll put them there."

"In the old shuttle? Why bother? Just store them with the rest."

"Phosphorus and potassium will explode in the presence of oxygen. I don't want anybody getting confused and bringing them into the station. That gives us a good locked location that is as far as possible from an oxygen source. Tell the guards I need to get in there on a regular basis, and I'll have some of the indentured workers in there as well."

"Okay, sure. I'll tell them. You know what? I think I don't need carbines. I'll bet we could do it with just revolvers."

"Easier to buy from what you said. Oh, and we need to have a fire drill."

"A fire drill? In space? You want to have a fire drill?"

"Fire is very dangerous in space, Mack. We can't spray it with water. We need to vent atmo, so we need to make sure everybody knows what the fire alarm sounds like, and knows how to get into their suit, and knows the fastest way out of whatever part of the station. And where to find suits."

"If they are too stupid, let them fry."

"Do you know where the fire exit is from your quarters, Mack? Do you know where the nearest suit locker is?"

"No."

"Neither does anybody else."

"I have my own suit. I don't need it."

"Not everybody does, including that doctor guy, and the folks who run the smelter. If we lost the smelter guys, no more goods. No more money. And what if your suit is damaged in a real fire?"

"Good point."

"I grew up on a station. I know things you ground-pounders don't. But there are lots of things I don't know, like where would you get ammunition for those revolvers you would buy to take over a station?"

"I know a guy with a warehouse full of it. And he gambles. We could set up a card game."

Jake finished his messages and slumped at his desk. Having located the needed radar and a buyer that would take the extra ore, he was now handling the repair and loading of the R&R. As Mack's operations manager, he had been allocated his own quarters. The furniture was standard metal legos, but he had lots of space—a sitting room, a bedroom, his own fresher, and a large closet. His personal clothes and items seemed lost in all that space. He also had a full desk computer, and access to almost all of the station's systems, except for security and the fusion plant engineering sections. Jake could have hacked into either system, but he didn't for good reasons. Hacking into the security system would invite swift retribution from Mack, and in theory, hacking into the fusion reactor control systems could kill them all.

The door bonged, and Jake yelled out, "Enter."

A one-armed old man carrying a tray entered. Jake had interviewed each of the sixty-five indents on the station. Martinez had been on one of the mining shifts, but he had experience in environmental maintenance and seemed to understand station electrical and plumbing as well. Jake had taken him off the shift and given him a list of items to fix, starting with the spare ration heaters. They were up to twelve working ones in the galley now. An entire shift could eat in fifteen minutes, rather than waiting hours for their turn. He had fixed two display screens as well, and Jake had streamed movies to them.

"Dinner, sir."

"Thanks, Martinez. Did you get your assigned skinsuit?"

"Yes sir."

"Make sure you keep it close. There will be a drill at some point."

"Yes sir. Thank you, sir."

"How are things?"

"Good, sir."

Jake looked at the old man. He was standing rigidly, and was sweating a bit.

He was terrified, Jake realized.

"Don't be afraid of me. I won't hurt you."

"Yes sir. Sorry, sir."

Jake sighed. "Be afraid of Mack. He'd kill you."

"Yes sir. But we're more scared of you."

Jake stuck his head up. "What? Why? What do you mean?"

Martinez realized he was in trouble. "Sir, we're scared of both of you. But more scared of you."

"Of me? Why? Why not Mack?"

"Sir, Mack ... he's scary. But he's only interested in what's in front of him. He might shoot you, or beat you to death, or something. But he'd have to see you. We know how to deal with him—stay out of his way."

"You think I'd shoot you?" Jake said.

"No, sir. Nothing personal with you. You're an accountant. But you might decide one day that it would be cheaper to turn off our air while we sleep, to save a bit of money. We can't fight that."

Chapter 26

The woman's mouth snapped shut when the elbow smashed her jaw. It wasn't clear which of the two women in red sports bras, singlets, and fishnet stockings had hit her, but it was hard enough to knock her down. She rolled onto her back and bounced down the hallway. She yelled a curse, rolled sideways to get her feet on the wall, then pushed off and shouldered into the two girls in front of her. She grabbed both their arms and somersaulted forward, dragging all three of them down.

The entirety of ring seven had been converted into a roller derby course for the quarterfinals between the local Mining Maimers and the Astro-glides. The match was broadcast live on the public screens around the station, but Dashi and Jose had gone down to a long, straight section of corridor to watch the pack skate by. They couldn't see the whole course from where they stood against the wall, but they had an up-close and personal action view of the squirming, fighting mass of skaters as they swarmed by their section of the corridor.

Which was why Dashi grabbed an overhead pipe and pulled himself up from the ground when he realized the pack was tumbling toward him.

The snarling pile caromed into the wall below his dangling feet with a flash of fishnet and a puff of glitter. He hung from the ceiling and regarded the mess. At least one punch was thrown, but the antagonists couldn't brace themselves well enough to make an impact. Instead, the pile rolled apart. A whistle blew twice. The girls untangled, rolled over, then skated off, cursing the whole time.

Dashi lowered himself to the floor. "Definitely a foul. Don't you think, Jose?"

"As you say, sir."

"The elbow, I mean. The somersault was quite permissible."

"The somersault? Of course. Sir, about Jake Stewart. He's not on High-22 anymore."

"Where is he?"

"He found a Free Trader that was moving some of the missing food. It appeared to have some sort of link to rogue Militia elements, possibly Empire Rising officers. He said while he was ingratiating himself with the crew of the ship, he noticed that the 'other party' you had briefed him on was interested as well. They were in the process of placing an agent on that ship."

"He used the word 'ingratiating'?"

"Yes, sir."

"The jammer will be here any second. Watch out," Dashi

said. He stepped back against the wall and put a preparatory hand on the overhead pipe.

Jose stepped back as well. "He decided to preempt their agent's placement by stowing away on that ship. He didn't tell us this ahead of time, of course. He just did it without asking."

"That's very unlike Jake Stewart. Stand back."

A woman in purple with a star on her helmet bounced around the corner. Her skate wheels struck a shower of sparks from the floor as she skated by. Dashi clapped his hands and cheered, then turned back to Jose.

"We need to buy a mining radar, sir," Jose said.

"Are you going into business for yourself?"

"Jake hid his report in a message to buy a radar. We need to appear to sell him one to keep the contact going."

"See to it. Tell me the rest."

"They were hijacked, sort of, by a group that has at least the tacit support of the Empire Rising group. He's on an abandoned mining colony that may be a former Imperial Scout Service base, and they are collecting metals and stockpiling strategic resources in anticipation of some future event. Possibly a disruption in orbital supplies."

"What would disrupt orbital supplies? And why?"

"He says that the Militia is stockpiling resources so that if they start some sort of orbital coup, they won't be beholden to the corps. They will be able to run on their own resources long enough to seize all of our orbital infrastructures."

"I see. Sounds pretty ambitious for the Militia."

"He says that he has evidence that Galactic Growing is

helping this rogue Militia element, and that the two of them are scheming to overthrow the current administrative regime on Delta and replace it with a military-corporate junta."

"Junta? Did you have to look that word up?"

"I did have to look it up, sir. Jake seems to be trying to expand his vocabulary. The only thing he doesn't know right now is how GG knew which shipments to have the Militia intercept."

"I told them," Dashi said.

"You told them?" Jose blinked. "Do you just have lunch once a week with the chairman of GG and give him secret TGI information?"

"Of course not. He has horrible taste in restaurants. When he's on-station, he always goes to that place on ring five. I am not fond of the food there, and the wine selection is atrocious." Dashi looked at the skaters on the display screen across the corridor. "I sell them the information. Indirectly."

"Indirectly, sir?" Jose nodded. "You know who their agents are, and you are letting them buy the information, so you control the flow."

"Yes. There are too many people involved to hide everything. I give them a reliable conduit that I can poison anytime I want. Step back."

They pressed against the wall. A mixed group of red and purple women in. There was a great deal of shoving and pushing, but no crashes as the mob flowed around the corner. Jose turned back to Dashi.

"Roller derby, sir? Really?"

"There is a great deal of strategy involved, Jose. What's Jake's status now?"

"He's in charge of their secret base, handling maintenance and operations. He's helping them produce more product, and selling it at a profit."

"He's in charge? How did he manage that?"

"He said he used spreadsheets."

"A man who has never gone to school may steal from a freight car, but if he has an education, he may steal the whole railroad," Dashi said. He smiled.

"Sir?"

"Old quote. Where are they?"

"Their orbit is such that he can't get off the asteroid for several weeks because of the orbital dynamics, so he's making himself indispensable to them. He has some very interesting suggestions as to what happens next. I think you'll have to review those."

"Send me your recommendation. But you haven't answered the best part of the question."

"What is that, sir?"

"Is this good news, or bad news?" Dashi turned to Jose and steepled his fingers under his chin.

Jose rubbed his own chin in an unconscious imitation of his mentor. "One of our operatives has potentially exposed himself, placed himself in a position of grave danger, possibly endangering himself and other allied operators as well as innocent civilians, and is actively helping our enemies steal resources to help them overthrow the legitimate administrative operator of Delta?"

"That's a good summary, Jose. Good news or bad?"

Jose stared at Dashi for a long time. Dashi had leaned back in his 'testing' stance.

"Jake Stewart is in grave danger," Jose began.

"Yes."

"He will possibly be killed."

"Probably, yes."

"And the others with him, if he is detected."

"If he's detected."

"It's great news. We are getting incredible intelligence from him. Even if he dies now, we know who our enemies are, which will give us the ability to counter them. Plus, since you didn't order this and Jake did it on his own, you— We have no exposure here. We can blame everything on a rogue agent and make it stick. This is a wonderful outcome."

Dashi nodded. "Very good, Jose. What about Jake?"

"I think he's a real operative now, sir."

"Indeed. What should we do now?"

"Send Jake the latest information that we have about this operation, and give him anything that he can use to get himself off that asteroid intact. Support his plans."

"Do that. This is your project now," Dashi said. "Get Jake home. Jake and anybody else he deems necessary. Stop the Militia from acquiring that stockpile. Get as many of those resources as we can acquire. Otherwise, destroy them. Don't start a war." He paused. A black-haired man with two days' beard growth had come around the corner. He was watching the skaters on the video screen. "What do you think, sir?" Dashi said. "Next point to the Mining Maimers?"

"No chance. Their jammer is weak."

"I disagree. What sort of odds will you give me on forty credits?"

"Two to one."

"Done." Dashi reached out and shook the man's hand. "I'm Dashi. This is my associate, Jose."

"Ali," the man said.

The three men watched the screen, then leaned forward to see the skaters as they came around the bend. Two women in purple led a group in red, and the purple jammer with the star on her helmet trailed behind. The two forward women braked their skates with a shower of sparks, banged into each other, and bounced off into their opposition. The maneuver created a temporary hole that the jammer exploited, running through the pack and passing ahead.

Dashi nodded with satisfaction. "Done," he said. He held out his hand.

"I've only got a hundred. Can you make change?" Ali asked.

"Of course," Dashi said. He reached in his pocket and produced a fixed-price credit chip and handed it to Ali.

"Good luck next time, if I see you," Ali said.

"We're usually here during the games. Myself or Jose," Dashi said. He flipped the received chip up into the air and caught it. Ali waved as he sauntered off.

"Sir, if I'm going to help Jake, I have a lot to do," Jose said.

"Then take this. You'll need it," Dashi said, and tossed the chip to Jose.

Jose caught it and inspected it. "What's this, sir?"

"Ten thousand credits."

"What? I thought it was a hundred."

"That's my— Sorry, *our* GG contact. Meet him at this game every month and make a bet. Make sure you win. He'll give you ten thousand credits, and you'll pass a twenty-credit chip back with attached information. I'll send you a list of what we supply them."

Jose got ready to go. "Sir, I know that you manipulated Jake Stewart into this position, but I'm still not sure how."

"That was easy. Have you looked at the bios of his compatriots?"

"Briefly, sir."

"Look at the pictures. One thing you can count on in this world is that a young man will do a lot of stupid things if he thinks it will impress a pretty girl."

Chapter 27

"Wake up in there. Professor Stewart is here to see you," the guard yelled. He had a shock stick that he banged on the door. It wasn't a cell, just two rooms at the end of a hall that had been walled off. They had their own head and cooking facilities, and for the most part were left to themselves.

Jake stepped in front of the viewport where he could be seen. He kept his face blank. Rick and Riley were standing in front of the tier of bunks at the back. Both were dressed in station coveralls. Rick looked pale, but otherwise well. Riley stood awkwardly. She still wore a walking cast on her right leg.

"Professor? They call you professor now," Rick said.

"They do. It's a nickname," Jake said.

"A nickname, huh. I can think of a better one: Emperor's Turd," Rick said.

"I don't care about nicknames."

"Good then, Emperor's Turd."

"Don't call him that. Be respectful," the guard said.

"I'll speak to them alone, thanks," Jake said. "Please, wait down there." Jake gestured toward the far end of the corridor.

"I ain't leaving."

"Then I'll just mention this to Mack. What was your name again?"

The guard coughed. "I'll be over there," he said, and turned and strolled away.

The three of them watched the guard go.

"Jake Stewart, you are a son of a bitch," Riley said.

"Sorry about that, Riley," Jake said.

"Sorry? I'll give you sorry." Riley ran at the viewport and slammed her fist against it. "Son of a bitch," she yelled again.

"Riley, I think—"

"Shut up. I hate you. You double-dealing dirtbag. Crook." Riley spat against the viewport and made a rude gesture with her finger. "I hate you," she said again. She turned away from the viewport and walked over to the wall, then she turned back. "You know what you are, Jake Stewart?" She began to tell him. In detail for several minutes, and without repeating herself.

Eventually she ran down and stomped back to the wall. Jake looked at Rick. "Did she learn those words from you?"

Rick crossed his arms. "So, you are a big boss here now, Jake."

"Kind of. They don't always listen to me. But they always listen to Mack, and Mack listens to me."

"We hear you're kind of running the place."

"Kind of."

"You are an Emperor's turd, aren't you? You left us here for weeks, and never a word."

"I didn't think you would want to talk to me."

"We don't want to talk to you now, either."

Riley broke in. "Why did you do it, Jake? Why are you with them?"

"I needed the money."

"I don't believe you. You never talked about money before."

"I wanted to keep living. Nadine was going to get us killed. You two were going to get us killed maybe. I changed sides to keep everybody alive."

"You tried to kill us."

"Better you than me."

"Screw you, Jake Stewart." Riley hobbled toward the bunk, climbed in, and rolled away from them. She pulled a blanket over her head.

Jake watched her for a moment before turning back to Rick. "You look good, Rick. It looks like the medical computer healed you. Why does Riley still have her cast on? Her break should have healed in a few weeks."

Rick blinked. "Complications in the healing. Not that you care. That medical guy, Pluto—Pluton, something like that— he put her back in the machine. They had to re-break it and straighten something that wasn't growing right. It extended the healing. It comes off tomorrow."

"I didn't know that. I should have been informed." Jake nodded his head. "I'll speak to somebody, and that won't happen again. I'm sorry about that. How's the food?"

"You didn't have to shoot us."

"I couldn't take the chance. I ordered extra rations for the two of you—high protein, extra calcium. It should have helped with the healing. I found a medical diet program. It was very helpful."

"We would just have walked away."

"I didn't know that. I couldn't take the chance. I had to look out for myself. Can you fly your ship by yourself?"

"We're not flying anywhere for you," Riley said from under her blanket.

"I can fly my ship by myself in my sleep. But why would I do that?"

"Do you want your ship back, Rick?"

"What?"

"Your ship. Big metal thing that holds eighteen full-sized containers. Good set of engines, good thrusters, functioning nav computer, and auto-pilot. That ship."

"Two of the thrusters are done. My control runs are flaky. The auto-pilot is unreliable. Why would you give me my ship back?"

"The same reason I didn't let Mack kill you after I shot you. The same reason I got you proper medical care, and proper food, and enough exercise so that you wouldn't be crippled. And the same reason I had two thrusters transferred from one of those hulks docked here. And upgraded your software. I've got plans for you."

"We don't want to be part of your plans," came the muffled response from under the blanket.

"We're loading your ship up with aluminum, iron,

titanium, tungsten, and some other bulk metals. We've got the refinery running a full twenty-four-hour day on two shifts to fill it up. There will be an excellent drop window in a few days. You can drop and hit some of the lower-level markets. There should be good money in it. We've repaired your ship as much as possible here. We'll give you 3 percent of the sale value of the metal, and another 2 percent if you spend it only on ship repairs. You need updated control runs from the nav computer to the engines, and you definitely need some sort of optical backup system for your radar—that could break again at any time. A sandcaster on the hardpoint would be a good idea as well."

"You want me to take a load down orbit?"

"Yes, a big load."

"Why? I thought they were deadheading containers. Just boosting them into orbit for capture with that mass driver."

"Yes, but the mass driver is very inefficient. We only get one window a week, and we don't have enough power to boost more than one container at a time. If we use your ship, we can move almost a year's worth of production at once, common and precious metals. And do it into a major market. A major market that we can sell into at full price. And when you get back, I have a list of supplies that you can bring back. Product should increase 230 percent once we have what we need."

"Why not use those little launches that you have in dock?"

"Not enough cargo capacity. Not enough range. They're only useful for meeting passing ships and moving maybe one container's worth of items at a time. It's just too slow."

"You want me to take a year's production of your stolen

metals and sell them on the open market for you. Why not do it yourself?"

"You have a reputation of striking it rich and then busting it out. This isn't the first time you showed up with a big score. People will think your prospecting paid out. They'll be interested, but not suspicious about the legality of it, and they already know that you won't answer questions about where it comes from."

"Uh-huh." Rick crossed his arms. "And it's my ship. There will be questions asked if it shows up without me."

"There would be questions, yes."

"And, I'll bet, Mr. Professor, that they don't trust you quite enough to let you off-station with a year's worth of production."

"I never asked. I'm not the right person for the job."

"Why do you trust me? We could just sell the goods, take the money, and fly off into the sunset."

Jake shook his head and looked at the ground. "I've been studying Francais in my spare time, and I really wish we were all fluent enough to have this conversation in it. English doesn't have a second-person plural pronoun."

Riley's head stuck up from behind the blanket.

"Jake Stewart, you are a pedantic twit. What are you talking about?"

Rick got it. "He means, sweetie, that when Jake says 'you,' he doesn't mean 'us.' He means just me. I'm taking the ship down, and you're staying in here, as a hostage."

A week later, the departure of the R&R went like

clockwork. A guard trailed behind as Jake walked Rick to the ship. Rick was professional.

"Full containers?"

"All of them. Inventory is in the computer."

"You repaired my thrusters? And the control runs?"

"The thrusters, yes. We couldn't get all of the control runs done. All of the primaries were replaced."

"You said you would fix them all."

"Parts issue. You have enough to drop, and your main engine is tested and working. Plus, you've got extra reaction mass."

They reached the docking truss and began to climb the ladder.

"Extra reaction mass?"

"Yes, we gave you two additional bladders, and they are full of water. We could spare some extra because we don't need it for the mass driver."

"And how do I move that water around?"

"We installed two extra pumps, so you can suck it from the bladders right into your tanks."

"Fair enough. Equipment? Provisions?"

"Some spares and a full load of food for three months for four people."

"There's just me."

"I believe in being prepared." Jake stopped at the platform in front of the airlock. He was breathing hard from the climb. Rick was sweating and favoring his leg a bit, but still moving.

"Thanks, Jake. Good to have you on our side," Rick said. His expression didn't flicker, but Jake caught the contempt.

"Suggested selling prices and markets are in the computer as well, but we are giving you discretion in how you unload things. We trust you."

"And if I screw up, my daughter is up here and will pay the price."

"Riley stays here." Jake walked to the outer door of the airlock and spun it open. "Here you go. Your window ends in several hours, but you can drop whenever you're ready."

Rick stepped into the airlock and turned to face Jake. "I liked you, did you know that? A great guy. Much better than the regular jerks that Riley met. You were different. Quiet, hardworking. I didn't expect this."

Jake stared at Rick. He turned his head—the guard leaned against the wall at the end of the loading dock, playing with his comm. He could probably hear them.

"Life is full of disappointments, Rick."

"I'll say. You were a big one." He looked Jake in the eye. "Don't hurt my daughter. I'll sell your stuff and get a good price for you and the rest. And I'll come back for more. But if you hurt her, I'll go looking for you, and I won't stop."

Jake shook it off. "Make sure you don't miss your launch window."

"I won't. But one question, Jake."

"Yes?"

"Why now? You could have had me out of here with most of this stuff weeks ago. It would've been an easier flight, and not as noticeable."

"It takes six weeks for a broken bone to heal."

"Mine were only fractures—I was ready six weeks ago."

Jake spun the door toward Rick. "I had to wait till everybody was ready." He slammed the airlock shut.

Jake watched the R&R drop from the operations room. The radar showed it accelerating to a new orbit. He checked the telemetry channels he had access to. All the new parts were working the way they were supposed to, and there were no alarms. Rick was safely on his way.

"Do they look good, Mr. Professor?" Mack asked.

"Yes, they are following the drop course. They'll be at the station and able to unload in about forty hours."

"How long till we get the money?"

"He's converting the bulk of it to certificates. Those he'll bring back here for distribution. Round trip will be about fourteen days."

"You sure he's going to come back?"

"He won't leave his daughter. And he's getting very well paid. A carrot and a stick."

"I guess that makes sense. Hey, have you ever seen a real carrot?"

"No, I've seen pictures on the vid, but never a real one. Have you?"

"Nope. Lots of turnips growing up. My farming factory did turnips and potatoes. I hate turnips."

"I've never seen a real turnip. I've eaten the trays. They aren't too bad."

"I hate 'em. All of us kids hated them. We spent too much time dealing with them. You spent your youth messing around a mining colony. I spent mine digging turnips out of machinery. Soon as I turned eighteen, I went to the big city."

"To Landing?"

"Yep. Went looking for work."

"How did you get to Landing?"

"Beat up a guy and stole his ticket."

"Oh. What type of job did you get?"

Mack smiled at him. "I got a job hitting people. I was good at that. Still am." Mack smiled at a memory. "You have kids?"

"No."

"Want any?"

"Not right now."

Mack laughed. "How true." He looked at the board. Jake had the telescope pointed at the R&R, but only the flare of the engine was visible now. "I have a kid. A girl."

"You do?"

"Yep. Back on the farm. And no, I won't tell you where. That's kind of why I took the monorail into town. I didn't want to be a father, not at seventeen. And I didn't want to be stuck in those third-rate jobs."

"Oh."

"She'd be ... fifteen now, I think. I've never seen her."

"Oh."

"You say that a lot."

"Other people than you tell me that. Why haven't you gone back to see her?"

"That guy I beat up for his ticket?"

"Yes."

"I didn't just beat him up. It was a little more serious than that." Mack walked to the wall and pulled a mug of basic. "There's no going back. And now here I am, years later. This job sucks, but the money is super good. Even better now that you're here. I figured I'd put in the year they wanted—mine this ore, make my nut, and get out of here. The payoff would have been great, and it's even better now that you've figured out how to move this stuff in bulk. We didn't think of hijacking the supply ship."

"It wasn't exactly a hijacking, and it wasn't exactly a choice."

"Too true. Well, it worked out for us."

Mack stood up and stretched. "Are you going to keep working those indents to death? I don't care, just asking."

"No. This crew will finish their shift in about two hours. The ongoing crews will meet up with them, and then finish up a few things at the refinery. Once we've done that, I'll give everybody a double meal ration, sixteen hours off, then it's back to two eight-hour shifts a day for the next few weeks."

"Why not push 'em?"

"Maintenance. We pushed the refinery and the mining tools as hard as we could to meet this window, and I'm worried about some of the drills. We'll shift back to regular schedule, and I can pull one drill a shift off for maintenance. I'm still going to be nervous until Rick comes back with spares."

"Whatever you want to do, Jake. You've certainly figured these things out. You handle mining. I'll break heads as needed."

"I don't need any heads broken right now." Jake got up and ran his own cup of basic. "But I do need some more skinsuits—I'll have almost everyone on both shifts out to finish off draining the refinery. I'll need at least two more."

"And where are you going to get two skinsuits?"

"Borrow them from the off-duty guards. Can you tell them to drop them off?"

"All the way down to the slave side?" Mack asked.

"I'll take care of that. They just have to leave them in my room, and I'll move them."

"Good enough. Let me know if you need any heads broken."

Chapter 28

"Mack, I, uh, was going to have the guards bring Riley up to my quarters later."

It was several days after the R&R launched, and they had been discussing its progress in Mack's office. Jake was talking about hydrogen purity levels. Mack was wondering if it was time for dinner.

"What? You were? You dog." Mack laughed.

"And, uh, I was thinking that I'd get them to bring Nadine as well."

"Both of them?"

"Yeah, uh, the two of them. I'd like them to, you know, be together."

Mack stared at him, his eyes wide. "Professor, I didn't think that you could surprise me, but there it is. I didn't think you would like that."

"Well, everybody has his thing, you know," Jake muttered into his cup.

"Sounds like a fun thing, actually. I should have thought

of it myself. Maybe I'll set something up later. Don't worry." Mack smiled. "It was your idea. You first."

"Thanks, Mack."

"Keep your gun handy."

Jake looked him in the eye. "I won't have any problems with them. I shot them once. I can do it again."

It was thirty minutes before shift change when the two grinning guards on shift pushed Nadine and Riley through Jake's door. Jake sat behind his desk and asked them to remove the restraints. He waited till they were done, then thanked them and waited till they closed the door.

Riley looked at Jake. "Why is she here? What do you want? How's Dad?"

"I needed to talk to the both of you. Your dad is on course heading away from the station," Jake said. "He's in an area with a lot of commercial traffic, so nobody can fire at him or board him without others noticing."

"I should ask the same question," Nadine said. "What am I doing here? And Jake, I hear you are Dr. Professor Stewart or something now."

"Kind of."

"You are responsible for this mess. You are going to get us killed."

"Actually, Nadine, I believe that it was you who got us here, and you were going to get us shot while escaping. I saved your ass."

"For what? I've been locked up for weeks. And no word from you all that time," Nadine said.

"I had things to do."

"Running a pirate slave station?"

"Kind of."

"Jake is a super pirate himself now, Nadine. Just like you were," Riley said.

"I was never a pirate. I was an operative for hire," Nadine said.

"Walks like a pirate, quacks like a pirate, smells like a pirate."

"You and your self-righteous dad can kiss my ass. Who do you think you were selling those supplies to?"

"We didn't know who we were selling them to," Riley said.

"You mean, you avoided finding out what any person with an atom of intelligence would have cared to figure out?"

"I don't need to take this from you, pirate girl."

"Enough, both of you. Please, listen for a moment," Jake said.

"What do you want, Jake?" Riley asked.

"I need you to get undressed."

"What? Undressed. Screw you, Jake Stewart. I'm not getting undressed for you."

"I just—"

"You are a sick little man. You know that, Jake? A sick little man. All that stuff you told Dad about taking care of me ... I believed all of that. You're just another pig, like the rest of these pigs."

Jake blushed. "Riley, I just need you to listen for a moment."

"And if I don't do what you say, then what? Are you going to shoot me again?" Riley crossed her arms and glared at Jake.

"Well, I...." Jake felt like he was losing control of the situation.

"What about me, Jake?" Nadine asked.

"Actually, I need both of you to get undressed."

Nadine blinked. "Wow, Jake. That's a surprise." She looked at Riley and gave her a broad grin. "Well, why not? I'm willing to experiment. What about you, missy? Should we give the boy a thrill?"

Jake blushed even more. "Let me explain," he said.

Ten minutes later, Jake was leading the two of them through the corridor. The three of them wore nondescript semi-hard suits, the same as those worn by the outside workers. Riley was limping a little, but she was able to keep up. From the insecure side that had the indents' quarters, food supply, storage, and connections to the smelting and control areas, they approached the airlock that connected the secure side of the station with the comms, docking trusses, and power.

"You could have told us, Jake," Nadine said.

"I couldn't take the risk of the guards overhearing. I had full control of the manufacturing side, but the computer section on the secure side was totally isolated from where I worked. I couldn't guarantee that somebody else wouldn't be able to read my messages."

"But if you had told me what to expect ahead of time, I could have helped out."

"Things kind of developed, Nadine. I adapted to circumstances. I took advantage of an opportunity."

"That was dangerous, shooting us. What if you had the wrong bullets?"

"I knew they were frangibles. I loaded them myself. Besides"—Jake turned and smiled at Nadine—"I wanted to shoot you. Now, we're even."

Nadine laughed.

"Was it fun shooting me and Dad too, Jake? Shooting him in the chest was risky. You could have killed him," Riley said.

"I knew those semi-hard suits can take shots to the chest. Especially from a revolver."

"And how did you know that?" Riley asked.

"Because I shot him in the chest with a shotgun while he was wearing one once, and he's still here," Nadine said, and laughed again.

"That didn't work out the way I expected, Riley. I'm sorry. I didn't expect to break your leg."

"Didn't work out the way you expected, Jake? That's it? You nearly killed Dad and I, and for what?"

"You don't get it, do you, merchie girl?" Nadine asked.

"Get what?"

"You are the reason he's doing things this way. We could have been out of here weeks ago, but Jake had to wait till your leg healed and you could move under acceleration."

"He didn't need to shoot me."

"He needed to shoot all of us. If he hadn't, those guys with machine guns would have killed us. He was right, and I was wrong. And even if we had somehow pulled it off—if we had pulled out of here on any of those ships—we would have been blown out of the sky."

"How?"

"By that." Nadine stopped, and pointed out a viewport. "See that track out there? You know what that is?"

"It's a mass driver."

"Right. It accelerates container-sized loads. Imagine what would be left of your precious ship if one of those hit it at two hundred meters per second."

They stopped just short of the main airlock junction. They could see airlocks that led to the secure side, the insecure side, the mill, and outside. A group of men stood hidden down the hall, where they couldn't be seen. All but two were in drab skinsuits or semi-hard suits. The two others wore an under-skinsuit leotard.

"Everything ready, Jorge?" Jake asked the leader.

"Yes, Mr. Professor," Jorge said.

"Please, don't call me that."

"Everybody calls you that. But we are ready. These two will take the guards' skinsuits."

"You two girls, wait here. Don't let yourself be seen around the corner. We need the skinsuits from the two guards," Jake said. "Ramon and Luis, follow me."

Jake strode around the corner, followed by the two suitless men. All three stopped at the outside airlock. The indicators flashed green, then the door swung open. Two suited men with shotguns strapped to their chest emerged from the door.

"Hey, professor," the lead one said. "What's up?"

"Second shift is going out to help third shift finish cleaning out the evaporator. As soon as we shut down the power, we only have an hour till the metal solidifies and starts gumming up the works, so I need everybody."

"Oh yeah, Mack mentioned that."

"I need your suits. Change out and give them to Ramon and Luis here, please."

"How come?"

"I need everybody out there. Unless you want to come out and chip solid lead out of the evaporator after it hardens, slip out. I'll take Ramon and Luis out there."

"You sure? What about security?"

Jake sighed. "First, where can they go? Run to the other side of this rock and asphyxiate? Second, I'll be out there, and I have my gun. And third, I say so."

"You're not the boss of me. I work for Mack."

"Too true. Want me to call him?"

"Nope, not necessary," said the second one. He had been quiet till now. "Franz, you know Jake is his golden-haired boy. Mack will back him up."

"And about that," Jake said. "Speaking of gold, the extra gold that is going in your pocket is coming from my operations. And it's going in Mack's pocket too. He won't like it if it's interrupted."

"Okay, okay." The first man put his hands out. "I'm just trying to do my job—keep an eye on things. We'll hit the airlock and get unsuited. How will you get the suits?"

"I'll come in with these two. We'll swap in there and get going. And that way, there will be a guard. Follow me, I don't want to wait." Jake turned around and strode down to the airlock that led to the secure side and swung the door open.

All five climbed in. Swapping suits didn't take long—just a few minutes' work. The guards returned to the secure side and locked the airlock's door. Jake and the others stepped out of the airlock. The last one out began to close the outer door but Jake stopped him. "Ramon, leave it open. Strip the emergency suits, and take the tools from the rack. Go to all the other airlocks open to this corridor, open the inside and outside doors, and dog them open." Jake stepped out into the hall and gestured. The group around the corner approached. "Jorge, is everything good?" Jake asked.

"Everyone is out on the surface, except us."

"Good. Please, help Ramon with the tools. Everybody else, seal your helmet and prepare for egress." Jake walked over to the opposite wall. "I just need to switch channels and start the fire drill."

Nadine and Riley switched to the same channel as Jorge. Just as they did, red and white strobe lights on the ceiling began to flash. Jake kept talking on the radio for about a minute, then switched back.

"Okay, let's go."

"Jake, what sort of escape is this?" Riley asked.

"We're all going outside, and the staff is staying inside."

"So what? They can still come out with guns and shoot us."

"Not if they stay inside, they can't. We've got all the regular skinsuits on workers right now, and everybody is outside."

"But they'll just go and find the emergency suits, or the bubbles, or whatever, and rig up something and come after us."

"All those are stored on the insecure side. They'll have to get over there. They have to go through this airlock for that."

"So what? We have to use the airlock to leave, so we'll just be leaving this area in pressure."

"Ah, well, Riley, that's what I learned from you. That's why we need the fire drill."

Nadine broke in. "Jake, stop being obtuse. Why do we need a fire drill?"

"So I can do this," Jake said. He walked to the wall and opened up a meter-square cabinet labeled 'EMERGENCY FIRE SUPPRESSION – ATMOSPHERIC VENT.' Inside was a large metal plate with four different handles on it. He rotated each of the four handles ninety degrees clockwise, then walked down the hall to another cabinet labeled 'EMERGENCY FIRE SUPPRESSION – CONTROL.' He opened it and pushed the button on the inside.

The panel in the other cabinet blew out. The atmosphere followed it. The corridor began spinning toward vacuum, as did every other area connected by the opened airlocks. It took almost a minute until the corridor took on the sharp-edged look of a vacuum with no oxygen to disperse light.

Jake switched back to the common channel. "Now they're all stuck in there. Let's get off this rock."

The group bounced along the surface of the asteroid, holding to a guideline so they wouldn't bounce right off into deep space.

"This is your genius master plan, Jake? Escape to the surface of an airless asteroid with no supplies so that we can suffocate when our O runs out?" Nadine asked over the radio.

"Just follow me. Riley, are you okay?"

Riley didn't answer, but Jake could hear her huffing over the radio channel. Jake stopped and went back to her and locked helmets. "Are you okay?" he repeated.

"Not quite. I haven't been on my feet much for weeks. This is hard. But I'll manage."

"We'll be in a ship in a few minutes. I'll need you to do some undocking."

"What ship?"

"That one over there." Jake pointed at a decrepit-looking ship near the edge of the mill. He led the group toward it. A line of indent workers was climbing into it. Jorge stood next to a pile of large crates, handing out small bars to each indent as they climbed on board. Jake arrived next to Jorge, and switched to a common channel.

"Jorge, speed it up. We have a drop window to make."

"We're going as fast as possible, Mr. Professor. Everybody wants to weigh it. But we'll be done in a few minutes. Only twelve left."

"What are you giving them, Jorge?" Nadine asked.

"Silver. Jake had us steal it from the mining production to pay out our wages."

"Silver. Why silver?" Nadine asked.

"It's easier to steal," Jake said. "Mack and company kept a close watch on rare earth metals, and gold and platinum. But they didn't really pay attention to silver yields. It was easier to drain off, and easy to purify."

"Yes, when Jake brought this to our attention a few weeks

ago, it was one of the big selling points. We get away from the asteroid, we get away early, and we get our wages."

"Your wages?" Nadine said.

"There are crates of silver in the back to top off our pay for those who are owed it. But the professor said he couldn't be sure where we are going to land, and it might be best if everybody had some money in their pockets."

"Jake, what is this thing? And where are we taking it?" Riley said.

"Well, first, we're going to get off this asteroid," Jake replied.

"In this thing?" Riley gestured at the ship next to them. "It doesn't have wings, so it isn't a shuttle. Those big nozzles in the back will make it scoot, but I don't see much fuel storage."

In Delta orbit, there were two general classes of ships—normal surface-to-orbit shuttles, and cargo and Militia ships. The former were giant wedge-shaped ships, with delta wings extending from the sides. This class of ships was basically big, flattened triangles streamlined for atmosphere with giant engines on the back. The delta shape functioned as an enormous wing to generate lift in the atmosphere. The engines put out enormous thrust, but only for a short time—they were only needed to reach orbit and dock there.

Cargo and Militia ships, on the other hand, were collections of metal trusses with modules bolted on. They had no need for streamlining because they were never in an atmosphere. Parts were just attached where convenient. And since they were never in a hurry, cargo ships usually had only one, or at most, two engines. They could generate thrust for a long time, as long as their fuel held out. They were more fuel efficient than shuttles.

This ship was streamlined—that much was evident. It was all smooth curves and rounded edges. It was shaped like a bullet that had been squashed flat on the ground. One side was almost, but not quite, flat. It was rounded up. The other side was some sort of complex, near-circular structure. In place of wings, the ship had rounded bulges on the sides, and there were round openings on each side.

"Those are big engines, but they will suck fuel. I don't see much in the way of tankage. We won't be able to hold acceleration for very long," Riley said.

"Don't worry," Jake said. "Look there." He pointed. One of the indents was winching a series of hatches closed on the bottom of the ship—standard containers were visible inside the bay. One was fuel bladder—collapsible tanks for H, and it included a frame for latching onto a ship, as well as pumps.

"That's a regular engine on the back. But what's that thing there—that extra opening?" Riley said.

"That's a ramjet," Jake said.

"A ramjet? What's that?" Riley said.

"It's a type of jet engine," Nadine said. "Very powerful, good at high Mach numbers. But it's air-breathing—you do know we are on an airless asteroid, don't you, Jakey?"

"Yes, Nadine, I know that. It has regular engines too. We'll use those to de-orbit. We're coming to perigee with Delta shortly. If we make our window, we have enough fuel to slow down enough to get caught in Delta's gravity. The asteroid will speed away, and we go dock somewhere else. But only if we go now." Jake began to climb in. As he did, he saw a hole appear in the bladder. Hydrogen started to vent out of it. Another hole appeared and began to vent. Then a third. What the heck was going on? Jake stopped and stared at the bladder. Why was it exploding like that? It was almost like somebody was shooting holes in it.

BANG. Something smashed Jake's arm, and it went totally numb. Oh. Somebody was shooting at them. Another bang hit his leg. He lost purchase and fell backward. There wasn't much gravity, so he kind of drifted toward the ground.

"Everybody, inside! We missed somebody. They're shooting at us. Move, move!" Nadine yelled over the radio. She shoved Jake ahead of her and propelled him up into the hatch.

"Riley, get up front and pre-flight us. Power the engines. Jorge, get all these guys inside now." Nadine paused. "Don't forget the silver. Bring the crate."

Nadine hustled Jake up and dumped him in a corner of the airlock, then she reached back and helped Jorge and another crewman in. She swung the outer hatch shut, and pressurized the lock. She and Riley raced forward, Jorge and the other crewman right behind them.

Jake laid on the floor of the airlock and rocked side to side. There was a large dent in his suit on his arm, and he had no feeling or control of his right leg or right arm. His breathing was becoming labored. His vision was filling up with stars. Was he in shock? Why didn't his arm work?

Jake looked up at the ceiling and addressed an uncaring

universe. "Somebody always shoots me. Why does somebody always shoot me?" He sighed, and then blacked out.

Jake wasn't out for long. He woke up and felt the ship vibrating. The engines must be spooling up. He flexed his arms and legs, and felt some control in his arm. His leg still hurt. He tried to put weight on it and collapsed, banging his head on the wall on the way down. He cursed some more, then dragged himself up with his hands. His leg didn't hurt anymore when he stood up, as long as he didn't put any weight on it. He started to drag himself to the control room.

The control room was crowded. Riley and Nadine were at the main stations. Jake dragged himself behind the auxiliary control board. Riley was running a check on the flight systems. Nadine was hammering calculations into her screen and had just pushed the acceleration warning gong. Jorge was in back but had sent one of his buddies up—an environmental tech. He was tinkering with his controls, setting pump flow rates.

"I said, we don't have enough fuel," Riley said.

"The fuel doesn't matter. Just get us off this rock before that shooter hits something important, like a control run. Tomas, what's the story?" Nadine said.

"Senorita, I am pumping as fast as I can, but we will lose most of the extra fuel before we can burn it off. We will only have the internal tanks."

"Just get us up and away from here. We'll be safe once we're moving," Riley said.

"Provided we don't get shot out of space," Nadine said. "Switch to my screen number five for a second."

"What am I looking at? What's this swinging red cone?"

"That's the mill. The red cone corresponds to the mass driver's area of effect. If you can stay out of that cone, they can't hit you."

"You think they'll shoot entire containers at us, just to knock us down?"

"I would," Nadine said. "Or at least threaten to. Shoot one just to show I'm serious, and who could tell the difference."

"I'm fine, girls, and thanks for asking," Jake said, slumping at the control station.

"It's not serious, Jake, we had Jorge check your vitals while you were out. He said you'll do for a while," Nadine said.

"Jorge is a doctor now?" Jake said.

"Stop your whining, Jake. Every time you get shot, you whine."

"I'll have to stop that, then."

"The whining?"

"No, the getting shot. I kind of like the whining."

"Right, okay," Riley said. She keyed the intercom. "Jorge, get everyone back there strapped in now." She turned to Tomas. "Tomas, you need to get strapped down somewhere."

"I will go back to the lounge and use one of the couches," he said and returned to the lounge.

Riley keyed the general intercom channel. "Liftoff in thirty seconds."

"No, no, merchie girl. I'm going to drive this thing. I'm the better pilot," Nadine said.

"You are not."

"I am. I'm taking over the board." Nadine began to swap

screens. She tapped a button. Nothing happened. She tapped it again, then a third time. Still, nothing happened. She turned around and saw Jake at the auxiliary board, laboriously typing with his left hand. She narrowed her eyes. "Jake?"

"I'm sorry, Nadine. You are a good pilot, but our fuel situation is critical, and you are very profligate with fuel," Jake said.

"Profligate? Jake, speak standard."

"You use too much fuel on your maneuvers. Too many radical changes. Riley was raised on a merchant ship—fuel costs money, and she's learned to conserve it. Her maneuvers are very efficient and precise. She'll take us out till we're on a docking orbit, then you take over."

"I'm a better pilot."

"Not at the short stuff you are not. You use too much fuel."

"And I knew what profligate means," Riley muttered, smiling.

"Shut up, merchie," Nadine said.

"Ladies, argue later. Let's get out of here," Jake said.

Riley pressed a button, and a bong sounded. She keyed her mic. "Lifting now. Everybody stay strapped in till we tell you otherwise."

Chapter 29

"I can just see them on the radar," the navigator said. "Look at screen three. Near that asteroid."

The pilot tapped his controls. "That's pretty far away, and they're moving fast. If we wait, I don't think we'll be able to catch them."

"We'll have to burn hard," the navigator in the cab agreed. He looked at the pilot. "Where's the major?"

"Sitting in the lounge drinking his hot cider, probably." The pilot smiled and looked at the navigator. The navigator grinned back, then put a hand above his screen, but didn't touch it yet. He held his other hand out with five fingers extended and made a counting motion—five, four, three, two....

The pilot placed his hands over the thruster controls and waited. When the count reached zero, the navigator pressed a button and an acceleration gong sounded. A split second after the gong started, the pilot keyed the thrusters, the ship pivoted on its tail, and then he fired the main engines. They were both pushed into their seats as they bled off speed, falling closer toward the moon below.

A howl of pain and then a stream of curses came from behind them. An officer climbed into the control cabin. He was waving a cup around, and his previously immaculate uniform was marred by a large wet stain on his chest. Cider dripped from his chin.

"Idiots. What are you doing?"

"Sir, we are in pursuit of a stolen ship." The pilot was very serious, and all traces of the grin had disappeared.

"Stolen ship? How do you know it was stolen? And why did you alter course without asking permission first? I should heave you out an airlock for your disrespect."

"Sir, the message said 'most immediate.'"

"Message—what message? I received no message."

"It didn't come over the ship's system, sir."

"What?"

"Gagnon here," the pilot indicated the navigator. "He got it on his personal comm."

"Ridiculous. Not on the ship's systems. What type of message was this?"

The navigator coughed. "It was an unofficial message, sir. Not from HQ."

"Unofficial? On your personal comm. You are taking direction from your friends, now?"

"From a member of the Officers' Council, sir," the navigator said. He stared at his screens and kept his mouth in a straight line.

The officer froze. He dropped the hand with the cup to his side.

"From the Council?"

"Yes sir. Most immediate. Pursuit. As we are now. Should we tell the Council that we are delaying executing their instructions until you confirm them?"

The officer coughed. "No, no, of course, anything for the Council. You did well." He looked down at his shirt. "I'll just go change my uniform."

The pilot spoke. "We'd rather you didn't, sir."

"What?"

"We need the freedom to maneuver as we pursue, sir. We might have to make split-second course corrections. If you were changing, we'd have to wait till you confirm you are prepared for acceleration. Of course, we could signal the Council that we're delaying."

"No, no. That's fine. I'll just go and strap into my couch."

"Thank you, sir. If you don't mind, could you lock the hatch shut behind you? It should be shut when we are at damage-control level three."

"Good idea. Of course. Carry on, you two. Good job." The officer carefully exited the bridge, swinging the hatch shut behind him. The crew waited a second after the hatch closed before breaking out laughing.

"Hey, they're pivoting," the navigator said a few minutes later.

"Why?"

"They're slowing. They're not trying to get away from Delta, they're trying for an orbit."

"That's good news. We should be able to catch them," the pilot said.

"For sure. We'll still have to burn hard, but we should catch up with them. Huh. That's a pretty low orbit."

"Will they be able to break out?"

"They've dropped from their original one already. If they wanted to go higher, they could. If they have enough fuel."

"Do they?"

"Not sure. I've got it in the telescope. It's kind of a weird-looking ship. Looks like a shuttle without wings."

"It's a shuttle? Are they going to land?" the pilot said.

"Nope. Definitely not. It is streamlined, but it's definitely not a shuttle. Just looks strange."

"How big is it?"

The navigator brought up a picture of their cutter and put the two side by side. "Smaller than us."

"Less fuel, then. Anywhere it can go, we can go."

"For sure."

"How long till we catch it?"

"We'll be alongside in about fifty minutes at this course."

"Alongside? What if they run?"

"They can't run from us if they can't see us. And I'm looking in the telescope, and I don't see any radar. Or weapons."

"What do we do then?"

"Don't know. Let's ask 'I-am-in-command' back there."

Chapter 30

"We need a course to a station," Riley said. She glanced out the forward viewport. It ran the entire width of the front of the control room, giving an excellent view of Delta, the rings, and the Dragon. "Our fuel won't last forever. We're out of that stupid month-long orbit. More like six hours. But it will decay. What next?"

"I'm not sure we need to go to a station," Nadine said. "Jake, you must have had a plan. Jake?"

Jake was lolling in his seat. He was very pale.

"Jake, are you okay?"

"My leg hurts. I'm sleepy. Shiny flashes."

The two girls looked at each other.

"Shit," Nadine said. She slid over toward Jake. "He's very pale. He might be going into shock."

"How can he be going into shock? He was talking a second ago?" Riley said.

"Maybe he's losing blood."

"He's not bleeding. There's nothing on his suit or on the deck, or anywhere. How could he be bleeding?"

"It could be internal."

"He was hit in the arm and the leg, not the chest." Riley locked her board, and then slipped back to bend over Jake. She was running her hands over Jake's suit. "Emperor's balls. Look at his leg."

Nadine leaned over to look. The leg of Jake's suit bulged out, and the suit had sealed over two bullet holes nearby.

"It went between two of the insets. He's bleeding into the suit. We have to get it off."

"Can we cut it off?" Riley asked.

"It's a Belter suit. Anything that can cut it will cut his leg off. We should be able to unzip it."

Riley fiddled with the suit. "The zipper is inside the boots."

"We take his boots off, then slip the zipper up, peel it back," Nadine said.

"And have ten liters of blood pool on the floor while he bleeds out."

Jake's mouth worked, "No, Riley, only five. Shiny flashes."

"Jake, just hang on, we'll sort this out. We need a med kit, Nadine."

"I'll get one," Nadine said. She scrambled toward the rear cabin.

"Just a minute, Jake. You'll be fine. We'll get you fixed up. What did you mean, what you said there?"

"Five liters, not ten."

"Jake," Riley said, "What do you mean, five liters?"

"Only five liters of blood in a person. Not ten. Floor won't get that dirty."

Nadine came in with a med kit. "How is he?"

"He'll be fine."

It took a few minutes to get the medical supplies ready. They found a full bottle of quick skin spray. It contained an organic compound that sealed over the skin. The spray functioned as a bandage, to keep the wound clean, and would dissolve in several days as the skin healed. In addition, it contained a strong antiseptic. Nadine had also returned with a medical stapler, a bunch of pads to soak up the blood that was bound to come out when they rolled up Jake's suit leg, and a bottle of blood fluid replacer. She also searched for 'what to do for shock' on her comm.

"Okay," Riley said. "I'll pull his boot off, then unzip and peel back the suit. You spray the bandage spray right into the wound, whatever it is, then we'll staple, and spray again."

"Sounds good," Nadine said. "Pull away."

Riley reached down and placed Jake's leg against her chest. She grasped the side of the boots. She squeezed hard. "Ready? Hey." The boot moved and clicked, and a compartment in the heel opened. Something fell out onto the deck.

"What in the Emperor's name is that?" Nadine asked.

Riley picked it up. "A chip. Course chip. In the heel of his boot. The boot is loose." The boot began to move, and blood started to well out from the cuff.

"Forget the chip. Get the boot off and peel the leg. Do it now."

Riley clicked the chip back into the compartment on his

boot, then pulled hard. The boot resisted for a minute, but then came free with a warm sucking sound. Blood flowed out onto the floor from under the cuff of the suit.

"Now, the leg. Go. Go. Go," Nadine said.

Riley reached down and pulled the plastic zipper. The suit split up Jake's calf, uncovering more blood. The blood pulsed rather than spurted, so it wasn't an artery, but a long, deep gash that ran up the back of Jake's calf muscle.

Nadine leaned over and sprayed a quick film over the wound, stopping the blood temporarily. Then she traded the spray can for the pads, and sopped up most of the blood over the gash.

"Squeeze the sizes of the cut together. I'll staple."

Riley pushed the sides of the cut together, hard. Nadine pushed the medical stapler up against the leg and began stapling. She shot four quick staples in, and then moved the stapler to put a fifth in. She hesitated.

Riley looked Nadine in the eye. "If you staple my fingers, I'll know it wasn't an accident. And I'll take that stapler and jam it right up your pretty little behind."

Nadine laughed. "Just a thought," she said. She moved her fingers slightly and fired a fifth staple, missing Riley's hand by a few millimeters. "Okay, move your hand."

Riley let go, and Nadine ran a second set of pads over before spraying the whole leg with a film of quick skin. Nadine looked down at Jake. "Okay, it's sealed. That will do for now. Riley, pull his suit back down and put his boot on. That will give extra support."

They zipped his suit back up over the quick skin. The boot

went back on, and the compartment clicked closed. Jake's head still lolled around, and he was barely conscious. "Five liters, not ten. Shiny flashes," he mumbled.

"He keeps saying that," Nadine said.

"He's delirious. Will he be okay?" Riley asked.

"He's lost a lot of blood. I would put him in the med-robot."

"If we had a med-robot, which we don't. Right, what next?"

Nadine read from her comm. "It says, 'After stopping the bleeding and sealing the wound, give the patient two liters of volume replacement.' That's this thing." She held up a plastic package with clear fluid in it, and an attached tube that ended in a needle. "It has a pain killer as well. They say to put this in and squeeze it into a vein in his arm."

Riley rolled up a sleeve, examined Jake's arm and located a blue vein. "Here, put it in."

This proved to be much harder than anticipated. Nadine messed up her first two tries, and ended up pumping the fluid under Jake's skin rather than into a vein. Riley took the needle from her and tried a third and fourth time in the other arm, finally getting it on the fourth try, and they began to slowly pump the fluid into his arm.

The improvement was immediate. Jake's color began to return, and he stopped mumbling. After only a minute, his answers became clearer.

"Jake, can you hear me?" Riley asked.

"Yes. But I'm kind of sleepy. And my leg hurts a lot."

"We'll give you something for the pain."

"Okay."

"We just want to make sure that you're okay. You were saying stupid things. Like how much blood is in a person."

"Five liters."

"Yes, we heard, thanks. And you kept talking about shiny flashes."

"That's the main drive."

"Our main drive is flashing?"

"No. The main drive of the ship chasing us."

"What ship chasing us?"

"The one I can see out the viewport. It's slowing down to match our orbit. See the engine flashes?"

Nadine and Riley turned to look out the viewport. Dead center was a flashing light. There was indeed a ship chasing them.

Jake was still a little woozy, but the argument was loud enough to keep him awake.

"We don't have enough fuel," Riley said. "Tomas has already pumped as much as possible. Tomas?"

"*Si*. Yes. The bladder mostly boiled off before I could pump it all out." Tomas and Jorge were crowded into the hatch to the lounge. "That's all the extra fuel we'll be getting."

"We can still climb above them. I can outmaneuver them and get to a higher orbit. They can't arrest us if they can't catch us. We'll shut down the engines and drift till we find a station," Nadine said.

"Which station? One with Militia? They'll arrest us," Riley said.

"They'll arrest you, merchant girl. They won't arrest me. I work for the Militia."

"No, you don't. You worked for Mack and his thugs. They are not Militia. The Militia will arrest you as well. We need to go to a Free Traders' station, or one that will fight Militia extradition. Like Galactic Growing."

"The Militia will probably shoot us," Jorge said.

"Whoa, wait a second, *signorina*," Tomas said. "Many of us have disputes with Galactic Growing. We cannot go to one of their stations."

"We can too. I'm going to find one," Riley said. She turned toward the computer. Tomas left the control room and climbed down to the passenger compartment. Riley began to type in navigation commands. "We just need to find one of their transfer stations and come close to it."

Jorge stood at the back of the cabin. "We cannot go to a Galactic Growing station. We must go elsewhere," he said.

"That's what I said," Nadine snarled. "But merchant girl here wants to go see her buddies."

"I heard you, but I don't care what you two say. I'm putting the course in," Riley said.

"Uh, ladies," Jake said. "If I could have a moment of your time."

"Shut up, Jake," both of them said.

There was a loud click. Jorge had drawn a revolver from a concealed holster. "We will not go to a Galactic Growing station. There are dozens of stations out there. Match orbit with any of them, but not Galactic Growing." He pointed the gun at the floor, not directly at her, but in the general direction. "I am very sorry, Miss Riley. Anywhere but there."

"Now that's what I'm talking about," Nadine said. "Give me the board, merchie."

"Are you going to shoot me, Jorge—really?" Riley asked.

"Miss, I will be in very big trouble if I go there." Jorge looked at the gun and put it in his holster. "No, I will not shoot you. But some of the others in the back—they might not be so gentle. They are young and excitable, and accidents do happen. Perhaps you should let Miss Nadine drive instead."

Riley rolled her eyes, but typed in a command and folded her arms across her chest. "Whatever," she said.

"I am sorry to bother you two with this, but we could not be diverted. Miss Nadine, where are you taking us?" Jorge said.

Nadine had started tapping commands into her board, but stopped, then frowned. She turned to Riley. "Which one?" she asked.

"You're so smart, you figure it out," Riley said.

Nadine glared at Riley. Riley glared right back.

"Which what?" Jorge asked.

"Station," Nadine said.

"Take us to the closet one, perhaps," Jorge said.

"Which one?" Nadine said again. Riley just grinned.

"What is happening?" Jorge asked. "Can we not just pick one?"

Jake felt a little woozy. He shook his head to clear it. His voice shook from the drugs. "It's not that simple, Jorge. We are moving at different vectors in three dimensions, and the moon and some of the asteroids are perturbing our course, and the other stations are also moving in three dimensions, so it is very difficult to calculate a course. The mathematics for each solution is very complex. We will have a different course to each one, and trying to find the closest one in time means we have to solve for all of them, and that takes more time, and then we will have to recalculate given the time that has passed. And we only have so much fuel."

"How does anyone get anywhere then?" Jorge asked.

"They teach shortcuts in navigator classes. Riley probably had made some guesses, or has some rules of thumb."

"Cannot Nadine do that?"

"Nope," Riley said. "She's purely a seat-of-the-pants pilot. She needs a course, or needs to see where she's going. She's not a navigator. She needs a destination."

"Bullshit, merchie. It just takes me longer," Nadine said.

There was a bang, and the decompression gong sounded for a few seconds. There were shouts from the passenger compartment, a banging, then the alarm went off.

"What was that?" Nadine asked.

Jorge had leaned back into the passenger compartment. He pulled his head back. "A small hole appeared in the hull. The guys patched it. What is happening?" he said.

Jake pointed out the front of the viewport. "Look there. Drive flare is gone. They've pivoted to point the bow directly at us."

"Why?" Riley said.

"To bring their mass driver to bear. They're shooting at us. Calculation time is up, ladies."

Chapter 31

"Gotcha," the pilot said. "We're at high guard now. We'll sweep above them every orbit."

"Pivot me for a clear shot. I'll use the laser—try to take out a control line. Then we can board if needed," the navigator said. They could see the shuttle on their screens.

The intercom beeped. The pilot ignored it. "Pivoting," he agreed. "You'll get your shot. Ah, shooting an engine out might not be a great idea."

"Why not?"

"This is a really, really low orbit. I'm already seeing some decay on ours, and they are lower. If we hit an engine, they might not be able to climb up out of there."

The intercom beeped again. They ignored it again. "I'll take a shot on the cabins then. They'll know we're serious." The intercom began to beep over and over again. They looked at each other. The navigator answered the intercom.

"Sir? We're kind of busy up here. This is tricky navigation. We need to maneuver to get a warning shot at this ship."

"No, you do not. Destroy that ship," the officer said.

"Sir? We normally fire a warning shot, then board. Ships are valuable, and damaging them is not a good idea. We can re-use their engines, if nothing else."

"The Officers' Council has an observer on the nearby asteroid. They are watching us. I have a communication from them. Destroy that ship."

The navigator looked at the pilot. The pilot punched the intercom and spoke. "Uh, sir, we can't really destroy it with a laser. Not enough power. We can damage exterior sensors and control lines, but we can't really blow it up."

"What about with the mass driver?"

"That would work, sir, if we can hit it. But they are still maneuvering, and the lag from our firing means that we're very unlikely to hit them."

"Get closer then."

"You idiots have missed," the officer snarled, looking out the viewport. He had climbed back into the control room as soon as they stopped maneuvering. "What sort of gunners are you?"

"Well, sir," the navigator began, "technically, we're not gunners. We've never received training. I've never actually fired the rail gun on this ship."

"I've never fired the rail gun on any ship, never mind this one," the pilot said. "I know that we're supposed to point the bow at them, but then the gunner is supposed to give us directions."

"So, give the gunners directions then. Or take them. Must I think of everything," the officer said.

"Sir, the gunnery program for the rail gun is locked up. You need a gunner's credentials to access them."

"Whatever for?"

"Keep accidents from happening. Save ammunition. I don't know, sir," the pilot replied.

The officer stared at the ceiling. "Very well. We have orders to destroy them. What do we do now, then?"

"You are in charge, sir. Your call."

"Can you simulate this gunnery program? Can you get close to them?"

The pilot looked at the navigator. The navigator shrugged. "Kind of. We can check their bearing in the telescope, and I think we can compute a closing course, but that's for the ship, not for weapons."

"The mass driver fires on the axis of the ship, yes?"

"Not quite, but close," the navigator said.

"If you see them in the center of the viewport, then we should hit them, shouldn't we?"

"Sir, they are so far away, at this distance, even an error of part of a degree will be a miss. And it takes time for the slugs to reach them. We have to aim at where they will be, not where they are now."

"But the closer we are to them, the less time it takes?"

"Yes, sir."

"Get close enough to make sure that a degree or two does not matter. Set up that closing course, and use it to shoot at them as well. Get to a lower orbit, quickly."

Nadine had taken the helm. Everybody else was strapped in. She kept them in the same orbit, and had added random drops, swings, and spins to make the mass driver miss them. Riley hadn't argued but was typing on the nav computer.

"We need to get away from them. Jake, you always have a plan."

Jake coughed. He felt better than he had a while ago, but he was still woozy, and his leg still bothered him. "There should be a TGI station almost intersecting our orbit in about thirty minutes," he said.

"TGI?" Riley asked.

"The insurance company?" Jorge asked.

"Jake works for TGI," Nadine said.

"You do?" Riley said. "What do you do for them?"

"He's a spy," Nadine said. "He was spying on you."

"You're a spy? You were spying on us. Is that why you stowed away on my ship?"

"No. I was spying on your dad. I stowed away on your ship because I thought you were pretty and wanted to spend more time with you," Jake said. *Did I just say that?* Jake thought. *These are pretty good drugs.*

Riley blushed. Jorge laughed. Nadine looked confused for a moment, but then her face blanked.

"Good deflection, loverboy," Nadine said.

"You, shut up," Riley said.

"Ladies," Jake began.

"Shut up, Jake," both girls said. Jorge began to laugh. Everybody looked at him. "What?" Nadine said.

"Nothing," Jorge said, hiding a smile. "I am just remembering what it is like to be young." He turned to Jake. "Mr.

Professor, I think if we go with you to a TGI station, we will be fine. Do you think they will let us go?"

"Yes," Jake said. "I can guarantee that they will let you and the guys go, Jorge. They have no interest in you. Nadine, you can run off like you normally do, and Riley, they won't stop you from going to meet your father."

"Like she normally does? What does that mean?" Riley asked.

"Never mind, Riley. Find us that station. It will come down from higher, but I think we can intercept. That was my original plan. We'll just need time. Nadine, how do we keep from getting killed by that mass driver?"

"Jake, that's not a Free Trader. That's a Militia ship. They have targeting software. It will know our capabilities and will calculate our course, and account for gravity, and drag." She stopped talking and looked at Riley. "How much drag does your ship have in atmosphere?"

Riley frowned. "A lot. We would never go this low— it would be dangerous. And why do you care? We're not in our ship."

Nadine smiled. "I know. Watch this, Jakey." She began hitting the screen, and they felt the maneuvering jets fire, then the thrusters.

"We're dropping," Riley reported. "We're going deeper into the atmosphere. It's slowing us down. What are you doing?" Riley said.

"Yes. But how much is it slowing us down?" Nadine said.

Riley looked at Nadine for a moment, then smiled. "Pivot us back, and get the telescope on that Militia ship," she said.

Riley and Nadine watched their screens for a minute. Then they smiled at each other.

"There's a flare," Riley reported.

"That's a shot," Nadine said. "Another. Three. Four. Five. No hits. They can't figure it out."

Riley and Nadine smiled at each other and exchanged a high-five.

"What is going on?" Jorge asked.

"We're in the atmosphere, and it's causing drag, which is causing us to drop, but this bizarre ship Jake stole is stream-lined. We're not getting nearly as much drag as we should. They're still shooting at us, but their computer is treating us like a regular merchant ship, so it's coming up with the wrong answer. They will keep missing, and they won't know why."

"That is good," Jorge said. "Jake, your girlfriends are quite smart."

"I'm not his girlfriend," Riley and Nadine said together.

They continued diving into the atmosphere. The air visible through the front viewport glowed red from the friction of their re-entry. Riley and Nadine flipped through screens.

"Crap. They're following us down," Nadine said.

"So much for your great idea that they wouldn't want to be this low," Riley said.

"Just give me a course to get out of here," Nadine said.

"I've found Jake's station. Just give me some time with the computer," Riley said.

Everyone in the cockpit was quiet. They felt the gentle sways and spins as Nadine's program gave them a random walk around their base course. A bong interrupted the silence.

"Okay, I've got a course to the station Jake wants. It'll be tight, but we can make it. I'm putting it into the computer."

Nadine watched her screen. "Okay, I have the course. We have to climb, and we'll move closer to that Militia ship if we do. They'll have a better shot. A much better shot."

"That's the best I can do. We're tight on fuel as it is."

"How much of a better shot? What are their chances of hitting us?" Jorge asked.

"We don't know," Nadine said.

"What do you mean, you don't know? You have computers here," Jorge said.

"We have computers, but we're missing software. We don't have any targeting software, and we don't have any evade software, so we have no way of tracking what they can or can't do."

"But they will have a better shot?"

"For a while," Riley said.

"Can't we wait?"

"We don't have unlimited fuel. We need to go somewhere. Up or down. Up there's a station," Nadine said.

"Nadine, could we—" Jake began.

"Jake, not now," Riley said. "The pilots are talking. Nadine, if you manually evade can you avoid getting hit?"

"Yes."

"Then do it. Fast. Before we lose that option."

"Hang on," Nadine said, and they were pushed into their seats as she accelerated to a higher altitude. She typed commands into the computer and was randomly swinging the control yoke back and forth while pulsing the main engine.

"Okay, we're coming up closer to them. In a few seconds, we should be by."

"Almost there," Riley said.

"Just a few more seconds, and we'll be safe," Nadine said. "Jakey, let's see if we can find your friends. Say, they should be paying for all the wages we lost. What sort of bonus can we expect?"

"Bonus, Nadine? I don't think they do bonuses, but I suppose I could ask," Jake said.

BANG!

Jake felt the ship lurch, and a number of gongs sounded. He was lifted out of his seat by negative g's, then slammed back into it, then negative again, then positive. Delta began to cartwheel across the viewport. First there, then gone, there, then gone. He felt Nadine cut the engines and the forces on him decreased, but the craft continued to pitchpole. Nadine was cursing, and she rolled the ship ninety degrees, then yawed it ninety degrees, and Jake felt her pulse the main engines to bring the tumble under control. She was using the main engines as maneuvering thrusters by spinning the ship around. Her cursing stopped as the ship's gyration slowed.

The three spacers ignored the retching sounds and the smell of vomit coming from the passenger compartment.

"Okay, that was bad. We lost a thruster, and we've dropped a lot. If we go up again, they'll have a better shot, and next time they might hit something important."

BANG. The ship lurched again. Jake was pushed back into his seat as Nadine revved the main engines up to full throttle.

"Going low. Real low," she said.

"We definitely hit them once. I saw them spin," the navigator said.

"Yes, but we're not getting as many hits as we should," the pilot said. "I checked the specs, and I'm using the computer's numbers for performance."

"Follow them down lower then," the officer said. "We have more fuel than they do, correct? We are a bigger ship."

"Yes, sir, correct on both counts, but it's just—" the navigator said.

"Just what? Just too hard for someone as unskilled as you?"

"No, sir. It's just odd. They are going way lower than I've ever seen any craft go. I've never been this low before—not in a regular ship." He looked at the pilot.

The pilot shook his head. "Me neither," he said.

"But you just told me that we can go anywhere they can, because they don't have as much fuel."

"Yes."

"Then follow them down. Get closer."

The pilot looked at the navigator. The navigator grimaced and shook his head.

"Sir, I'm not sure," the pilot said.

"This is an order. I order you to follow them down."

"Sir, I respectfully decline," the pilot said.

"You decline? I will have you court-martialed. You will be dismissed from service," the officer said.

The pilot laughed. "Probably not. My cousin's wife is a major shareholder. They won't dismiss one of their own on the word of the second son of the second son of a minor shareholder—a nobody like you." He looked at the officer.

"Bad for business, and for corporate loyalty if you don't look after your people. The only justice I will face is a letter of reprimand, and get grounded for a year or two. It's better than dying."

The officer opened his mouth. Then he closed it. He looked at the navigator, who shrugged and turned away and began to type on his screen.

The officer smiled. "Very well. I will just log my order, and we will argue about it later. Of course, I will send a copy of the log to the Officers' Council. They may have their own thoughts on the matter. And their own feelings on what is appropriate justice."

He grinned at the pilot. The pilot's face had gone blank. He shook his head once, then reached for a button on his screen. "Everybody, prepare for a rough ride. We're dropping into atmosphere."

"Riley, what's our status?" Nadine asked. Nadine was trying not to drop any lower while keeping away from the pursuing Militia ship.

"Not good. They're following us down. They'll have a good shot in a few minutes."

"How many minutes?" Jake asked.

"Jake, shut up. We don't have time for your number-crunching. Nadine, if we don't break past them soon, we won't have enough fuel to match orbits with that TGI station. And if we go lower, we won't have enough fuel to break orbit at all."

"Okay, what do we do?"

"How low do we have to go for them to not be able

to recover, not be able to break back up to a safe orbit?" Jake asked.

"What?" Nadine said.

"It doesn't matter about them. It matters about us," Riley said. "We have to keep away from them, or they'll break us into little pieces." She turned to Nadine. "What if we do a maximum burn? Try to blow right past them?"

"We can do that, but they'll still get a shot. What will that do to our fuel?"

"Kill it," Riley said. "We'll be drifting away at very high velocity."

"Which means we'll slowly starve to death on our way out."

"Ladies," Jake began.

"Shut up, Jake," they both said.

Jake looked at them both for a moment. Then he shook his head and screamed, "LISTEN!"

Everybody shut up and turned toward him. "Nadine, go lower," Jake said, in a normal voice.

"Lower? Are you nuts? We can barely get out of this orbit as it is."

"I know what I'm doing."

"You? You are the one that got us in this mess," Riley said.

"Yes, yes, I am. I'm the one that figured out that you were trading with a rogue station by your cargo. I'm the one who figured out how to get there. I'm the one who kept us all from being killed by those thugs. I'm the one who got your dad off the station with a fortune in ore. I'm the one who made sure you were well enough to travel before breaking out. I'm the one who recruited Jorge and his guys to help us escape.

I'm the one who figured out when the drop window was. I'm the one who arranged how to steal this ship and provided the extra fuel for it. I'm the one who got us this far!"

Jake's voice went up an octave as he spoke. He shouted the last part. Everybody was quiet. Riley's eyes were wide. Nadine had tilted her head and was looking at him oddly. Jorge was smiling. Jake took a deep breath.

"Now, if things had been left up to Jorge, he would still be stuck there. If it were up to you, Nadine, we would have died in a blaze of glory during that first shootout. If it was up to Rick and you, Riley, you two would be apprentice miners and Mack's guys would be crashing your ship into a dock some-where—that is, if you hadn't all died when the atmosphere plant gave out because they didn't do the maintenance on it."

He took another deep breath.

"So, yes, I'm the one who got us here. And I'm the one who will get us out of here. If everybody just shuts up and listens."

He turned to Nadine. "Go lower. They will follow, and they won't be able to climb up. Their orbit will decay, and they will break apart in the denser atmosphere."

"So will ours," she said quietly.

"No, we're streamlined. We can de-orbit successfully."

"Jakey," Nadine said, then started again. "Jake, you know that we're not a shuttle, right?"

"We are not a shuttle."

"From a ground point of view, we're just a rocket."

"Yes."

"If we de-orbit a rocket, once we're in atmosphere, we

can't maneuver. We'll just crash into the ground and build a big crater. I don't want to do that."

"We'll use the ramjet to control our landing. There is a checklist. I'll send it to Riley's screen."

"We don't have wings. If we go into the atmosphere, we'll just start tumbling, and we'll burn up."

"We don't need wings, Nadine."

"What sort of aircraft doesn't need wings, Jakey?"

"One that isn't an aircraft. One that's a lifting body," Jake said.

Three minutes later, Riley and Nadine were examining a screen Jake had brought up.

"You think this will work?" Riley asked, turning to Nadine.

"It should. Jake's right," Nadine said. "Once we start the de-orbit, as long as we're careful, it should fly kind of like a glider. The computer can get us partway, but once we're in the thicker atmosphere, somebody will have to take over. I've never seen this 'lifting body' thing before. It doesn't have wings, but it does generate lift. And if we can get those ramjets working, we'll be able to go wherever we want on the surface once we're down low enough."

Riley punched a button on her screen. "I have a checklist for the ramjet. But it won't work the whole time. We need to be going fast for it to fire. Too fast to land. At some point, it will flame out as we slow down. We have control surfaces for when we're in the atmosphere, but I don't see how we can fly it with no thrust."

Jake spoke up. "Nadine will fly it once we're in atmosphere. She can fly a glider, and this will act a little like a glider."

Riley looked at Nadine. Nadine nodded. "How did you know that, Jake?" Riley asked.

Jake just shook his head. "Never mind. You two follow the checklist. I have to send a message."

"Wow. This checklist is strange. I've never seen anything like this," Nadine said.

"It's a very old system. These lifting bodies were shifted out with some of the colony ships because they were cheaper to build than shuttles," Jake said.

"Okay, but can we get to the shuttle landing dock?"

"We're not going to the shuttle dock," Jake said.

"We're not?"

"No," Jake said. "I had a few communications from TGI while we were upstairs. They have acquired a ground-based processing plant."

"We're going to land on a food plant?" Nadine said.

"Not exactly," Jake said.

"We're in trouble," the pilot said.

"Emperor's balls! Really?" the navigator said.

"What is all this shaking? What is going on?" the officer yelled.

"The atmosphere. It's denser than we thought. We're heating up, and we're going to take structural damage soon. We're not designed for this type of resistance," the pilot said.

"We have to destroy that ship," the officer insisted.

"They have destroyed themselves. They're lower than we are. They can't climb out of that orbit now. They're going to crash. Or explode and burn up. Something," the pilot said.

"We're going to explode and burn up if you don't get us out of here," the navigator said.

"I'm trying, but every time I pitch up to fire the engines, the shaking gets worse. I'm afraid something might come off."

"Do something, you idiot, or you will get us all killed!" the officer screamed.

"You know what," the pilot said, "I'm pretty tired of you. When we get out, I might just send my own message to the Officers' Council."

"Peasant!" screamed the officer. "Do not speak to me like that." He reached forward and smacked the pilot on the side of the head. The pilot jerked away, pulling the control yoke. The jerk pulled the ship to one side, and the unbalanced forces caused it to begin tumbling through the atmosphere.

"The Emperor's scrotum," Jake said. He looked up from his screen.

"What now?" Nadine said.

"The Militia ship just broke up. I saw it in the telescope. It rolled over and snapped into pieces." Jake looked closely. "They're burning up. Nice light show."

"We'll be a light show soon. Riley?"

"We have to correct our orbit. We need to line up for that lake Jake picked out."

"It's not a lake. It's an estuary," Jake said.

"We don't care. For us, it's a lake," Riley said. "Nadine, we need to pivot and make a correction. It will use most of our fuel. Once we're on course, we need to flip back on our belly and use the atmosphere to slow us down. We turn off the main engine and do something called an S-turn to bleed off speed. The parameters are on your screen."

"I know what those are. I can do them."

"We need to slow down enough so that we don't burn up. Then, when the atmosphere is thicker, we can fire the ramjet and head for Jake's lake."

"Starting when?"

"Now would be good, before we burn up or break into pieces."

"Maneuvering," Nadine said.

The ship pivoted. Jake was pushed back into his seat as the main engines fired. The movement rocked him from side to side as Nadine alternately pulsed jets and engines to bring them closer to the correct orbit. The ship shook more and more. An alarm bong sounded.

"Best we're going to get," Nadine said. "Pivoting back."

Jake felt negative g's again, and Delta spun through the viewport. It was bigger now. Nadine throttled the engines off. The entire ship began to shake, and the viewport glowed red. The ship was digging into the atmosphere.

"S-turns soon. We need to drop more speed," Riley said.

Nadine began a complex series of turns that rocked the ship from side to side. The shaking didn't slow down, and the glow outside got brighter.

Jake let his mind drift. He had done all he could. They would either make it or they wouldn't. After the ramjet came on, they would have control to maneuver a bit more, then it would shut down when they got too slow. At that point, Nadine would land them on the lake. Or estuary. It was an estuary. That was important. Why was it important? He frowned as he listened to them talking.

"Atmosphere is thickening," Riley said. "We should be able to start those ramjets."

"Soon. I'm not getting much in the way of lift here. We've slowed down a lot, but we're starting to drop faster," Nadine said.

"I just have to swap the fuel pump. Stand by." Riley typed a few commands. "Igniting." She tapped a control. Jake felt a tiny jerk. "It's on."

Nadine moved the yoke back and forth, and pushed some other controls. "I've got some control. I have to disengage the thrusters. Yup. Now we're an airplane."

Jorge spoke up while cleaning vomit off his shirt. "An airplane?"

"Yep," Nadine said. "The ramjet pushes us through the air, and even though we don't have wings, this ship's weird shape generates lift. The control surfaces steer us, at least until we get too slow. At which point the ramjet fails, and we glide in for a landing on Jake's lake."

"Estuary. It's an estuary. Ah, crap," Jake said. "What time is it?"

"What time is it? Why does that matter?" Riley asked.

"I need to check the state of the tide."

"What's a tide?" Riley asked.

"Depending on what time it is, it's a problem. A big problem."

Chapter 32

Jose had run all the way from the hotel container, but he stopped before rounding the corner. What would Dashi do in this situation? Not run, that's for sure. He took several deep breaths, smoothed his shirt, squared his shoulders, then sauntered around the corner like he was going to lunch. About one hundred people wandered around the plaza in front of the monorail. The station took up one entire side, while an actual building, which looked like a Galactic Growing office, took up the other. The third side had rows of bunkhouse containers, and the fourth was something he had never seen. Jose looked at it in bewilderment as he walked across, until he saw the cross above it. It was a church. He'd never seen one, but he'd read about them. He shouldered his way up to the door, where a TGI security agent was arguing with a GG ticket clerk.

"Who is in charge here?" Jose said.

The two women looked at him. "Who are you?" the GG ticket clerk asked.

"This is the assistant sector director, Mr. Jose," the TGI security agent said.

"Oh. Well, I guess you are, sir. How can we help you?"

I'm in charge, thought Jose. *When did that happen? Never mind.* "Everyone here was supposed to be on the monorail for Point-37 twenty minutes ago. What went wrong?" he asked.

"Sir, I don't have full authorization for cost-sharing from your company here. My office has put a hold on all transfers until they deal with some internal cost accounting," the ticket clerk said.

"You won't ship us out? We have an agreement with your company to move these people," Jose said.

"I understand, but I'm not really the one to yell at. I'm just the ticket clerk. I can't release the cars without a ticket, either from my office or somebody else's."

"There will be trouble if you don't. We will complain to your officials, and it will go hard on you."

"The auditors will give me more trouble if I let you go without tickets, and I see the auditors every month—I'll only see you this one time."

Jose glared at her, but she just shrugged her shoulders. Jose looked at the TGI agent. She nodded. "We're all ready. All packed. We can be on board in a few minutes if she releases the car. They even have two cars over here ready for our cargo, but she won't let us on."

Jose frowned, then looked around. He ran his fingers through his hair. What to do? A man approached the ticket clerk while he was thinking.

"Rosita, I need to buy a ticket on the next mono to Landing," he said.

"Give me a minute, Ricardo, I have to deal with these people first," the ticket clerk said. She turned back to Jose. "Look, sir, if you can't get the authorization, you'll have to wait."

"We have things to do. We need to go now," Jose said. He looked at the ticket clerk. "You sell tickets?"

"Yes."

"Do you charter cars?"

"Sure, for a price."

"What's the price to charter those two cars," Jose said, gesturing at the two empty cars on the sideline, "to take us to Point-37?"

The ticket clerk blinked. "Um, with cargo loading, or what? And when?"

"We'll load everything ourselves," Jose said. He looked at the TGI agent, who nodded. "Immediate departure and direct to the end of the line. No delays."

"Delays won't be a problem—there are no cars down that end of the line. I have to calculate the price." She began to play with her tablet. "Immediate departure, no advance booking, discount for self-loading, here you go." She showed him her tablet. An exorbitant figure was listed on it.

Jose looked at it. Well, he was in charge, right? Dashi had said his promotion was effective now. He swallowed, and handed the agent his corporate credit chip.

"I authorize the charges. I'll sort it out with your senior people later."

The ticket clerk shrugged, took the chip, and pushed it into her tablet. Jose turned to the TGI agent next to him. "There is a shuttle maintenance crew somewhere in this mess," he whispered. "Make sure they get on, and put somebody on to take care of their stuff. They will have work right away when we get there. And assign them a guard or two." Jose looked back at the ticket clerk, , who was frowning. "Assuming we get on, of course."

"That's a lot of money, sir. Are you authorized to spend that much on your say-so?" the TGI security agent asked.

The clerk's tablet binged. She nodded, then turned to yell to the yard crew.

"Yes," Jose said. "I got a promotion, haven't you heard?"

"Let me get this straight," Riley said. "Not only do we need to land on this stupid lake, but we need to land at a particular time and in a particular direction. Said direction not being the one we'll be traveling when we get there. All because of this tide thing."

"It's not a lake, it's an estuary. But yes," Jake said. "Right now, the river is gushing out into the sea, going east—going out to the ocean. If we land in the river with the current going that way, once we stop, we'll just get swept out to sea."

"So we'll get hit by some water. Why is that bad?"

"We'll get swept over a ten-meter waterfall, sink, and drown."

"We'll just hit water. Water is soft," Riley said.

"No, water is pretty dense. Hitting water from ten meters up is kind of like hitting concrete. If we get a hole in anything, we'll fill up and sink."

"And waiting will help us how?"

"The tide is coming in up the estuary. It moves up in a wave, and once the tide gets high enough, it will cover the waterfall and move upstream, to the west. Then if we land, the current will carry us inland, and eventually we'll be able to tie up to a dock, or get caught by a fishing boat, or anchored. No drowning."

"You're saying we're going to need to recalculate our course, stay higher longer, then cut down lower, have the engine go out, and then glide in at an exact time."

"It doesn't have to be exact. Any time after 15:33 will be fine. That's when the wave goes past the waterfall."

"I hate planets," Riley said. She shook her head. "This might be a problem."

"I see that mountain you said to look out for, Riley," Nadine said. "We're headed right for it."

"Put us on a minimum-fuel glide. We have to maintain a minimum speed to keep the ramjet working, but we'll need to conserve fuel."

"We have to go over that mountain, or we'll crash."

"If we burn too much fuel climbing, we'll run out and start to drop. And if we're going too fast, the atmosphere will burn us up. Not to mention when we crash, we'll be nowhere near Jake's lake."

"It's an estuary, not a lake."

"Shut up, Jake," both girls said.

Jake sat behind them. There was nothing he could do. He looked at the two girls. Riley was biting her lip and staring at a navigation screen. Nadine had sweat running down her neck. Nadine sweating? That was a first.

"Riley," Nadine said.

"What?"

Nadine swallowed. "I need help. If we're going to get down, I can't take my hands off the controls even for a second. I can't change screens. You'll have to call the course changes."

"But you're the pilot."

"I don't care. I need you to help me. Can you do that?"

"Yes," Riley said. "Yes, I can. Let's do this." She began to cycle through her screens.

"Nadine, how many times have you landed a glider?" Jake asked.

"I've done it a number of times, Jake," Nadine said. She didn't take her eyes off her controls.

"A number of times?"

"Yes."

"A number of times. More than once?" Jake asked.

"One is a number, Jake, now shut up. Riley? Call it."

"There is a mountain in our path."

"I'm going to gas it to get over," Nadine said.

"Not too much," Riley said.

"Can you use the radar, find a better way?"

Riley flicked through some screens. "Not on a moon.. It doesn't point in the right direction."

"Here we go," Nadine said.

"Up, up, up," Riley said. The mountain grew large in their screens as they drew closer.

Nadine pulled on the controls. The mountain shifted.

Nadine flicked her hands, and the mountain disappeared from view.

An alarm bonged. "Fuel alert," Riley said. She turned off the alarm and typed something on her screen. "Okay, new course. Left, left, almost, left, there," Riley said.

"That takes us out to sea," Nadine said.

"Yes, we need to make a big loop, then another, to avoid that tide thing."

"Okay." Nadine manipulated the console slightly. The mountains dropped, then the land disappeared, and the sea appeared below them.

Jake could see the fields of green algae floating on the sea. The terraforming of the oceans had been quite successful here. Not only did the algae produce oxygen, they were also a food source for some fish and edible for humans. Their course wove around, and Jake saw the mountains reappear in the distance. The land opened into a bay, and a churning line of froth showed the returning tide starting up the estuary.

"Nadine, we have to go over that bay. Circle around and then come in behind that wave thing, and land on the water," Riley said.

"What happens after we land on the water?"

Jake spoke up. "I've arranged for crews to come out on fishing boats and tow us to shore after the tidal bore passes."

"How did you do that?" Riley said.

"I had help from my head office."

"Do you have confirmation of that?" Nadine asked.

No, Jake thought. He hoped that Jose had gotten the latest message.

"Nadine, just do your thing and land the plane. I've taken care of the rest," Jake said. He tried to sound authoritative, like he knew what he was doing.

"Okay," Nadine said.

Wow, Jake thought. Was it really that easy?

"We trust you, Jake," Riley said.

That made Jake feel even worse.

"Lower, Nadine, lower," Riley said.

"We need to get over those mountains."

"We're going to run out of fuel," Riley said.

"Emperor's balls," Nadine said. "I'm turning now. I won't be able to get over those mountains. We'll turn out and come back in."

"Nadine, we need more time."

"I'll go farther out to sea on the loop," Nadine said. She turned the control wheel. Another alarm went off. Riley punched it.

"Fuel out, stand by for— There it is. Fuel's gone. Engines shutting down. Now."

The engine noises faded. Nadine maneuvered the controls.

"Good times, everybody," Nadine said. "We're in an un-powered glider. We have no fuel for our engines. We seem to be dropping faster than I expected, so I don't think we'll make our time window. And our course is heading us out to sea." She paused for a moment. "Great plan, Jakey."

"I won't do it," the fisherman said. "The tidal bore is due in about seven minutes. We stay tied up here behind the break-water till it goes by, then we can motor out. I'm not moving until after that, then we'll go and pick up your friends."

Jose looked at the message he had just received from Jake.

"They say they'll be on the tidal bore almost exactly, and the boat has to be standing by in mid-channel to take them under tow, otherwise they'll sink."

"If I'm out there, I'll sink—along with your crew."

"But surely some of you ride this bare thing in?"

The captain crossed his arms and shook his head. "It's called a bore, and yes, I've had to do it from time to time, but it's very dangerous, and I'm not interested."

"Look, I'm from TGI, and we're the new owners of the plant. Don't you want to do a favor for the new boss?"

"New boss same as the old boss as far as I'm concerned. The old guys screwed us on everything they could. Didn't pay the contracted rate, overcharged us for fuel, promised everything under a reflected moon, and then blamed it on head office. Nope, I don't believe in TGI, or GG, or any of those companies."

"What do you believe in then?" Jose said.

"Us here, we believe in hard cash. That's what we believe in."

Jose looked around. He was speaking to the oldest fishing captain present. The man appeared to represent the entire fishing fleet. The other captains eavesdropped nearby. Most of them were nodding, but not all of them. The crews behind them grinned at each other, enjoying the entertainment. Jose looked back at his crew of shuttle techs. There were four specialists in servicing standing next to him. About twenty others had dragged down a load of gear they said they needed. Giant magnetic grapples for anchoring and maneuvering the shuttles, large plastic things he heard were called balloons—filled with air and used to float them somehow. Lines and ropes and special tools to open hatches. Two men wore skin-suits with special air tanks for underwater use—divers, they were called.

He looked back at the captain, then pulled out his tablet. He pushed a chip into the side of it and began to type on it. He had to confirm it three times before it beeped at him. He pulled out the chip and turned to the head shuttle tech.

"What's that thing there?" Jose pointed. "The one that you said was the most important to get attached first?"

"It's called an anchor," the tech said. "We have to get these attached to the shuttle before it runs up the river and crashes on shore."

"How many do you need?"

"Two is good, four is better."

"And that second thing? How many of those do you need?"

"The flotation bags? Four at least."

Jose looked around and saw a table. He walked over and jumped on it. He stuck his hand up and waved it around. "Listen up," he yelled. "Ten thousand credits to the first crew to get four anchors and four flotation bags on that shuttle. Double if they are out there ready to start before that tidal bore comes in."

In the ensuing rush to the docks, Jose was picked up and carried bodily to the dock, and thrust onto a ship. He kept getting knocked down as more crewmen swarmed aboard. By the time he managed to stand up, all of his crew was stuffed on board, and the boat was pulling out into the channel.

"Jake, how fast do these things go?" Nadine said.

"Things? The tidal bore?" Jake said.

"Yes, the boring thing. How fast?"

"Twenty kilometers an hour."

"Okay. We just have to adjust a bit. We're dropping too fast. Turning now."

Riley pushed an alarm for hard landing, and strapped herself into her seat. Nadine did likewise. Jake was already strapped in, so he just watched as Nadine pulled back on the controls and began to follow the estuary in. They were still going fast, but they were sinking fast too. The tidal bore was behind them. Jake played through his cameras until he saw an aft view, and he could see it gaining on them.

"Okay, everybody, hang on. We're going in." Nadine eased back on the controls, and the shuttle began to pitch up a bit.

Jake looked at his screen again. "Nadine, that tidal bore thing is gaining on us."

"I know, Jake, I know."

"Nadine, we're supposed to land behind it, not in front of it."

"Jake, gliders land when they want, not when you want. Besides, if we're airtight in space, we're airtight in water, right?"

"Sure. Why?"

"So, we'll just get bumped around a bit. Emperor's balls. What's that doing there?"

"What now? Oh, crap," Jake said. "That's our recovery boat."

"It's right in front of us. We're going to hit it if we don't land now." Nadine hit a control. "Brace for impact," she said over the radio.

The shuttle pitched up, then there was a whoomph, and Jake saw steam in all his camera views, after which he felt the shuttle settle. They floated around for a second.

"There. That wasn't so bad, was it?" Nadine said. She turned to Riley and held up a hand. The two girls shared a high-five.

Then the wave hit them, and they flipped upside down.

"Brace yourself on that stanchion," a crewman said.

"What?" Jose said.

"The pole. Hold on to the pole."

Jose held on and watched the shuttle begin to descend. It looked like it was on a final approach, but the lack of engine noises confused him. Was it actually gliding in? Jake hadn't said anything about that. All he'd told him was that he would be landing around a certain time—particulars of which were out of his control—along with details of this tidal bore thing, and the complete urgency to have a shuttle-ground crew there immediately, or else they would be destroyed.

Another crewman hurried over to Jose holding something red. It looked like a bag or a cushion with a hole in it. "Can you swim?" he asked.

"Swim? What's that?" Jose said.

"Put this on," he said, and handed him the cushion.

"Or what?"

"Or you'll die," he said and hurried off.

Jose strapped it on and looked back. That was a very funny shape for a shuttle. No wings. And there was that tidal bore behind it. It was a wave. A big wave. Jose ran up the stairs to the top of the ship where the captain was. This captain was the youngest of the group of captains he had spoken to back at the dock, and his crew looked the roughest. They seemed competent, though—they were dumping some sort of heavy-looking things off the front of the ship and running out some chains.

"That's a big wave," Jose told the captain.

"The biggest," agreed the captain, and continued yelling instructions at his crews. They were upset about something and yelling back. Chains rattled, and things were thrown overboard. Winches spun. The boat jerked to a stop and pivoted toward the wave. The very large wave.

"Are we going to die?" Jose asked.

"Everybody dies," the captain said.

"I meant today," Jose said.

The captain turned to him and nodded. "So did I." He held the look for a few seconds then laughed. "Got ya. Nope, not today. We've got our anchors out and holding, and the crews are ready on those grapples, and we've got your divers ready on the flotation bags. We'll be fine, as long as they land close enough," he said. He looked up at the sky. "They look plenty close enough."

Jose turned forward. The shuttle was landing. "They look close enough," he agreed. Then he frowned. "Say, they look really close. Won't they hit us?"

The captain ignored him and began yelling at the crew again. A man next to them spun a huge wheel. Jose felt the engines surge, and the ship swung to the right. A giant winch on the front of the deck began to play out rapidly, and another began to pull in. There was yelling, and an alarm began to sound. "Collision. Collision. Collision."

Jose grabbed hold of the railing. He saw the shuttle flare up and do a perfect belly landing. Then the giant wave behind the shuttle hit it and flipped it up on its nose, and it began to fall off the wave toward them.

The boat slewed sideways, and Jose saw one of the crew pull a lever longer than his arm. A chain rattled free off one side. The ship corrected and pointed right into the wave, and Jose felt the engines roar below him and the ship raced forward. Was this idiot actually riding into this wave? He was, and they screamed forward up and up and up on top of the wave. They swung to the right, and Jose saw the shuttle tumble nose-first beside him. The crewmen fired magnetic grapples out to lock onto the body of the shuttle, then the wave spun the boat sideways, and the captain was yelling again, and Jose saw the other anchor crew pulling the chain in.

The wave churned underneath them, lifting them high. The captain waited till they were at the very top.

"Pop the chain!" the captain screamed. "Meet the helm." The crew at the front of the ship hit the windlass with a hammer, and the anchor and the chain released. The boat was attached to the shuttle, and the magnetic grapples pulled the bow around to follow it. The captain turned to the stern. "Sea anchors!" he screamed. Another crew on the stern pushed what looked to Jose like two mattresses with metal crosspieces lashed to them overboard. The ship pulled to the end of a long chain attached to them, and Jose felt the drag begin to slow them down. The wave passed underneath them, and the boat slid down the back side.

"Full reverse!" the captain yelled. The boat's engines screamed, the engines and the sea anchors pulled back, and then the shuttle appeared from the white froth forward. It floated on the surface, but was slowly sinking.

"Floaters, second anchors!" the captain yelled, and more lines shot out toward the shuttle. Two were just anchors, but four of them had large plastic things attached to the front, along with trailed hoses. The floaters inflated and expanded, and the shuttle stopped settling.

One of the grapples had wrapped all the way around the shuttle, but the whole mess was holding. The shuttle was slowing down. One of the sea anchors broke off, but the captain dumped a regular anchor off the stern, and that line stretched, and stretched some more.

The boat hung on the end of the anchor line, creaking, but then jerked to a stop, rocking gently in the current. The shuttle was attached, and the four floaters were holding it on the surface. It bobbed on the surface about ten meters ahead of them—upside down.

"I believe," the captain said, "that you owe me twenty thousand credits."

"Everyone paid off then?" Jake asked Jorge, gesturing to the empty bag Jorge held.

"Yes, with the silver I gave them on board, and the credit chips your Mr. Jose gave them. We are square," Jorge said.

"Good. What are you going to do now?"

"Some of the guys are signing up here. Mr. Jose said he

is hiring people with agricultural experience, and the rates are good. And as you know, most of us had some sort of issue with Galactic Growing, so we can't go there. And one of the guys lived here before, and he had a few good things to say."

"That's great, Jorge," Jake said.

"How is your leg?"

"The doc looked at it and said the girls did things perfectly. He gave me another shot, put this bandage on, and said it should heal up nicely. I feel pretty relaxed right now. I've got to send the skinsuit in to be repaired, though."

They turned to watch the shuttle being pulled onto land.

" TGI is going to use our stolen ship as a surface-to-orbit shuttle?" Jorge asked.

"Seems like," Jake replied.

"What's that thing there? Those metal rails that run into the water?" Jorge asked.

"They use them to fix the fishing boats. They put them on that carriage thing and use a winch to haul the boats out to work on them." They watched as the shuttle was pulled up the rails.

"One of your girlfriends is coming," Jorge said.

Nadine approached them, stopped, and looked at the estuary. "Interesting spot here, Jake," she said.

"How so?"

"Nice wide east-west lake—perfect for receiving shuttles coming in from orbit. Perfect direction. Mountains to cut down crosswinds. Water for fuel."

"Yup, plenty of water to land on, even at low tide. Just

have to watch out for that tidal bore. Can't land if it might hit you."

"You almost screwed that up, Jake."

"Next time I arrange to land in a stolen shuttle pursued by a Militia cutter, I'll try to take that into account."

Nadine laughed. "Actually, it was a pretty good plan. Your plans keep getting better, Jake. You've become moderately competent at this sort of thing."

"You did a good job gliding us in."

"I have some skills."

"At least you didn't shoot me this time."

Nadine's face clouded. "I didn't enjoy that part."

"We discussed this. I didn't have time to explain everything to you. And after I shot you, it was too late."

"Next time, explain it to me first."

"I will. Are you going to stick around?"

"Why would I do that?"

"Well, you're kind of ... fun to have around. Exciting."

Nadine regarded Jake for a moment. "That's true. Do you think you could take more excitement, Mr. Rule Book?"

"I'd like to find out."

Nadine smiled. "That could be interesting. But not now, Jake. I have to go."

"Ah."

"But first." She leaned toward Jake and put her arms around him in a big hug. Jake was completely surprised but hugged her back. She held him for a minute, then dragged her arms down his side and stepped back. "Thanks for all your help, Jake. You did not do totally horribly this time. I'll miss you."

"Thanks, Nadine. I'll miss you too."

She smiled. "There was some talk of a bonus? A girl has to eat."

"Right. I have something to make you feel better."

"What's that? Gold? Silver? Platinum?"

"Fertilizer."

"What?"

"Right here." Jake gestured. "Four crates. A ton of fertilizer."

"You almost got me killed a dozen times, and you're giving me fertilizer?"

"Yes. Francisco here will help you load it up." He gestured to one of the guys who was standing by. "He'll help you put it on the monorail. That one up there is leaving in a few minutes, but it'll be back, and he'll make sure you're loaded up before it goes."

"Last time you gave me something to take, you screwed me out of a lot of money."

"I don't think I gave it to you that time, but it doesn't matter. This is yours free and clear. Some valuable chemicals there."

"Thanks, Jake. I'll get that sorted out, then we'll talk some more."

"Sure, Nadine," Jake said.

"Oh, and I'll be taking this." She held up the Gauss gun she had pulled out from his holster during the hug. Then, she turned and followed Francisco up to the station.

"She's a firecracker, that one," Jorge said.

"You have no idea," Jake said.

"And here's your other one."

Riley was approaching him. She stopped a few feet from Jake. "What happens now?"

"Jose is having the shuttle pulled up to monorail. See, they've extended the rails up to the monorail line. Then that crane lifts it onto that modified flatcar. The monorail will act like a modified mass driver. It's not as powerful, but that shuttle is lighter, so it will still be able to reach orbit. TGI has its own orbital capabilities now."

"I meant what happens to me."

"Galactic Growing and the Militia aren't too happy with TGI right now, but they have nothing against Free Traders. You can do what you want."

"Jake, you were a total bastard to me."

"I'm sorry, but I had to do it."

"You broke my leg."

"If I hadn't done that, we'd all be dead. I've been shot in the leg before, and it didn't break my leg. You need to eat more calcium."

"You shot me, put me in jail for months, and all you can say is I should eat more calcium?"

"It wasn't months. Your leg is fine. Your dad has his ship back. He's made enough profit off all those metals to prob- ably pay off the entire mortgage and send you to engineering school at the university, and nobody at Galactic Growing or the Militia knows that he was involved, so he's in the clear with everybody."

"That's it?"

"Emperor's balls, Riley. I did what I had to do. I'm sorry if I hurt you. But I had to do it. Um, will you be sticking around for a while?"

"Jake Stewart, you are the most infuriating man I have ever met. You know, I really liked you."

"You did?" Jake said. "Well, I liked you too. A lot. That's why I stowed away on your ship."

"I know. But what sort of girl is going to hang out with a guy who doesn't trust her?"

"I couldn't tell you. I'm sorry, Riley. Do you have to go?"

She turned in a circle and nodded. "How do I get out of here?"

"Go see that guy over there." Jake pointed. "That's Jose. He's my boss's assistant, or perhaps my assistant boss now if what I'm hearing is correct. He's in charge of things here."

"That's a nice suit he's wearing."

"Yes, Jose is a great dresser. Snazzy."

"Has he ever shot anybody in the leg?"

"I don't think so," Jake said.

"Well then. Free trades, Jake Stewart," Riley said. She extended her hand. Jake took it, and they shook vigorously. She then marched over to where Jose was standing, and grabbed his arm. Jose turned to see who it was, and she began talking to him. But she didn't let go of his arm. Then she smiled, a brilliant thousand-watt smile.

"She didn't smile like that before," Jorge said.

"I think she spent too much time with Nadine," Jake said.

Francisco arrived and stopped before the two of them and then extended a credit chip.

"Well?" Jake asked. He didn't take the chip.

"It was like you said—she talked to me and was very nice, and she talked to some of the other guys there who remembered her from the station. She gave us two hundred credits to unload those four boxes you gave her, and switch to the ones we brought down."

"She stole your silver?" Jorge said.

"It's sort of TGI's silver, but it's not really important. You keep that, Francisco. Thanks for your help."

"*De nada*," Francisco said, pocketing the credit chip and turning away.

"Jake!" a voice sounded behind him. He turned.

"Hello, Jose."

"He wants to see us," Jose said. There was no doubt who 'he' was.

"When?"

"Soon as we are squared away here. Is everything off the shuttle?"

"Yes."

"Good. That Riley girl is much more interesting than you mentioned."

"Oh?"

"Yes, very friendly too. She's invited me to tour her ship when we're in orbit."

"She has?"

"Yes, great fashion sense too. We talked about scarves."

"Scarves."

"She has some great ideas. I think I'll take her shopping when we're up there. She'll love it," Jose said.

"I'm sure. Where is she now?" Jake asked.

"She said she wanted to get back to the station right away, so I put her on the monorail."

"She's up there now?"

"Yes, there she is. With your friend Nadine."

Jake turned, facing the monorail. He could see Riley's back as she boarded, and Nadine just behind her. Nadine stopped and looked back, and saw the three men looking at her. She blew them a kiss and smiled.

She was the last on board. Jake watched the door close behind her, and a second later, heard the hum as the monorail lifted, and then it began to move and gather speed as it swept toward Landing.

Jorge started laughing.

"Emperor's balls," Jake said.

"What?" Jose said.

"We were just talking about how Jake was going to die alone," Jorge said.

Nadine stared out of the train window. She and Riley had seats together.

"You did well on that de-orbit, merchie," Nadine said.

"You didn't do too badly either—for somebody who can't navigate," Riley said.

"Maybe we'll fly together again."

"Maybe."

Nadine turned back from the window. "You're meeting your father up at the station?"

"Yes, he'll dock and meet me up there."

"That's good," Nadine said.

"I've invited that Jose fellow to tour the R&R," Riley said.

"Jose, really? I thought you were into Jake."

"Kind of, but he's a little geeky. He doesn't dress well. He doesn't trust me. And he shot me."

"He does that a lot. Be careful when he pays you—sometimes he shorts you. Once, he gave me aluminum instead of platinum."

"You did mention that. Didn't you steal all that cargo from him thinking it was platinum? But he outsmarted you by hiding the valuable stuff?"

"He did not outsmart me. And I didn't steal it from him. It wasn't his."

"But it wasn't yours either, right?"

"Well no, but he shouldn't have told me it was platinum."

"He says he never told you, that you just assumed it was."

Nadine looked at her for a moment. "That is kind of true. Just be careful with him. How did this work out for you?"

"Dad already sold the cargo and got an excellent price, so we're covered for a long time. What about you?" Riley asked.

"He offered me a ton of fertilizer, of all things. But I'm wise to his tricks. I bribed some of the guys to replace the four crates of fertilizer with four crates of silver. I'm making bank on this one."

"Fertilizer?"

"Precursors, the guys said."

"You mean phosphorous and potassium? He gave you a *ton* of phosphorous and potassium?"

"Yes."

"Do you know how much that's worth?"

"Not much. It's just fertilizer."

"It's incredibly expensive. Delta has a shortage of that in the crust. All the Old Empire plants need it. The farms recycle as much as they can, but they have to have extra to keep operating. And with the population growth, there is a huge demand for it. It's probably worth five to ten times as much as silver," Riley said.

"What?"

"And if it's purified in orbit, and delivered dirtside, it's worth even more. The recycling is very difficult. That would probably double the price again."

"Oh." Nadine stared out the window. "Damn you, Jake Stewart," she said, and paused. "Again."

It took longer to get things sorted out than Jake had expected. It was more than a week before he was able to get up to orbit and see Mr. Dashi. When he arrived at Dashi's outer office, there was nobody there, which was unusual. Jake stopped, uncertain, until Mr. Dashi himself stepped out from the inner office. "Good to see you, Mr. Stewart. Come and sit down." Jake followed Dashi into the more luxurious wood-paneled interior.

"Things have worked out well, Mr. Stewart. You are to be congratulated."

"Thank you, sir."

"I am especially impressed with the way you were able to conceal your messages in the reports you sent from the Militia station."

"Thank you, sir. And thank you for trusting me with that information about the new shuttle-landing area. That helped in developing the plan."

"Yes, we had thought to buy one of the old ones and refurbish it, but once you identified that lifting body, we changed our plans."

"Thank you, sir. How are the lifts going?"

"Oh, we only do about one every two weeks, just to keep in practice."

"Sir?" Jake said.

"We still use the mass driver and the Militia shuttles."

"They let you do that?"

"There are many other corporations on Delta, and they are not all on the Militia's side. And now that we have the capacity to loft our own equipment and supplies up, those other games have stopped. Sometimes, Mr. Stewart, it is more important to be able to do something, than to actually do it."

"I see, sir. And what about the Militia ship that we destroyed?"

"You mean the Militia cutter that suffered an unfortunate navigational accident while attempting to dock with a newly discovered Old Empire scout base and disintegrated on re-entry? A wretched occurrence that has nothing to do with us."

"Just so, sir," Jake said.

"But most of the senior management are excited about it. Imagine—a real Old Empire station! There is some evidence that rogue elements occupied it recently and were doing illegal mining before the Militia occupied it, but they were gone by the time official elements arrived. In fact, the concession is up for auction right now. We may bid."

"I see, sir. What happens next?"

"Well, you've done some excellent work. I think you deserve some time off."

"Thank you, sir. I'm not sure what I'll do with myself."

"Perhaps you could find some projects to amuse you for a while. Oh, before I forget, here are your boots and your old skinsuit." Dashi reached behind him and produced a large package.

"Oh, thank you, sir. I wondered where they had gone to."

"Yes, the doctor gave them to Jose while you were running around dirtside. He had them repaired for you. And of course, here is the course chip that you kept in your boots."

Dashi weighed the course chip in his hand.

"Clever hiding place in the boots there. The course chip is encrypted, of course. I assume a family key. If the boots came from your father, I'm sure you have some way to decipher what's on there. Perhaps that course will lead you to something interesting."

Jake looked at Dashi for a moment, and nodded. "I see, sir. I'll do that. Perhaps that will be my project while I'm on leave."

"It sounds like a very engaging and illuminating way to spend your time. I'm sure you'll enjoy it."

Jake recognized a dismissal. "Thank you, sir," he said. He stood up and walked toward the door, then paused. "How old are you, sir?"

"Older than I look, but a gentleman does not discuss such things," Dashi said.

"Did you know my father, sir?" Jake asked.

Dashi nodded once. "We met in passing, many years ago. I did not know him well. I was very surprised to see your name on the school roster."

Jake nodded and stepped out to the outer office, then turned and said, "Where is Jose today, sir? Did you give him the day off?"

"No. I need to hire a new assistant. Jose has been promoted. He has a new job, and he is out looking for his new office. He will need space of his own."

"Good for Jose."

"Yes. He took his girlfriend with him."

"Girlfriend, sir?" Jake asked.

"Yes, redhead lady. They were going to go clothes shopping."

33

BOOKS BY ANDREW MORIARTY

Adventures of a Jump Space Accountant

1. Trans Galactic Insurance
2. Orbital Claims Adjustor
3. Third Moon Chemicals
4. A Corporate Coup
5. The Jump Ship
6. The Military Advisors

Decline and Fall of the Galactic Empire

1. Imperial Deserter
2. Imperial Smuggler
3. Imperial Mercenary

Get a Free Ebook

Thanks for reading. I hope you enjoyed it. Word-of-mouth reviews are critical to independent authors. Please consider leaving a review on Amazon or Goodreads or wherever you purchased this book.

If you'd like to be notified of future releases, please join my mailing list.

https://dl.bookfunnel.com/utkw99vv1s

I send a few updates a year, and if you subscribe you get a free ebook copy of Sigma Draconis IV, a short novella in the Jake Stewart universe. For updates on new releases, you can also follow me on Amazon, Bookbub, or Goodreads.

Andrew Moriarty

34

ABOUT THE AUTHOR

Andrew Moriarty has been reading science fiction his whole life, and he always wondered about the stories he read. How did they ever pay the mortgage for that spaceship? Why doesn't it ever need to be refueled? What would happen if it broke, but the parts were backordered for weeks? And why doesn't anybody ever have to charge sales tax? Despairing on finding the answers to these questions, he decided to write a book about how spaceships would function in the real world. Ships need fuel, fuel costs money, and the accountants run everything.

He was born in Canada, and has lived in Toronto, Vancouver, Los Angeles, Germany, Park City, and Maastricht. Previously he worked as a telephone newspaper subscriptions salesman, a pizza delivery driver, a wedding disc jockey, and a technology trainer. Unfortunately, he also spent a great deal of time in the IT industry, designing networks and configuring routers and switches. Along the way, he picked up an ex-spy with a predilection for French Champagne, and a whippet with a murderous possessiveness for tennis balls. They live together in Brooklyn.

Please buy his books. Tennis balls are expensive.